# THE
# WIZARD OF
# LA-LA LAND

**Books by Robert Campbell**

*Jimmy Flannery series:*

The Junkyard Dog
600-Pound Gorilla
Hip-Deep in Alligators
Thinning the Turkey Herd
Cat's Meow
Nibbled to Death by Ducks*
The Gift Horse's Mouth*
In a Pig's Eye*

*Jake Hatch series:*

Plugged Nickel*
Red Cent*

*Whistler series:*

In La-La Land We Trust
Alice in La-La Land*
Sweet La-La Land*
The Wizard of La-La Land*

*Other titles:*

Juice*
Boneyards*

*Published by POCKET BOOKS

# THE WIZARD OF LA-LA LAND

## Robert Campbell

POCKET BOOKS

New York   London   Toronto   Sydney   Tokyo   Singapore

POCKET BOOKS, a division of Simon & Schuster Inc.
1230 Avenue of the Americas, New York, NY 10020

Copyright © 1995 by Robert Campbell

Campbell, R. Wright.
   The wizard of la-la land / Robert Campbell.
     p.    cm.
   ISBN 0-671-70321-8
   I. Title.
   PS3553.A4867W59  1995
   813'.54—dc20
                                    94-14615
                                         CIP

First Pocket Books hardcover printing January 1995

10  9  8  7  6  5  4  3  2  1

*For LaVonne,*
*Beautiful lady of the bright and loving spirit*

"There are things human beings do to other human beings that are worse than murder, because when you're dead that's the end to memory and pain."

—*Bosco Silverlake*

*1*

*Driving* south from Hollywood on one of the twelve clear days of the year, the top down on his Cadillac convertible, Mike Rialto—pleased that his good eye was just as dry as his glass eye in the remarkable absence of air pollution—reflected upon the days when he'd first arrived in Hollywood from the East Coast back in 1945.

He'd been twenty-four, just mustered out of the army on a medical, still getting used to the loss of one peeper, which had been plucked from his head by a flying stone kicked up by the tire of a passing Jeep on 16 April while slogging along the road to Nuremberg with the XV Corps, US Seventh Army. It gave him a Purple Heart and the swagger and dash of a combat veteran. He bought a Cadillac convertible with some of his poker winnings and drove west, running out on a girl he'd knocked up in Bethesda, Maryland.

Hollywood, back in those days, was a place where you could buy a cup of fresh-squeezed juice—strawberry, mango, pineapple, papaya and passion fruit—for a quarter.

You could drive around in an open convertible without withering from the pollution in the air.

It was a small town. In the evening, couples, old and young, walked up and down Hollywood Boulevard looking in the windows of the furniture stores. Farther west the streets of Beverly Hills and Westwood were almost empty.

The air and the girls smelled as sweet as honey; the girls quick to jump into bed, without reservations, hidden agendas, or fear of consequences, especially with a war hero like himself.

He rented a little garage apartment in West Hollywood and hunkered down to practice the card shark's craft with a sideline in the skin game, having no overpowering desire to be in the "Industry."

He proved to be better at fronting for bimbos—not exactly functioning as their pimp but more by way of being a subcontractor and talent agent—than at making a living with cards. So he played cards only sometimes, trying to improve his skills, hoping that one day he would be good enough to make his living at what he considered his true calling.

Now, driving the San Diego Freeway on the way to Artesia Boulevard and the town of Gardena, where years ago a badly written statute had allowed gambling at five-card stud and the establishment of card parlors that added greatly to civic revenue, he remembered that Maryland girl's black, curly hair, the sweet, awkward eagerness she had, staring up into his face with eyes wide open as he mounted her, watching him when he neared climax and then turning her head away as though the contortions of his face were frightening to her, more than she could bear.

He couldn't remember her name.

Right there on the freeway he was nearly overwhelmed with bittersweet regret, a longing for that girl he might have married. The girl who'd probably gone ahead and had the child he'd given her—abortion being no option to speak of back then—and married some raw-necked, rough-handed farmer, older than herself, just so the kid would have a name. Or maybe she'd never married at all—raising that child all by herself.

She'd been eighteen then and would be—my God—sixty-seven now, grown old and overweight, just as he'd grown old and fat . . . if she were still alive. And the kid would be forty-eight with kids of his or her own. And some of those kids might have kids. Children and grandchildren and great-grandchildren, a whole goddamned family that would gather on the Fourth of July and other holidays, kissing and hugging their grandpa. It was enough to make you cry.

He turned off on Artesia Boulevard and drove east to Western Avenue, where he turned again and went north a block and a half before entering the parking lot of Jack Queen's Ace High Club, the card parlor he'd first visited nearly half a century before, loyalty to his own traditions being a principal quality of Rialto's character.

Inside the club, he saw them all gathered, the people who were as much his family as anybody had ever been family, the young slickers trying to sharpen their game, the criminal types, the retired folks, men and women, shuffling the cards, dealing them out, betting on the turn of the cards, anticipating the sweet taste of success, their eyes looking through the back of their heads at the long years of losing.

Wally Keep spotted him from across the room and threw up a handful of waving, snapping fingers, calling Rialto to his table.

Dewy Messina, his long sad face looking like the trailing horse in a twelve-horse race, smiled in anticipation on one side of his mouth, knowing that Rialto would be good for a fifty-dollar contribution to his winnings. Messina, the poker wolf; a man who never anted up when holding a small pair just to be friendly; a man who rarely drew a card in hopes of an inside straight; a man who nearly always walked away a winner, commiserating with the losers how this one or that one had ravished Lady Luck that day, never attracting the automatic aversion card players had toward anyone who walked out of a game winning big.

"Long time no see," Abe Forstman said in greeting, a remark that was usually ignored, since it was the remark Forstman made each and every time he met a friend, even if he'd seen him just minutes before while in the men's toilet having a pee.

But, discombobulated by his reminiscences and suddenly valuing accuracy in a matter so precious as the passage of time, Rialto said, "What're you talking about? I seen you just last Friday and here it is only Monday."

"What've we got there? Three days? Seventy-two hours? A lot can happen in seventy-two hours. You take the Berlin Wall. They cracked that baby and knocked most of it down in seventy-two hours. You take Poland—"

"Are we going to have a political discussion here?" Chuck Wissy asked.

"—became a democracy practically overnight. Who's talking politics?" Forstman said. "What we're talking here is a little metaphysics."

"Never mind the Ex-Lax. You sitting down, you're standing up, Mike?" Messina asked.

"I'm sitting down," Rialto said.

"So, it's your deal, Abe. Let's play cards."

"All I was saying is the world can change in seventy-two hours," Forstman said. "A million people get born and a million people die."

"I don't want to hear about it," Wissy said. "I don't want to think about such numbers. I can count up to the ace, that's all I want to think about."

"It's all I can do thinking about one person, maybe two persons at a time," Rialto said, sitting himself down.

"So, there you go," Forstman said. "I'll give you one person and what seventy-two hours could mean to him. I'll give you Kenny Gotch."

"What's a Kenny Gotch?" Wissy asked.

"Kenny Gotch is a kid what came to town ten years ago a dreamer and is now dying inside a nightmare."

"I know this Kenny Gotch," Rialto said. "Calls hisself Harriet LaRue sometimes; wears purple dresses and rhinestone shoes on the Hollywood stroll."

"No more. Don't wear dresses and don't wear rhinestone shoes. Don't want to be called Harriet anymore. Afraid, he says, that God won't be able to find him when he dies if everybody keeps on calling him Harriet LaRue."

"He's dying?"

"Karpov's sonoma. One of the terrible things what comes with AIDS."

"So, what are you telling us?"

"I'm telling you he could be dead inside seventy-two hours. I stopped over to see him at Angeles Hospice and that's the news they give me."

"How come you're over there visiting this fairy?" asked Messina, who talked that way because he was said to have been mob connected back in Philadelphia, where he came from and thought it expected of him.

"The kid ain't a queer," Forstman said. "He swore to me he wasn't so inclined."

"Purple dresses and rhinestone shoes sounds to me like a person of that persuasion."

"Merely the accoutrements of the enterprise upon which he was engaged," Forstman said. "He allowed certain liberties for certain cash considerations, but just because a man works in a sewer don't mean he's got a taste for shit."

"Never mind splitting hairs," Wissy said. "You ain't answered the question. How come you were playing angel of mercy at the Angeles Hospice?"

"Kenny Gotch's related by marriage to my wife. Don't ask me how. He's a third cousin through marriage, three times removed. Something like that. What do I know? My wife tells me the boy's dying and I should go pay him a visit, show him a little human kindness. I tell her I never even met the kid except once at a funeral, a wedding, but she insists."

"Just like that, she asks you to go visit this gazooney? Out of the blue?"

"She's at that age."

"What do you mean at that age?" Messina asked.

Forstman looked up from his cards and focused his watery eyes on Messina. "Well, you know," he said. "She's at the age where she wants to spread a little kindness because she figures she's going to be needing some of it for herself pretty soon."

"I can understand that," Rialto said. "I'll open."

"So, you listen to his confession?" Messina asked. "I'm in."

"Do I look like a priest?" Forstman asked, tossing in his chip.

"What do you Jews do in place of asking for absolution for your sins?" Keep asked, tossing in his.

"We regret."

"I guess this kid had plenty of regrets," Wissy said, putting up his ante too.

"Who ain't got regrets when you're looking at the great by and by?" Forstman said.

There was something in the way Forstman made the remark that sang in Rialto's ear and he looked up with his good eye to see Forstman looking right back at him as though he had something on his mind.

They played out the hand, which was a dull one, and Rialto said, "Deal me out, I got to take a pee."

"It's about time for me to wring out my sock too," Forstman said.

"So, we'll wait for you," Messina said, and leaned back to give both of them a look of his own, always sensitive to the flow of rivers underneath the surface and words left unspoken.

In the john, at the white porcelain urinals, Rialto said, "You got something on your mind, Abe?"

"I don't know."

"You don't know if you got something on your mind?"

"I don't know if I should talk about it, break a confidence."

"That's up to you, Abe. All I come in for was to take a leak, you was the one wanted to—"

"I had to relieve myself, too. I been—"

"—have a talk. So, you didn't want to have a talk, that's okay."

"Well, I don't know. Kenny Gotch wanted to relieve his soul—"

"So maybe you want to relieve yours?"

"—but I don't know if I got the right to pass it on."

"You give a promise to a dying man?"

"Nothing like that. He didn't ask me to promise anything like that."

"So, I'd say he left it up to you."

"You remember seven, eight years ago, there was a little

girl found dead lying across a tombstone over to Hollywood Cemetery?"

Rialto felt a chill, the way it happens when the past comes back to haunt the present.

"If it's the one I think you mean, it was Isaac Canaan's niece, Sarah, and it was ten years ago. I was in on the search for her. Unofficially."

"That's the name. Sarah Canaan. Kenny Gotch knows something about who done it."

They were quiet after that, finishing up what they were doing, zipping themselves up, washing their hands, drying them on the roller towels, smoothing their hair back with their hands, staring at themselves in the stained mirror, a horror out of the past coming back to shake them up.

"So, who?" Rialto finally said.

"That much he didn't give me. Just that he knew who did it to her."

"Oh," Rialto said, finding himself much relieved.

"You got any ideas what I should do about it?" Forstman asked. "I don't want to get involved, you know what I mean?"

"Sure. Nobody wants to get involved."

"So, you got any ideas?"

"You mean you want *me* to get involved?"

"Well, seeing how you're in the trade. Seeing as how you're practically a cop, so to speak," Forstman said.

"You don't have to drown me in chicken fat," Rialto said. "I know a couple of the individuals involved in the matter, who were in on the search. I'm acquainted with the man who was changed by what happened to the little girl. You might even say Isaac Canaan, the uncle, is more than just an acquaintance but—"

"That's all I'm saying."

"—I don't know if I should get involved."

"Well, I didn't say you should. I don't know what to do, I just wanted to get it off my chest. So, now I got it off my chest. You don't want to do nothing about it, that's okay, too."

That's what Forstman said but that wasn't what he meant.

7

What he meant was that Rialto went around telling stories of what a daring private eye he was, wrestling around there in the down and dirty, but when it came to doing a little something, extending a helping hand, using a little of his know-it-all know-how, he came up empty like any sucker welching on a bet, unable to back his play.

"I'll go over and talk to this cousin of yours—"

"My wife's by marriage."

"—three times removed, and see if he's just having delusions," Rialto said.

"They get delusions when they die of this Karpov's sonoma?"

"Who knows? It's a possibility."

# 2

*The* last time they counted, New York had 28,595 cases of AIDS. LA had 10,194. But that was yesterday. Don't ask about today and don't ask about tomorrow.

No telling how many of them came out of La-La Land, a center of what might be called promiscuous behavior but, nonetheless, still thought of in some quarters as a small-town beauty.

The truth is, of course, Hollywood's no longer the innocent little town at the end of the yellow brick road that Rialto found full of juice stands and willing women nearly fifty years before. Now it had every earmark of being a corporate town filled with bottom liners and Japanese takeover specialists, a variety store filled with curiosities and perversions every bit as plentiful and various as those available in cities of ancient decadence.

Angeles Hospice, just off Franklin Avenue, mere blocks

from the corner of Hollywood and Vine, has the biggest charity AIDS ward in the city.

On the floor where Rialto was looking for Gotch's room, practically everybody was walking around with surgical gloves and masks. All he could see were worried eyes and scared eyes and eyes that looked like these people were about to run screaming down the halls and out of the death house.

For a minute there he wondered what the hell he was doing walking into such a place at seven-goddamn-thirty in the morning.

He'd spent the night sitting on bus stop benches and in all-night coffee shops so that he could avoid the loneliness of his apartment and the fear of the dark it contained. When dawn had lightened the sky and it was time to get to bed, he'd decided to start the day with the good deed he'd more or less promised Abe Forstman.

So here he was, seven-thirty in the morning, an hour when the graveyard shift was fagged out after a long night and the morning shift was still rubbing the sleep from their eyes, walking unnoticed along corridors echoing with the squeak, squeak of crepe rubber soles—like a bunch of goddamn mice—his own leather heels laying down a sharper *paradiddle* on the vinyl floor.

When he opened the door to Kenny Gotch's room and saw Gotch lying there all scrunched up and facing the wall, what he could see of an arm, a neck and the side of a head looking like something already buried and dug up, he almost backed off and said the hell with doing the favor for Abe Forstman.

Then he remembered that he wouldn't only be doing a favor for Abe Forstman, he might also end up doing a favor for Isaac Canaan, the kiddie vice cop, a man of considerable influence among the brethren in blue.

For a man who occasionally transacted a little business with the hookers along the stroll and who might come in contact with the police in some unfavorable and unfortunate sequence of events, it behooved Rialto to make a little deposit in the Cosmic Bank of Good Will in expectation of future interest, dividends, and withdrawals.

The skeleton under the sheet lay there motionless.

Rialto was reminded of how, when he was a kid and woke up scared in the middle of the night, he'd go into his mother's bedroom and stand there staring at her to see if she was breathing, afraid of what would happen to him if she wasn't.

He stood there staring at Gotch.

A little breeze gusted through the window, stirring a paper napkin on the bedside tray table, where the remains of an old meal dried up and shrank, stirring the thin strands of hair combed across the emaciated skull lying on the pillow.

It seemed to Rialto that Gotch had moved a little.

He went closer and bent over the bed, looking down into the sick man's face. The kid couldn't be more than twenty-five, twenty-six, but he looked a hundred and ten. His eyes were half open, the way some people's eyes do when they're dozing.

Rialto straightened up, not wanting to startle Gotch. He sat down in the wooden chair, figuring he'd give it five minutes, hating to disturb a sick man who was having himself a little nap, remembering how important sleep had been to him when he'd lost his eye, wanting to forget about the damage to his looks and well-being, escaping the truth in sleep just like Gotch was probably doing most of the time.


There were centuries during which Pan, the ancient god most likely to have been the spiritual ancestor of the Christian Satan, was depicted as a child or a youth, half human and half goat, a symbol of unbridled sexuality. Religious authorities of nearly every persuasion condemned Pan's nature as a manifestation of evil. Pan was, according to some, the father of Satan.

In succeeding centuries Satan was variously pictured as a demon with horns and tail, a virile male of great guile and sophistication dressed in a frock coat or cape, consort of naked witches, and ravisher of innocent women. In America, he was known as a Yankee peddler with the persuasive skills of a horse trader, a mature seducer of considerable charm and menace.

During the twentieth century Satan aged considerably, the

general fear and loathing about growing old infecting every aspect of the culture; old age and its natural decay becoming the new face of evil.

Walter Cape might have been cast in the role of the devil, having a tendency toward a flaccid lower lip, watering eyes, a runny nose, occasional loss of memory and bursts of temper, and other signs that the machine was breaking down.

Senility had come upon him suddenly in a singular moment when a hoodlum by the name of Whistler, who called himself a private detective, accompanied by a one-armed brute, a southern cracker in a soiled white suit and a Jewish cop rumored never to sleep, burst into his home on the hill during a dinner party and tossed a rotting human head into his lap.

He'd fought against his physical and mental decline, having survived worse than rotting heads during the years when he'd amassed his fortune in one enterprise after another designed to exploit the most shameful weaknesses of men; committing all the sins to which flesh is heir and reinventing a few not much practiced since the Marquis de Sade tried to live the nightmares that thrilled him in the haunted nights.

There was no doubt that when Cape awakened between satin sheets that once pleased his senses but that now seemed merely too slippery and cold for comfort, his mind was filled with what is considered evil in this and every society: images of small children, boys between seven and fourteen, piled naked in a cage, waiting for him to choose among them; images of any who opposed him strung up on a dozen different devices of torture, their bodies running red with blood.

Sometimes his head was filled with images from his own boyhood; the few happy times, holidays, Christmas, the Fourth of July, and Halloween when the women of the whorehouse in Wilkes-Barre, Pennsylvania, in which he'd been born and raised, worked double shifts and bought him gaudy presents and candy with their windfall profits.

And sometimes he awakened weeping, knowing that for all his wealth, which still commanded the service and loyalty of people who loathed him, his strength and potency were spilling from him like the life's blood from a severed head.

\*     \*     \*

Rialto sat there thinking about what Abe Forstman had told him about Kenny Gotch, information gathered up by Forstman's wife who, though she might have been only a cousin three times removed, seemed to have a pretty good handle on the dying man.

Kenny Gotch had been born in Chicago to a hardworking butcher, Manny Gotch, and his pious Catholic wife, Harriet, whose only sins were marrying a Jew in the first place, the wild, even passionate, love she had for her firstborn, and the indulgences she showered upon him.

There was talk in the family about how she'd kept him in dresses until he was three and four years old, but the grandmothers said that was just her old-fashioned way. He was started on piano lessons at five and enrolled in dance classes when six.

Harriet had dreams of her Kenny becoming an entertainer, her grandfather having been an actor in New York City years before.

When he was ten she rented a room at the community center and Kenny gave a recital during which he played a piano piece by Mozart, danced a pas de deux with his shadow to the accompaniment of a number from *Swan Lake* and gave a dramatic recitation called "The Horse."

The kids in the neighborhood, the sons and daughters of the grocer, the candy store owner, the manager of the five and dime, the fifth-grade school teacher, the rabbi from the local shul and others, bludgeoned by their parents—who themselves had been forced by commercial ties or friendship to make the effort—suffered through the hour and a half and later beat the crap out of Kenny in the empty lot behind the movie theater on the boulevard.

Only the priest, Father Mahoney, the pastor of St. Mary's, showered lavish praise on the performance, but everybody knew that was because he was fighting for the souls of Harriet and her son, afraid that they might be lost to Mother Church forever, living as they did inside a Jewish neighborhood.

Some months later, in the same empty lot where Kenny had been roughed up, Manny Gotch, searching for Kenny because he'd not come home on time for supper, came upon Phil Kropotnik down on his knees behind the bushes by the back fence with Kenny's pecker in his mouth. Kropotnik was sixteen and already a notorious *fageleh* in the neighborhood, the fault clearly lying with a masculine mother who owned and managed seven slum dwellings on the South Side and a feminine father who sold furs at Carson Pirie Scott.

In that neighborhood, among those simple people, you didn't have to look far for the reasons behind homosexuality and other such offenses against nature. Dressing a boy in skirts for too long a time, coddling him with hugs and kisses past a certain age, teaching him how to dance on his toes, urging him to recite pieces about horses in public, allowing him to listen to a man in a skirt preach about a place called heaven where creatures that you couldn't tell were they men or women went flying around on Technicolor wings, all but guaranteed the twisting of a boy into a person of a certain sexual persuasion.

Manny kept his eyes peeled after that, but Kenny had developed a taste for it and it wasn't long before he was cutting school and turning daytime tricks with queer johns trolling the streets down around North Welles. Not long after, hardly fourteen years old, he ran away from home, devastating his mother's life and relieving his father of considerable worry and shame.

According to Abe Forstman, Kenny had apparently hit the stroll at Hollywood and Vine running, a new kid on the block, with all the sass of a big city tooter and the apparent innocence of a half-Jewish altar boy.

That was in January of 1984.

It was in August, Rialto remembered, that Isaac Canaan's seven-year-old niece was snatched off the playground down the block from her house.

It wasn't until the following December that she'd been found, lying broken across a tombstone.

There was no date of record when Kenny Gotch took to wearing purple dresses and rhinestone shoes and calling himself Harriet LaRue.

\* \* \*

Rialto was getting very bored and restless sitting there. Was the schmuck going to sleep his life away, Rialto wondered. He leaned a little closer and saw the edge of a pink piece of paper sticking out from under the pillow. Being a curious man and having nothing else to do, he captured the corner neatly in two fingers and drew out an envelope of the sort that comes with a greeting card . . . which it turned out to be. A greeting card with a sugar-sweet painting of a woodland scene on the cover and some birds inside, along with a sentimental verse and the words "I love you, but I'm afraid," inscribed in purple ink. It was signed "Pooch."

Rialto grabbed the seat of the chair between his legs and dragged it up a little closer to the bed.

"Hey, how's it shaking, kid?" Rialto said, soft and low.

When there was no response, he got up into a crouch, bending over the bed again, trying to get another look at the kid's face to see if anything was stirring, shoulders hunched, the way people approach somebody dying, not wanting to stand up too tall in case death makes a mistake and snatches the one most visible.

"Not shaking hardly at all," Rialto said to himself.

He staggered a little from the effort of bending over and steadied himself on the mattress with the hand that still held the card and envelope.

Kenny Gotch emitted a little sound like a groan or a gasp.

"So, listen, kid, you probably don't remember me. We met once or twice down on the stroll around Hollywood and Vine. You and me are sort of in the same line of work. I mean I do a favor for a friend every now and then, introduce him to one of the ladies on the stroll. You know what I mean? Book a couple of acts for a party now and then? I don't book your speciality; I book female specialities but nothing otherwise. Still and all you could say we were business acquaintances."

After that first sound there was nothing else forthcoming from Gotch.

"The reason I thought I'd stop in to see how you was doing was I play cards with a relative of yours. Abe Forstman. Well actually it's his wife who's a relative of yours; third cousin on your aunt's mother's side, three times removed. Something like that. So anyway, Abe tells me you told him something about a little girl what was kidnapped and killed about ten years ago. They found her body on a tombstone in Hollywood Cemetery. You know what I'm talking about?"

If Kenny Gotch knew he wasn't saying.

"You named a name. You named the name of the little girl who was in the newspapers. Sarah Canaan. Abe tells me you told him her name. I don't think you dreamed the name. I don't think you made up any lies about that little girl what was used, abused and tossed away like a piece of garbage."

Rialto moved in close. It was very hard to do, getting so close to the dying man, the odor of him rising up in a sickish sweet cloud, but Rialto had done a lot of hard things in his time and this wasn't the worst of them.

"You believe in souls? You believe in heaven and hell and life everlasting?" he asked. "They tell me you was raised a Catholic."

Rialto moved in yet a little closer, figuring he had a little something going here.

"Somebody's giving you the time to wash yourself in the blood of the lamb. Make your confession. Clean yourself up for the big interview, if you get my meaning. It's up to you," Rialto said, shifting his weight as though it was his intention to leave, as he reached out a hand and tapped Gotch on the shoulder.

"Why don't you give me the name of the one who stole that baby and did those terrible things to her?" he said.

He took hold of Gotch's shoulder and started gently, very gently, pulling the man over on his back, leaning down close. Suddenly the balance tipped and Gotch came around fast, falling onto his back, his eyes popping, mouth flying open, a glut of blood suddenly spewing out of his maw.

Rialto jerked his head back, stumbling to his feet, but some of the blood landed on his cheek and ran down his neck just as the door to the room opened up. The next thing he knew a nurse wearing a tee shirt with a one-eyed Popeye on it was screaming at him, asking him what the hell he was doing making unauthorized visits to a dying man.

Rialto stood there shivering like a whale in terminal terror.

The nurse went to the bed and gave Gotch a quick look. Then she turned to Rialto.

"You got any cuts, abrasions, or razor burns on your face and neck? You get any of his blood or body fluids on your hands? Did any fly into your eyes? Take off your jacket and your shirt, anything else that's got blood on them. Drop them on the floor where you're standing. Then go into the toilet there and I'll wash you off."

Rialto didn't protest or ask any questions. He just did as he was told and allowed the nurse to lead him by the hand into the toilet and over to the sink, where she washed his face and neck and hair as carefully and tenderly as could be.

He stood there while she dried him off, just staring at her face, not wanting to ask but wanting to know.

She read his mind, which wasn't hard.

"He's dead," she said. "What the hell were you doing in here?"

"I just came to visit."

"Don't you read signs? Didn't you read the signs that tell you that you're supposed to check at the nurses' station, get masked and gloved, before you go in to see one of the patients on this floor?"

"I didn't notice."

"You family?"

"I know one of his relatives. I said I'd stop by and say hello."

"So, that's all right, then. You said good-bye."

There was a discreet knock on the door and then it opened. A young woman in a candy-striped smock breezed in, not shouting any good mornings in case Kenny Gotch might still be asleep, a big smile on her face. When she caught sight of him lying there with all the blood, she turned so pale a splash of freckles appeared across her nose and cheeks.

"Oh, fachrissake," she said.

"Sit down and put your head between your knees, Diana," the nurse snapped. "Don't you go fainting on me."

# 3

*Isaac* Canaan awakened with a bar of light lying diagonally across his face, cutting it more or less in half. It flooded one eye and warmed the corner of his mouth where a little drool of sleep had dried.

He'd joined the police force late in life, lying about his age by nearly a decade and forging a birth certificate to support the deception, but the harsh, hot sunlight made him look every day of his sixty-three years.

They said that Sergeant Isaac Canaan rarely slept. Medical mavens hanging around Gentry's Coffee Shop—where there was always at least one expert on any human belief, profession, pastime, or enterprise—maintained that something had shocked his pituitary when his niece had been abducted, and was the cause of his chronic insomnia.

The discovery of her poor little body, draped over a tombstone in Hollywood Cemetery, had done nothing to heal the damaged balance of his hormones. He was still sleepless for nights and days on end, prowling the alleys, boulevards, and streets where the baby hookers displayed their wares, trying in a stubborn, unsmiling, bitter way to save their lives.

They said he never took off his hat because he'd made a vow to wear it constantly until he'd found his little niece's killer, in much the same way that some priests were known to wear a rosary wound around their hands, even when they took a bath, or religious Jews wore the *t'filin,* the cords that held the box containing the six prayers, tied about their arms at all times.

The truth was that Canaan wore an embroidered skull cap on his balding head day and night; nobody's business but his own. He had been known to lift his fedora to age or great beauty, but that was a very rare occurrence.

By work and nature, and by reason of the abduction, abuse, and murder of his niece, he was a solitary soul, having no friends with whom he went to boxing matches or movies. He was not known to date the ladies, although unsupported rumor had it that he and Shirley Hightower, a waitress at Gentry's Coffee Shop down along the Hollywood hookers' stroll, sometimes shared a bed. He had no family with whom to shelter, since he avoided his brother, Max, and his sister-in-law, Ruth, because he felt that he had failed them in some fundamental way.

When a police officer, a vice detective—which was a profession an Orthodox family like his own thought little of— wasn't even able to use his power and his skills to save a little girl, a child of the family, Isaac saw it as a terrible betrayal. He thought his family disdained him; he'd joined the cossacks and still had not been able to do his family any good when evil stalked them.

Isaac believed that, even though his brother, Max, an intelligent man, knew that just being a policeman gave no guarantee that the policeman's family would be immune from the terrors and tragedies of life.

Still and all, Canaan had been unable to feel free and easy with his brother or his brother's wife, not only because he'd failed to rescue little Sarah but because he'd failed since to avenge her murder, denying them what comfort they might have drawn from justice and retribution.

He saw little of them and lived the life of an outcast, as solitary as any of the alienated nomads on the stroll.

The closest human relationships he had were with the nighthawks, snowbirds, tired prostitutes of a certain age, petty thieves and lost souls who frequented Gentry's. Of those only Whistler, Bosco, and the waitress, Shirley Hightower, rushing around in her nurse's shoes, tending the customers as though they were patients in her exclusive care, might, by any stretch of imagination or language, be considered friends.

His hours at home alone were spent doing housekeeping

chores, watching late-late-night movies or afternoon soap operas on a thirteen-inch black-and-white screen, napping in his green Naugahyde BarcaLounger, reading the Torah and the Talmud and otherwise contemplating the mystery of God's hard love.

The only other entertainment he allowed himself—if it could be called entertainment—was the calligraphic reproduction of quotations from the Talmud done with antique writing instruments on real parchment in colored inks he ground and prepared himself.

No one, not even his family, knew of the dedication and skill that he gave to his calligraphy.

One of the very first he'd ever penned and illuminated was the one by Simeon ben Gamaliel, who wrote, "All my life I grew up among the sages and have found nothing better for anybody than silence."

4

*The* Big Two had been Rialto's war and Canaan's war. Vietnam had been Bosco Silverlake's war and the man they called Whistler, having been of an age that fell between conflicts, had come to find his war with himself, as ninety-nine out of a hundred of us do.

He'd come to Hollywood in 1974—before it became known as La-La Land—looking for a tumble in the hay with the bitch goddess Success. Though why she should be a goddess and not a god has always been a puzzlement, except that men, more than women, are prepared to kill—and commit other acts like rape and betrayals even more horrible—for fame, honor, power and fortune.

In 1981 an accident—like Fred MacMurray's famous trench

coat catching the attention of a director who wanted to buy such a coat and ended up giving Fred a part in his flick or Lana Turner getting picked up and picked out by a talent scout who saw her resting her sweatered tits on the marble counter of a drugstore soda fountain, sucking up a strawberry ice cream soda from the straw between her strawberry lips— dragged him out of the ranks of the wannabes and made him the host of a morning show for kiddies, anonymous behind a clown's suit and a painted face.

It was a sad face, as befitted a clown in La-La Land, and the stories he told between cartoons, though amusing to the kids, struck chords of sweet melancholy and longing in grown-ups. The next thing he knew he was a late-night story-teller, putting the kids to bed and spinning dreams for tired single mothers.

Not long after he went late-late, telling stories, taking calls, offering little tags and rags of street smarts during a midnight rap that attracted, seduced and comforted the lonely, lost and insomniac, making him a local star.

Soon he was Sam the Sandman, the Sad Man, counselor to the flotsam and jetsam of the nation gathering in the streets, alleys and gutters of La-La Land, living the life, loving the life, doubting the life, just the way ninety-nine out of a hundred of us do; waiting for real life to happen. He found that one girl out of four million all men dream about and lost her to a homicidal hillbilly from Appalachia.

The next year he took a call from a woman wanting to say good-bye to the only friend she had in La-La Land—a television clown—and he hadn't been able to hold her on the line long enough for the number to be traced and the police to arrive. He was later told the cops were at the door when they heard the shot. He'd been ten seconds less persuasive, less mesmerizing, less compelling than he would have had to be in order to do the job and save a life that perhaps really wanted to be saved. It had been a little microcosm of the missed opportunities that littered La-La Land like the leaves that would have covered the streets if there'd been any trees to speak of.

It was good-bye to show business for the Sandman.

He got a private cop's ticket, just to make a dollar, poking his nose into other people's dirty laundry, pawing through the stained panties and soiled Jockey shorts of a thousand illicit love affairs. Plenty of work in the town that was said by many to be the cheatingest town in the country, perhaps the world.

He'd never been a stranger to the bottle, but somewhere along the way he married it. He grew older five days to one, caught in the amber of time and whiskey, but didn't grow a day wiser. Never even sure about the day and date when the drinking went out of control. Only sure of the day and date he put the bottle away.

So, figure ten years saved, but another ten never to be recovered. Always playing catch-up, running like hell toward the garden gate and never getting there, trying to win back the lost decade, even while knowing it could never be won. Nothing makes up for the loss of time. Absolutely nothing.

Whenever he dreamed, he was always ten years younger than his calendar age; in his dreams of childhood he was a phantom not yet born riding his bike down a tree-shaded street back home.

And here, ten years after he'd recovered his sobriety, he was still out in the streets. He'd found the war everybody found out there on the hookers' stroll, the battle being fought on as many battlefields as there are cities and towns large enough to support a population of hungry, lonely men, exploited women and desperate children. A war that was tougher and more deadly than the one America had fought against that Arab, several thousands of miles away.

Whistler was a good soldier because he fought when almost all hope was gone.

If you suggested such a thing to him, he'd deny it; would say he believed in practically nothing, least of all the hope of salvation, and that he did what he did in order to feed his face and keep the roof of the rickety house he owned on Cahuenga Boulevard overlooking the freeway above his head.

On this perfect day he was dozing in his favorite booth next to the big window of Gentry's Coffee Shop and Snack

Bar on the corner of Hollywood and Vine. The door was open, inviting in the miracle of fine weather.

Nobody else was sitting inside. The few twangy boys, grifters, pimps, cops, strollers and jack-rollers not yet chased home by the morning light stopped in to buy containers of coffee now and then, but were gone in a minute, scarcely making a ripple, disappearing out there on the street of dead neon and yesteryear's trash still lying in the gutter. One or two sat on the curb, drinking from their cups and taking the unaccustomed sun.

The only other soul in the place—except for the cook napping in the kitchen—was Bosco Silverlake, the one-armed counterman, sitting on his stool by the register, reading *Jung and the Lost Gospels.*

"Ho-hum," Whistler crooned, his eyes closed and his cheek resting against the cool glass.

Bosco marked his place, tucked the book into the pit of his lost arm, hooked a china mug with his thumb, snatched the coffee pot from the electric warmer and went over to Whistler's table to refill his cup before pouring one for himself and sitting down. "Was that a protest, a comment or a purr of appreciation?" he asked.

"I've got spring fever. If Sigourney Weaver walked through that door and invited me up for an afternoon in bed, I'd have to turn her down. I'd have to take a pass."

"A rain check."

"I'd have to say come back tomorrow and then regret it for the rest of my life."

"How's that?"

"Sigourney isn't the kind of woman you can say no to even once."

"She'll never know what she's missing."

Jonas Kilroy looked like a tall, skinny Howdy-Doody, red hair, freckles, open, friendly, silly grin and all. Every morning he stood at the top of the short flight of stairs leading to the entrance of the humanities building and reflected upon that portion of the population of the University of California, Los Angeles, that swarmed in squads, companies and light divisions along the paths, across the foot-worn grass, into this and that hall of learning, wondering where his enthusiasm and passion for preparing feasts of learning for such cattle had gone.

His disciplines, comparative religion and mythology—in spite of the kick-in-the-ass jumpstart Joseph Campbell's PBS series had given them—were no longer considered requirements in the education of the well-rounded man and woman, and he, as a high priest of the knowledge, was no longer a figure in the academic landscape but merely an anachronism, like the professors of English literature and archaeology, affectionately regarded as the caretakers of old-fashioned pursuits and accomplishments suitable for students looking for an easy B and some entertaining bullshit.

Looking at them churning up the grass in their thousands, adding their own exhalations to the air pollution and breathing in more than their share of smog, he reckoned how many were taking remedial English, how many pottery making, and how many some other craft or skill that would be better taught in some apprentice program out there in the real world rather than behind the walls of an institution of learning that should be, by all rights, not only cloistered but sacred to intellectual pursuits.

Once a minute, standing there, he returned a greeting offered by some young man or woman. Once every two or three he was mistaken for another student.

He turned around and slouched through the door, held open by a thin girl with glasses who called him Professor Kilroy, and looked at him with blinking adoration. He had half a dozen such student acolytes who treated him with a certain awe and respect, and it struck him again, as it had more than once, that Jesus Christ hadn't started with many more disciples than he enjoyed.

Nobody except Mary Bucket, the nurse who was head of the graveyard shift at Angeles Hospice, the one who had walked in on a terrified Mike Rialto, knew that Diana Corday, the candy striper, was a hooker.

Nobody in the hospice except Mary Bucket knew that her

real name wasn't even Diana Corday. Her real name was Dotty Bojack and she'd been born and raised in Pittsburgh, Pennsylvania. Her father had been a drunk and her mother a casual Saturday night slut. Her brother, Harry, had copped her cherry when she'd been thirteen. Her father had had his drunken way with her at least once a week over the next four years. She ran away to Newark, New Jersey, and got a job in a factory testing condoms.

The women in the factory gave the things to their littlest kids to blow up like balloons. They used them to tie back their hair. They carried them in their purses and pockets and scattered them on the tables in the local taverns on Saturday nights just for the hell of it. They were missionaries of the safe way even before AIDS reared its ugly, deadly head.

Dotty allowed certain men to have her standing up in the corridor leading to the outside shed where the garbage cans were kept, just beyond the men's room of Stosh's Tavern on Elizabeth Avenue. They provided her with all she could drink and sometimes gave her money to buy herself a present, a scarf, a hat, a new pair of shoes. Letting them do it to her also did something to dull the loneliness and the feeling that her life was going nowhere, like her mother's life had gone, never realizing at the time that she didn't have to stay on that particular train.

When she was laid off at the factory in the middle of one of the cyclical recessions that show up as aberrant blips on financial charts, leaving the wreckage of unnumbered lives in their wake, she went to the tavern six nights a week instead of two—Sundays being kept for church, two masses and a devotion, morning, noon and night—and she accepted a little help with the rent, utilities and groceries now and then.

Because she wasn't altogether dumb, she finally figured it out that if she regularized these more or less casual bouts of passion with the working men who frequented Stosh's and other taverns, she could make two, three times the take-home pay she used to make at the condom factory. And no deductions.

She learned about the takings available in hotel lounges

and the better restaurant bars where businessmen whiled away their solitary hours between the appointments they often dreaded to keep, bending the knee and kissing asses for their livelihoods, picking up hotel hookers during the idle hours to prove to themselves that they were masters of the universe and not just grubby delivery boys and messengers.

Dotty changed her name to Diana right about then, having first intended to call herself Sheena in imitation of "Sheena of the Jungle"—a television series made in the fifties and often rerun in the years that followed—which she'd loved when she was a small child and the television set had been her only nonthreatening companion. But since she wasn't six feet tall, blonde and superbusty, the way the actress in those now-ancient melodramas had been, she twisted and turned it until she came up with Diana, the goddess of the hunt, a name, she said, that wasn't too exotic for her chunky Polish ass to carry but that still conveyed a certain message.

One Saturday night she went to some wrestling matches in Jersey City where she met a man who hired her services to celebrate Hulk Hogan's victory over the Masked Menace. Afterward, he tried to stiff her—in the financial meaning of the expression—calling her a Catholic Polack bitch and slapping her in the face. He got a razor cut across his throat, which took his life by way of reply.

Diana left for Hollywood that same night, deciding that the weather in New Jersey, though down around the teens, was bound to get too hot for her since she'd been seen leaving the arena with the john she later killed in self-defense by a vice cop named Mick Malone, who bore her a special grudge because she'd refused him any free samples.

First night out in Hollywood she paid off the bartender of a cocktail lounge on the Sunset Strip, the maître d' of a restaurant in Beverly Hills and the owner of a coffee shop in the Melrose district. She was back at work with scarcely a skipped beat, affirming once again that writers, whores, preachers and private dicks can do business from their hats.

She went to church on Sundays and confession some Saturdays. She made novenas when she wanted something very bad, but wasn't surprised or particularly disappointed when she didn't get what she prayed for. She volunteered some of her time to free clinics, hospitals and other such institutions and ended up a candy striper at the Angeles Hospice because people she knew were dying there.

Diana and Kenny Gotch had been street friends.

Diana was sitting on a cot in the nurses' lounge.

Mary Bucket was standing in the doorway with her arms folded under her breasts, head cocked to one side, the way she did, measuring you out, taking your temperature, gauging your blood pressure and general condition.

"You feeling all right?" Mary asked.

"Feeling a little better," Diana replied.

"Taking early shift after working all night might not be the smartest thing in the world," Mary said.

Diana looked up sharply, ready to fight, but saw that Mary wasn't making a judgment call, she was simply saying.

"I wasn't up late. I made it an early night."

Bucket wondered if an early night meant two customers, three customers or maybe only one. She knew that Diana wanted her to believe that she was a high-class escort girl, a sort of sexual surrogate, an unlicensed therapist treating dysfunctional men, an entrepreneur, a young businesswoman who wore silk teddys and lacy garter belts instead of tailored suits and sensible pumps, who carried a purse full of condoms instead of a briefcase filled with papers and a calculator, but what you are, Mary thought, regarding Diana's bowed head, is an uneducated beauty with a taste for the lowlife who got lucky in your trade when you came to Hollywood.

"You don't look good," Mary said.

"It was a shock."

"You've seen blood before."

"I knew Kenny. I knew him from the streets."

"I didn't know."

"He used to wear purple dresses and rhinestone shoes sometimes." She gave a short laugh of affectionate remembrance. "He called hisself Harriet LaRue when he dressed up. He couldn't make up his mind." She frowned slightly. Her face showed everything she was thinking and feeling. "Men and women, boys and girls, cats and dogs; he loved everybody and everything, just because he wanted to have somebody or something love him back."

Everybody had somebody else to blame for their weaknesses and sins, Mary thought. Everybody had reasons. Too great a capacity for love, unrequited, was prime.

"All that indiscriminate loving did him in," Mary said, hard as nails, not making a judgment but just stating a fact, having heard the self-pity in such sentimental songs before. "You ought to go on home."

Whistler was grinning foolishly, his eyes closed, as a breeze skipped through the door and brought with it the smell of distant salty seas and frangipani blossoms rotting on some exotic shore.

"That's a nineteen-seventy wind just blew through the door," Whistler said, his eyes still closed.

"No, that's Mike Rialto, wearing somebody's hospital greens," Bosco said.

Whistler's eyes snapped open as Rialto slipped into the booth.

"Can I have some of that?" Rialto asked, looking at the coffee pot.

Bosco shoved his own untasted mug closer and said, "You look like you need it."

Rialto grabbed the mug in both hands and drank it down, not caring how hot or black it might be.

"This is an act of mercy. I won't forget you," Rialto said.

"I'm not sure I want to ask," Whistler said, "but even though that blouse is an improvement over the horse blankets you usually wear, I've got to admit it's an unexpected fashion note."

"I just came from Angeles Hospice where a man died all over my face."

"Come again," Bosco said. He was sitting alongside Whistler and both were facing a frightened, sweating Mike Rialto.

"Puked his life's blood right in my face," Rialto said.

Whistler and Bosco both winced in sympathy.

"And that ain't the worst," Rialto said.

"What's the worst?"

"The poor sonofabitch died of AIDS."

Bosco and Whistler backed off an inch at the sound of the word as though they feared contamination.

"Is this somebody known to us?" Bosco asked.

"He used to be in the parade out there from time to time. Dropped in and out over the last seven, eight years. You ever know a kid named Kenny Gotch, sometimes dressed up and called hisself Harriet LaRue?"

"Wore purple dresses and rhinestone shoes?" Whistler said.

"That's the one."

"That she was a he?"

"Name of Kenny Gotch. From Chicago."

"Is that significant?" Whistler asked.

"Only that he died a long way from home."

"Was he a good friend?" Bosco asked.

"Only met him once," Rialto said, then added as an afterthought, "and he threw up on me," as though at once indignant and curious about why fate should have done such a thing to him.

"Are you all right?" Bosco asked, filling up Rialto's mug again.

"There was this nurse explained it all to me. About me not having any cuts or scrapes. How his blood never contacted my blood. How it was a million to one I was going to be perfectly all right. Then she told me to come in for a blood test in six months."

"It gets very complicated," Bosco said. "Gestation periods and windows of negative testing and things like that. You could get a clean bill and still have the HIV virus."

"What's that?" Rialto asked, as though Bosco was visiting some new horror upon him.

"Human immunodeficiency virus. It's what you get before you get AIDS, which is a very complex disease complex."

"I got lost there," Whistler said.

"I just mean the disease is complicated and there's several opportunistic diseases what can take you out once you get it."

Rialto was staring at Bosco as though the one-armed man

was a cat who'd suddenly decided to start talking. Even knowing that his nose was always stuck in some book—many requiring rare scholarship and understanding—it still came as a shock to many, even some who'd known him a long time, that Bosco, whose speech was slangy and ungrammatical, had such a wealth of information crowded into his head.

"Remind me not to come to you the next time I'm in need of comfort," Rialto finally said.

"I'm only saying," Bosco said.

"So, tell us how come you were visiting a person you never even met," Whistler said, trying to get Rialto's mind off the horrors of the disease he'd been exposed to and also because he was much intrigued by the thought that Rialto would ever commit an altruistic act.

Rialto recited the events that had dropped him beside Gotch's bed in Angeles at the moment of his death throes. And then he hesitated when he came to the point of it all, casting glances over each shoulder in turn before leaning closer to Whistler and Bosco—who leaned in closer as well, knowing that some great revelation was about to drop from Rialto's lips.

"Isaac Canaan ain't anywhere around, is he?" Rialto murmured.

"You see him?" Bosco whispered right back.

"He could be in the pisser or taking a catnap in a booth back there. He could be coming in through the kitchen even as we speak. The man's got a nose like a hound and ears like a fox. Some people say not only does he never sleep but he also reads minds."

"Don't make yourself crazy, Mike. Take a look," Whistler said, poking a thumb toward the window and the street beyond. "There's the man in question himself."

The other two turned to see.

Isaac Canaan was standing across the boulevard talking to a trio of the oldest of old-timers, Bitchie Boo, Dee-Dee and Miami Magic, the three Heavy Metal Fates, all decked out in crotch-length leather skirts and spun-aluminum wigs, doing the dozens with old Canaan, the kiddie vice cop, laying kisses on his cheek.

"So is it about Isaac that this Kenny Gotch delivers news?" Bosco asked.

"It's about the matter closest to his heart. The one they say keeps him awake through the long nights," Rialto said, still speaking softly, as though afraid that Canaan could hear them right through the plate glass, the width of the boulevard and a river of traffic away.

Like the passing of a veil across his face, Whistler's color paled and he ran his tongue across his lips, as though fighting back a sudden wave of nausea.

"This Kenny Gotch had news about Sarah?" he said, his voice scarcely audible.

"He told his relation, my friend Abe Forstman, that he knew the man who stole her."

"Did he say he was there with whoever did what they did before they murdered her?"

"I don't know about that. I didn't have a chance to ask him anything. He was dozing when I went into the room. I sat there talking to him for a while, hoping to wake him up. Then I nudged him a little bit to hurry it along and he rolled over and threw up in my face."

"So he actually never told you what he told this friend, Abe, of yours?" Whistler said, trying to pin things down. "Did he tell you anything?"

Rialto shook his head.

"Did he speak?"

Rialto shook his head again.

"So you don't really have anything to tell Isaac if you were thinking about telling Isaac anything?"

They all relaxed, falling back against the vinyl of the benches, as though a decision had been made. If you had nothing to say, you had nothing to say.

They all looked out the window again. Canaan was crossing the street, turning his head right and left, talking to this one and that one, well out of normal earshot. He was in his shirtsleeves and vest, his jacket over his arm on this fair day, but the hat, which few had ever seen removed and which even fewer knew concealed a yarmulke, the headwear of a pious man, was still firmly on his head.

"Should I tell him as much as Abe told me?" Rialto asked.

"There's only enough there to drive him crazy," Whistler said. "Take a piece of advice, just forget all about it. Just forget you ever heard Kenny Gotch's confession from your friend, Abe. I'm certainly not going to say anything to Isaac. You can bet on that," Whistler said, just as Canaan stepped up on the sidewalk. A couple of seconds later he was through the door.

"Say anything to Isaac about what?"

"About nothing," Whistler said. "I was just seeing if your famous ears were still working."

They didn't know what only Canaan knew; he had been losing his hearing over the years and had taught himself to read lips, little by little, which created the marvel of a man who seemed to hear much more at greater distances than ordinary men, even if he sometimes failed to answer a direct question up close because his mind was apparently elsewhere.

"I can hear a fly fart across the street above the traffic," Canaan said. "So, don't fool with me. Tell me who is this Kenny Gotch and what did he confess?"

"Jesus Christ, you're a number, you are," Bosco said. "You want coffee?"

"I want fresh and I want a clean mug."

"Something to eat?"

"A hamburger and beans."

"Burger on a bun?"

"Put the beans on the bun too," Canaan said, giving Rialto the old one-eye. "You just escape from a hospital for the mental, are you masquerading as a doctor or is this the latest costume for pimps?" he asked, finally deigning to remark upon his attire.

"Jeez, you don't have to talk to me that way, Sergeant Canaan," Rialto said. "I've had a bad day and insulting me just makes it worse."

"So, shove over and tell me which part of what I said was insulting."

"I got to go. I'm not feeling very well," Rialto said, hauling himself up out of the booth. "You sit down and enjoy yourself."

He lumbered out of the coffee shop and half-trotted down the boulevard and around the corner on the way to the parking lot in back.

"Wild hair?" Canaan said, folding his coat and putting it on the bench. "Something to do with what you ain't going to tell me?" He sat down beside his coat, folded his hands on the Formica, leaned forward and said, "So, Kenny Gotch?"

"Do you know a Kenny Gotch?"

"The name rings a bell."

"How about Harriet LaRue?"

"The twangy boy what wore purple dresses and rhinestone shoes?"

"I didn't know he was a twangy boy until Mike Rialto told me he was dead," Whistler said.

"You thought he was a sister?" Canaan asked.

"So did Bosco."

"Yes, it's true," Canaan said, "he had a sweet face and good legs. He told me once he didn't even have to shave them, just bleached them every now and then."

"Well, he's dead."

Canaan grunted softly as though he'd just taken a slight blow.

"Over to Angeles Hospice," Whistler went on.

"How'd you hear?" Canaan asked.

"Mike Rialto knew the kid's uncle or cousin, something like that, and stopped over as a favor. The kid had AIDS and not many visitors."

"Rialto did that?" Canaan said in a way that sounded as though he once again believed in miracles. "Visited somebody he didn't even know just to do a favor for a friend?"

"Mike's got a good heart," Bosco said, coming back with the coffee.

"I'm not saying he don't," Canaan said, "but such good deeds strike me as unusual."

"Hamburger coming," Bosco said, sitting down to join them.

"So, is this twangy boy dying what you didn't want to tell me about?" Canaan asked.

"This kind of weather," Whistler said, "days like we've been having, we didn't want to spoil it for you. We didn't want to have to tell you that you lost another one to the street out there."

Canaan had turned his head at mention of the weather and was looking out at the stroll, where the hookers, hustlers and grifters walked around with faces raised to the sun, as though the fineness of the day had escaped him. He grunted again and was turning back to ask yet another question, clearly unsatisfied with the answers or excuses he'd been given, when Shirley Hightower—who'd come to work while they'd been sitting there talking—arrived with his beef and bean sandwich and momentarily turned his attention elsewhere.

"This kind of weather," he said, as though reminding himself and everybody else that, once upon a time, it had been the weather that had lured them all away from home and, though degraded beyond recognition, it was the hope of days like this that lured them still, "is like a glass of vintage wine."

Everybody looked startled, a remark like that coming out of Canaan's sad mouth.

# 5

*It* was eleven o'clock in the morning and Chester Waltz was finally getting to work on the two new corpses that had greeted him when he'd come to work at the morgue of Angeles Hospice that morning.

He was a nervous man with fingers that looked as though they'd been stretched. When not otherwise occupied, one hand was always actively engaging the other one, his fingers in constant play. That habit and the habit of tilting his head and turning it sharply to one side or the other from time to time, along with the green hospital surgicals he always wore, down to the booties covering his shoes, gave him the look of a large praying mantis anticipating a meal.

How he'd ever gotten into waste management—which is what he called his work when trying to impress some bar fly of the flip and casual courage with which he approached his work among the dead—was something Waltz had never been able to figure out. One day he'd been a high school boy running small errands for the mortician down the block, the next he'd been doing night work over at the UCLA Medical School morgue, where fresh cadavers for the anatomy classes, with modified ice tongs in their ear holes, were stacked up on overhead conveyors in the fridge like so many sides of beef. The next he was working the morgue in this hospice, which was probably the most infectious morgue in the city.

He looked over the charts. The old woman taken by liver cancer didn't require much more than a quick bath; there'd be no autopsy required, since the surgeons had already been in there while she was still alive to see what they could see. But he intended to take special care of her, even combing and setting her hair a little, rouging up her cheeks a trifle, in case anybody from the family came along with the undertaker's assistants to pick up the body and maybe offered him a little gratuity for the nice way he'd treated their old mother, sister, aunt or whatever.

The other body, the young male lying on the channeled preparation table, the bloody one who'd vomited up his lungs, the Karposi's sarcoma, the AIDS, would require gloves and a Plexiglas full-face mask and extra garments, making certain that not one drop of blood or other bodily fluid landed on his skin, even though he had no cuts and abrasions.

At first he thought he'd just bag it up and send it on to county for preparation, since they had laid down protocols for the handling of AIDS victims that they were better able to follow than he was at the hospice. Then he thought he'd at least wash him down, do them the favor, put the technicians in his debt. You could never tell when you'd need a favor in return.

He could see that most of the blood was all over the body's chin, neck and chest, now that he'd removed the folded towel that had partially obscured it. It looked as though somebody'd painted him with a big brush.

Waltz put on the necessary gear, picked up the hand spray and started washing the body down, making sure the fan of water struck the body at a shallow angle to reduce the chance of spatter. He never noticed the little cage of steel imbedded in the hollow of Kenny Gotch's throat.

# 6

*There* are towns that are promises, seductions, dreamscapes; blackboards written on and then erased so many times that they wear a haze of chalky gray. Very few people bother to read the stories that have been wiped away; they're too busy writing their own stories, which they sincerely believe will last a thousand years.

Bosco Silverlake knew and remembered all the stories and understood the consequences of retelling them and dwelling upon them.

He'd once loved a baby prostitute and had lost his arm to the blast from a shotgun in the hands of the child's pimp. But that hadn't been the truly crippling wound. The fact that she'd cried about the pimp he'd killed with a blow of his uninjured fist was the thing that broke his heart. So, if ever he was asked outright how he'd lost the arm, he'd say he lost it in Nam or under a truck or in a drunken brawl in a

Tijuana brothel, for as far as he was concerned the truth was a story best left untold.

If he were asked for his advice he would advise one and all to take things as they came and leave the worst of their stories unremembered and untold.

Canaan had finished his burger and beans on a bun, washed down with three cups of coffee, and was back on the stroll trolling for information, looking for sinners to be saved.

Bosco caught Whistler staring out the window and it was clear that the beauty of the day had lost its savor.

"No more, no more," he heard Whistler murmur.

Bosco went over with the pot, knowing that Whistler was saying no more pain for his friend, Canaan; no more pain for himself.

"You want to leave this one alone," Bosco said. "You start it up all over again, with nothing but a mention from a dying man to a relative who maybe didn't hear so good and you'll fall back into the obsession. You'll be at it day and night. The sun won't shine no more. You'll become a ghost like old Canaan out there."

Whistler didn't reply, but just stared at him as though wondering from what source Bosco drew his immunity to the poisonous world in which they lived.

"I'm telling you," Bosco said, "there's no good in it."

"Are you going to tell me the one about how it won't bring Sarah back?"

"I'd never say anything that dumb or that smart," Bosco said. "If I thought you could find the one who done it after all this time, I'd go looking with you. If I thought you'd find him on the word of a dead man and prove to yourself, without a doubt, that he was the one who done it, I'd hold your coat while you cut the sonofabitch up into one-inch cubes and put him through a meat grinder. I ain't one to preach against vengeance. I'm just saying you got nothing. I'm just saying ten years have passed. I'm just saying you should take the advice you gave Rialto and forget all about it."

"Sarah was stolen and murdered," Whistler said, separating each word as though carving it in stone.

"I understand what you're saying and I can imagine what you're feeling, thinking about what they put that baby through before they killed her."

"It's hard to get it out of your heart," Whistler said.

"I know. It's the worst. There are things humans do to other humans worse than murder, because when you're dead there's an end to memories and pain," Bosco said.

Whistler pushed his coffee mug back a few inches, signaling his departure.

"Going somewhere?" Bosco asked.

"Taking a walk. Maybe take a drive."

"Going where?"

"Maybe down Sunset to the Coast Highway. Maybe up the highway to Trancas and beyond."

"You'll only bump your nose into Oxnard and Ventura."

"Maybe I'll go over to Griffith Park and rent a horse."

"You'll only get mugged. Somebody'll jump out of a tree and smash you."

"Maybe I'll go out to Forest Lawn Cemetery."

"Well, you might find some peace and quiet there," Bosco said, grudgingly.

Jeanne Millholme had nervous hands and a way of slapping at a lock of hair that insisted on falling over her right eye. She was crowding fifty, her figure still very trim, but her neck and the backs of her hands were beginning to turn into crumpled tissue paper. She'd never been a pretty woman, but there was a nervous intensity about her that could've easily been misinterpreted by a man as sexual agitation, which made her exceptionally attractive.

The man sitting opposite her looked to be about twenty years younger than she until he moved into the slanting morning light and the network of lines around his eyes and the little purse marks at the lips showed up like small nets of scars.

He was good-looking, his dark, neatly trimmed beard bracketing his mouth and underlining a smooth white face adding to the illusion of youth, or, rather, agelessness. His black hair was pulled back and caught up with a twist of scarlet cord, giving his face the drawn look of a saint under torture. His black eyes had curious flecks of amber in them, which gave him a compelling stare. It was surprising how few people caught on that the special effect was molded into the contact lenses he wore to correct his vision. He dressed in black, emphasizing his slender build, intensifying an air of mystery about himself. His gestures, in contrast to hers, were graceful and languid.

His name was Raymond Raditski, the blade-nosed, ax-jawed grandson of a Montenegran mountain man whose son, Raymond's father, had emigrated to America, settled in Dayton, Ohio, married and had a son just at the right time for that son to grow up and have his ass dragged into Vietnam.

A war for everybody. This war, which became the con merchant's war where eighty thousand grunts put their asses on the line in jungles so rank trees fed upon trees while four hundred and fifty thousand support troops fucked the fragile sloe-eyed native girls, traded smoke, dope and choke, and complained that the movies flown in for their entertainment were not fresh off the griddle of La-La Land.

The Vietnam War bred crazy men with delayed stress syndrome, a stranger, more complex dysfunction than the one they called shell shock back in World War I and battle fatigue in World War II and the Korean Police Action. It bred druggies and deserters, pushers and thieves, rapists, sadists and murderers. It bred misologists, who hated reason, argument or enlightenment, misogynists, who hated women, and misanthropists, who hated all of mankind.

Self-indulgence was Raditski's only religion, the con a way of life, and life itself a bitter joke worth nothing but pennies.

He didn't call himself Raymond Raditski.

A black attaché case, discreetly imprinted with the name BENNU RAHAB in gold, sat on the floor near the chair in which he sat.

*Bennu* was taken from the ancient Egyptian religion, the name given the soul of Ra, the supreme deity, and guide of the gods in the underworld, identified with the phoenix, symbol of immortality. *Rahab* was the raging monster, the dragon of darkness, the crooked serpent formed by the hand of God as noted in the Book of Job.

It was a conceit, an amusement not much different than the film fashion for names like Touch, Rock, Tab and Lance that once swept the ranks of movie hopefuls.

Between Raymond Raditski, Dayton, and Bennu Rahab, Hollywood, there'd been a dozen aliases, half a dozen countries, a hundred and one schemes and scams, everything from blackmail, procuring, child stealing and burglary to contract murder.

They were sitting in Jeanne Millholme's studio, a sunny slice of the living room crowded with an easel, taboret, sketch pads, paints and vases filled with brushes.

There was a mummified monkey's paw and a human skull painted with complicated ornamentation sitting on the coffee table between them.

Photographs of a child, a boy of six or seven, in frames of silver and leather and wood were lying everywhere, on counters and tabletops.

Beautifully executed paintings, disturbing visions of women beleaguered by serpents, exotic animals and leering demons holding threatening spearlike cocks in their hands, small children with arms outstretched in supplication flying backward through the troubled air into black vortexes, were hung on the walls and piled against one another on the floor.

Her eyes flickered from paintings to photographs to Rahab's face without pause.

He was laying down a series of four-by-five photographs, portraits of the artist.

"These are important to me, you know," she said. "The one I choose is going to be used on the brochure announcing my one-woman show."

"I understand," he said. "Take a look."

She slapped the lock of hair out of her face and bent over to examine the photos, the lock falling right back into place. It took her awhile to study them all.

"Do you retouch photographs?" she asked.

"I can if you want, but most people don't like the effect. It can look a little phony."

"Have you got a loupe with you?" she asked.

He picked up the case and placed it on the table, snapped the locks and opened it up. It was fitted with sponge rubber carved out to accommodate a camera back, auxiliary lenses, a portable telephone and other gadgets.

She leaned forward and reached out a finger to a collection of small tools and knives.

"Please, don't," he said.

She pulled her hand back.

"What are they?" she asked.

"Tools to repair my cameras."

He plucked a jeweler's loupe from its tiny cradle of foam and handed it to her.

She slapped at her hair without effect, placed the loupe to her eye and bent over to study the first of the portraits. He studied the top of her head with a look of quiet speculation.

When she straightened up she stared at him directly and said, "Did you retouch this photo?"

"What do you mean?"

"Someone's marked it up. The mouth is too sad and the eyes are full of horror."

Keeping his eyes on her until the last second, he took the loupe from her fingers, placed it to his own eye and bent over. He was a long time at it, though he was paying no attention to what he was looking at.

"Those are your eyes and your mouth, just as they are. Why would I want to mark up your photo?"

"It could be someone else. Do you develop your own negatives?" she asked.

"Usually I have them developed at the photo lab."

"Well, then," she said, as though he'd made her point and confirmed her suspicions.

"Why would anyone at the photo lab want to retouch your photograph?" he asked.

"That's something to wonder about, isn't it?"

She was definitely a Loony Tune he thought, out there on the edge.

"We can have another sitting if you like," he said.

"There'd be a charge?"

"Not as much as for the first sitting, but something. There are costs. Material and my time."

"Besides, even if I'm imagining things, the mouth is too sad and the eyes too haunted," she said, repeating the phrase almost exactly as she had just seconds before.

"I asked you to smile but you wouldn't," he reminded her.

She slapped at the lock of hair, as though impatient with him for putting the blame for the melancholy portraits on her.

Was it just common vanity that prompted her displeasure? Just that she wanted to look younger, fresher, more beautiful than she really was?

"I'll try to smile at the next sitting," she said. "And will you develop and print them yourself this time?"

He hesitated. "If you like."

"Indulge me in this. I'd just rather have you do them yourself."

"Why's that?"

"I'd just rather nobody had the chance to have pictures of me around that I didn't want them to have."

He was about to ask her why she thought a technician in a photographic lab would want pictures of her but thought better of it. He recognized free-floating, indeterminate paranoia when he came across it. He'd used it to turn a quick buck in a con game more than once.

"You think I'm unduly suspicious?" she asked.

He shrugged.

"This isn't the first time someone's tried to get pictures of me."

"It's happened before?"

"Oh, yes. Pictures of people can be useful to other people."

"In what way?"

She suddenly smiled, as though all they were doing was having a playful conversation. "You know some tribes in Mexico and the Americas still believe that taking a picture of them steals their souls. Do you understand?"

"Yes, I understand," he said, reaching across the table and touching her hand.

41

She pulled it away and slapped at the lock of hair as though wanting to slap his face.

"Don't," she said.

"I didn't mean to offend you," he said, leaning back in his chair.

"I'm not going to pay you now. I'll pay you when everything's been done to my satisfaction. Okay?"

If he'd been looking for innuendo she was spreading plenty of it around. "Ah," he said noncommittally, and smiled.

"You really can't expect me to."

"No, no, of course not."

She stood up and went to stand against a tall chest covered with framed photographs of the child. There was another photograph on the wall alongside her head.

He had the feeling that she wanted him to make some comment. "Who's the boy in the picture?" he asked.

"He was my son."

"He was?"

"He's dead." The lock of hair was in her eyes again but she didn't slap it away; she stood stock still, staring at him.

"I'm sorry," he said. "Tell me about the painted skull," he said, as though changing the subject because he was sensitive to her pain.

"I got it when I lived in Mexico," Jeanne said. "Have you been to Mexico?"

He stiffened, his eyelids fluttered—she would have sworn it—but he was trained to wariness and dissimulation—you could bet on that—and he recovered in an instant, before anyone but the most discerning would have noticed any change.

"Just the border towns," he said. "Tijuana, Nogales."

"Never in the interior? Never around Chihuahua?"

"Is that where you lived?"

"No. That was just the nearest city of any size. I went there twice a year to do my shopping. We lived, my son and I, higher in the mountains among the Indians. They brought me the head."

They stared at each other, both aware that there was a subtext to the conversation going on between them, the way people about to make love or kill one another speak on several levels at once.

"I'd painted the skull of a deer I'd found," she said. "After that they brought me quite a few animal skulls to be painted. Ferrets and jaguar and deer and wildcats. Asked me to paint them with symbols. They were followers of Espiritismo."

"Oh, yes," he said, and smiled, understanding a little more now, her fear of having her soul captured in a photograph and altered by someone out to do her harm.

"Later they brought me some heads for myself, which I decorated and sold in the tourist shops when I went into Chihuahua."

"You say they brought you the heads? Before you said they brought you the skulls," he pointed out mildly. But there was an edge to his voice, as though he were a schoolteacher expecting a student to be precise in her recitation.

"After a while they would bring me the heads when they were still fairly fresh. I'd boil off as much of the flesh as I could, then bury them in a bucket of quicklime."

"That head, the human head, was it brought to you fresh?"

She hesitated for a long moment, turning her face away but looking at him from the corner of her eye.

"It was the head of a man who'd committed a terrible crime. He was executed by the villagers."

"Without a trial?"

She smiled, still looking at him sidelong.

"They knew he was guilty," she said.

"Of what?"

She hesitated, then turned her head away, slapping at the unruly lock of hair.

"He was a child stealer," she said. "He stole children and sold them across the border. They brought me his head. I couldn't refuse it. There was a great deal of meaning in the gift because my son had been stolen."

"You said he was dead."

"They found the bodies of children along the road. The child stealers had killed them and thrown them aside. Perhaps the children were slowing down their escape once the child stealers understood that the Indians were after them. The animals had gotten to the bodies."

"Was there more than one child stealer? More than the one the Indians beheaded?"

"There were more than one that gathered up the children. The buyer was elsewhere."

"Did anyone tell the authorities?"

"What could they do? What would they want to do? They were stealing Indian children out of the hills. That wouldn't have been worth more than a shrug of the shoulders. Besides . . ."

"Yes?"

"The Indians had killed one of them. They were afraid that would bring the authorities down on them. These were simple people, you understand. They understood right and wrong, good and evil, but they didn't understand courts and judges and trials."

He put away the loupe and closed the case, then stood up. "I'm sorry about the portraits. We'll do better next time."

He took three steps toward the door, then paused.

"Among the Indians, did you believe in Espiritismo?" he asked. "Did you believe in the witchcraft?"

She widened her eyes and caught her breath.

"If I were you I'd make certain to burn any hair left in your comb and brush after you've used them," he said. "I would burn any fingernail parings and cover the mirrors."

His mouth was quirked in a mocking smile as he advised her of ways to protect herself against the malevolence of magic.

His attaché case buzzed, startling them both enough to make them laugh. "My telephone. I'll take it outside," he said.

After he left she began to tremble. She didn't know how much she'd given away throwing out the bait, trying to entrap him into making some revealing comment. She was still not absolutely certain that after ten years she'd found the man she'd been hunting for. There was a way to be absolutely certain that he was the child buyer. The man the Indians hacked to death had told them of the spider mark between the child buyer's buttocks.

Whistler didn't go to Trancas or Griffith Park or Forest Lawn Cemetery.

He drove over to the Angeles Hospice in his old beat-up Chevy, parked it at the back of the lot and went inside where visitors presented themselves before going in to see the dying.

Whistler took one of the molded plastic chairs along the wall in the reception area and sat down. Nobody paid him any attention for a long time, and then an old woman sitting two chairs down touched his sleeve and said, "I haven't seen you here before."

"I've never been here before."

"My name's Rose Magiore."

"My name's Whistler."

"How do you do? Who did you come to visit?"

"Who?"

"Mother? Father? Your wife?" she asked.

"Nobody. I've got nobody here."

"I understand."

"Do you?" It startled him that she should say that because he certainly didn't understand what had brought him here, unless it was the overpowering desire that had suddenly come over him, sitting there in Gentry's, to do something about this Gotch's revelation, anything, even if it was only picking lint.

"You'd be surprised," Mrs. Magiore said. "People come here for other reasons besides visiting friends or relatives."

"They do? Would you give me an idea what those other reasons could be?"

"Well, for instance, I've met one or two who came just to see if they'd be scared by being so close."

"So close to sick people?"

"So close to people dying. You know it's a big mystery to most of us nowadays, the whole business of dying. When I was a little girl people in my neighborhood were buried from the house. The body in the coffin was put in the living room and the oldest son or daughter sat the vigil all night. People kissed the corpse on the forehead. Even on the lips. You don't see a lot of that anymore. And you don't get as many wakes and funerals. People are cremated and stuck in a jar. No fuss. Maybe a memorial service a year down the line. Maybe not."

"You think it was better the old way?" he asked, really wanting to know what she thought.

"I think maybe it made it easier on the people left behind, you know what I mean? Maybe it taught us not to be so afraid of it." Then she thought about it and said, "Maybe not."

"Who are you here to see?"

"My husband. He's got a cancer. My two children are in there with him right now. One of them came in from Florida and the other one came in from Texas. I want them to be able to say whatever they want to say to him without me being around."

"What do you think they'll say that they wouldn't want you to hear?"

"They're both boys. How would I know what boys got to talk about, they wouldn't want a mother to hear?" She looked at him and smiled. It gave her face an impish look.

Whistler smiled and she patted his hand.

"Some people find a lot of comfort just sitting here. Maybe one of these days you'll feel like going inside and talking to somebody who hasn't got anybody to visit them."

"A person can do that?"

"There's a lot who volunteer."

Two big Italian-looking men came into the waiting room from the corridor. They were in their late fifties. They looked like lost children. Their father was dying in a strange place and it frightened them. They looked at Whistler oddly, as though searching for signs of fatal disease.

When their mother introduced them, they shook hands almost shyly, as though not wishing to intrude on the grief that Whistler might be carrying around with him, and then one of them said they'd wait outside in the car while Mrs. Magiore went in to see her husband.

After Mrs. Magiore and her sons were gone, Whistler sat

down again and then popped right up when a nurse in greens and a white tee shirt, with the head of Popeye printed on it, came striding over.

She was short and stocky, but the way she carried herself—the way she stopped in front of him, just a half inch inside his space, looking up, measuring him, judging him, as though he wasn't just a stranger but somebody there to do her an injury or a service—made her seem tall and graceful, as sure of herself as any woman Whistler had ever met.

"You're not visiting anyone," Mary said, making a statement of it.

"No."

"You're not just curious." That almost became a question, but not quite.

He shook his head.

"You didn't come to volunteer your services?" she asked.

"No."

"So what's your business?"

"You had a patient died today."

"We had two."

"His name was Kenny Gotch."

"AIDS," she said.

"That's right."

"Did you know him?"

"No."

"So, what's your interest?"

"I was asked to come by a friend," he said.

"Are you a friend of the man who was here when he died?" she said. Again it hardly qualified as a question. She was the type, Whistler thought, who didn't really ask questions. She'd already made up her mind about most things. All she sought was confirmation.

"I know him."

"He ran out of here without leaving his name, address and telephone number."

"He was scared."

"We'd like to follow up. We don't want somebody running around too afraid to get tested for HIV."

"That's part of why I'm here."

"What did he tell you?"

"Just that Kenny Gotch sprayed blood all over him with his dying breath."

"Did he tell you that Kenny spoke to him before he threw up and died?"

"Does it matter?"

She shook her head. "Last words. Everybody's curious about last words. One man asked for a ham on rye. His stomach was almost eaten away and he was asking for a ham on rye. Another time a man said, 'Baby Girl in the fifth at Hollywood Park, on the nose.' "

"Hallucinating?"

"There was a horse by the name of Baby Girl running that afternoon. It seemed like an omen, you know what I mean?"

"Did you lay a bet?"

She made a wry face. "What do they call it? A cee note? I bet a hundred dollars on the nose with our friendly bookie who works in the morgue."

"How'd Baby Girl do?"

"I'd like to say she came in dead last. It was worse than that."

"How could it be worse?"

"She came in second."

"That's worse," he said, and they both laughed.

"So you tell your friend he's probably got nothing to worry about but better safe than sorry," she said. "You want a cup of coffee while I explain the risks involved?"

"I could use something to eat. Can I take you somewhere?"

"You want to buy me lunch?" She grinned, the corners of her mouth tipping up so sharply she looked like a pretty Halloween pumpkin head.

Funny-looking woman, Whistler thought.

"The commissary food's good here," she said, "but I could use a change of scene. Nothing fancy. It won't bend your wallet."

"Hell, there's always plastic."

"I better get a jacket."

"It's warm out."

"I don't want to go walking around outside dressed like this."

She stuck up a finger, telling him to wait, and marched away like a drum majorette leading the high school band.

She took longer than a minute.

She came back wearing a peach linen jacket and white slacks. She still wore the Popeye tee shirt, a fashion statement. She'd changed her nurse's shoes to low-heeled peach-colored pumps.

"If you're going to buy me lunch, I should know your name," she said.

"Everybody calls me Whistler."

"That's not your name."

"It's the one I answer to."

"Like a rock star? 'Sting?' 'Prince?' 'Madonna?' That's okay. What do you do for a living?"

"I'm what you'd call a private eye."

"I wouldn't call you a private eye," she said, smiling playfully again.

"What would you call me?"

"I don't know, but I wouldn't call you a private eye. That sounds old hat."

"That's me, just an old hat."

They were outside. She tucked her hand in the crook of his elbow and tried to match her stride to his. "We can walk," she said. "It's just down the block. Hey, take smaller steps. You got a pair of legs on you."

"What's your name?" Whistler asked.

"Bucket. Mary Bucket. Ain't that a hell of a note, a name like mine?" she said. "Mary Bucket. I don't want to tell you the rhymes some smart-ass kids in grammar school made out of that."

"How about the high school kids?"

"By the time we got to high school, they'd learned better. I'm small, but I'm mighty."

"I was going to say."

"I'm not scaring you, am I?" she asked.

"Not much," Whistler said, wondering what she was offering.

"Well, that's good. I wouldn't want to scare you off."

# 7

*Kilroy* was driving west along the sweeping curves of Sunset Boulevard in a little red rag-top Mazda two-seater, a suitable car for an underpaid associate professor, a suitable car for a man with red hair that could take the wind, another mask in a collection of masks he wore. It was a very unhandy car for cruising Westwood Boulevard, teeming with students, pretending to be one of them, a youngster without a worry in the world except getting a rock or getting laid. For that masquerade he had a curly blond wig and a black 1965 Chevrolet convertible with red leather seats.

He also owned a vintage Bentley, a classic Thunderbird, a Corvette and a three-quarter-scale reproduction of the famous Cord runabout. They were all garaged in a barn up against a hillside in Agoura on ten acres he had been given by a patron. Ten acres, a house and outbuildings, belated payment for services rendered, extracted when he became old enough and strong enough to assert his will over a very, very old man.

He collected automobiles. He also collected rare books on ancient religions and master prints of torture, all carefully locked away in the house he occupied on weekends, holidays and vacations.

The spread was taken care of by a live-in handyman, a kid by the name of Sultan, who looked to be about twenty but could have been much younger. He had the brown body and the bleached white hair of a surfer or a cowhand who went around without wearing a hat and eyes like a streetwise ancient high on crack. But he never went to the beach and he never rode a horse and he hadn't been on the streets in a year. He stayed on the acres in Agoura and never strayed.

The few people living nearby and the merchants in the village thought there was something very odd about Sultan. Though affable enough, he never had much to say, and there was about his halting manner the look of someone lost in dreams.

He was simpleminded, naturally flawed or somehow brain damaged by drugs, abuse or other cause, part of the arrangement with the man who gave gifts but who had always tried to extract a benefit for himself, one way or another.

During the week Kilroy occupied a modest condominium on the fringes of Westwood, from which he ventured forth on weekend nights, before driving to Agoura, often not alone.

The morning had been ill spent and irritating, his weekly seminar on early religions, with an emphasis on that one known as *la vecchia religione,* the old faith that predated the Druids by several thousand years, being even more sparsely attended than usual, and those few sprawled in the seats so inattentive that they might as well have leapt out of the windows through which they stared, freeing themselves for the adventures their young blood craved.

As he approached the San Diego Freeway he thought about the crowded highway he'd encounter when he passed Will Rogers State Park and took the long plunge to the Pacific Coast Highway, Santa Monica State Beach and the sea. No telling how long it would take him to beat his way north to Malibu and beyond.

He swept down the on ramp of the freeway going north and minutes later picked up the Ventura Freeway heading west again, having decided to take the back way through Agoura, making a stop at his house and then going southwest past Lake Sherwood on 23 and then on south two or three miles to the Coast Highway, where he could ease along in the light traffic moving toward Trancas and the southern beaches.

He pulled up into the gravel courtyard in front of the ranch house about one o'clock in the afternoon.

Sultan came out of the cool shadows of the barn to see

who had arrived. When he saw it was Kilroy, he raised a languid hand, then turned away, returning to whatever solitary pursuit occupied him there.

Kilroy stood for a moment staring into the blackness into which Sultan had disappeared, then went into the house to change his clothes.

# 8

*The* lunchroom Mary Bucket took Whistler to was like herself, plain but very pretty, inexpensive but not cheap, everything up-front, no secrets, easygoing but not shallow; value for money all the way along the line.

"The chicken salad sandwich on sour dough is something you won't forget," she said.

He let her decide for him. The waitress went away to get two chicken salad sandwiches and two glasses of mint tea.

"This'll be the healthiest meal you've had in a month," she said.

He was amused. "How can you tell?"

"Your complexion's none too good. You're getting a little crepey around the eyes. Poor nutrition. You don't exercise. You're a man without a woman. Your house is probably a mess. You probably let the laundry pile up until it starts to smell."

"You think I'd be better off with a wife?"

"You'd probably be eating better."

"A little sexism there?"

"Nothing wrong with a little sexism as long as it doesn't stick its nose in where it's not wanted. I won't argue the finer details but, pound for pound, you might be stronger than I am but I could probably keep going farther and last longer than you could. Also I'm undoubtedly neater and cleaner than you."

"Hey!"

"Fastidious. That's what I meant to say. More fastidious."

The sandwiches and iced tea came.

"While we're eating this healthy food," Whistler said, "I suppose it'd be better not to talk about what we're going to talk about."

"It won't bother me if it won't bother you," she said, taking a big bite out of her sandwich.

"How do you do it, day after day?" Whistler asked.

"How do *you* do what *you* do day after day?" she countered.

"I see hard things now and then but not every day."

"You mean all the dying? Well, that's not the hardest thing in my business."

"What's the hardest?"

"Seeing the hope fade away. You think our opposing thumb or the ability to laugh and blush is what makes us human? It's hope that makes us human. When that disappears you might as well jump in the hole and let them hit you in the face with a shovel."

Whistler thought of Isaac Canaan and how the soul in his eyes—because wasn't that what she was talking about here?—seemed to have faded away, slowly but surely, ever since his niece had been mutilated and murdered.

Rahab had learned some tricks in his years of making his living on the edge by illegal and violent means.

There were times when you broke through to the killing ground, did your work and then stayed behind to forage. More often it was better not to linger too long, not to delay that extra minute or extra five, daring time to catch up with you and catch you red-handed.

It was better to go away and then return, an innocent bystander, one of many spectators in the crowd, someone who had just happened near or on the crime scene, finishing up what had to be finished up as though you were another person altogether.

He knew what the world, by and large, didn't seem to know—or knew but didn't act upon.

Each of us was not one but many. Nam had taught him that, revealed his many faces, many hearts, many minds to himself, and he came to understand that saint and sinner, Christ and devil, could occupy the same body at the same time.

Jeanne Millholme was clearly running wild, her many selves at war, focused about the loss of her child down in Mexico. Ten years ago, she'd said?

He remembered that filthy, sweaty, heart-breaking venture, buying children from the child stealers and transporting them north across the border to be sold. A child, boy or girl between six and twelve years of age delivered on some pervert's doorstep, twenty-five hundred dollars COD back then, no questions asked.

He remembered Harry Atlanta, hacked into stew meat by the machetes of a backward tribe that had pursued the kidnappers of their children down the jungle trails, catching Harry but not catching Jack Gaggle and Red Monty, who'd left the bodies of children behind to slow down their pursuers.

He remembered how they'd arrived where he waited with only half a dozen in their hunting bag, tied together with cords looped from neck to neck, frightened children well past crying who'd stared at him with great round eyes, seeing in him a savior that must be obeyed as they made the journey north across the border, tucked away in the false bottom of a truck that forded the Rio Grande in sight of border guards who'd been paid to turn their eyes the other way.

Even if her hints and glances meant that she suspected him of being the child buyer, had sought him out and hunted him down somehow over ten long years, she was so captured by other aspects of herself that she was lost to madness, more common in this world than anyone suspected, vulnerable, curious, open to persuasion and manipulation.

She might have sought him out to do him harm, but he'd have her in the end because he could call up the many who lived inside his shell at will—killer, clown, con and lover— and give her anything she wanted, the mate she dreamed of even when she didn't know she dreamed.

around the corner near the service alley. He left his briefcase in the car but slung his camera around his neck. It was an expensive Nikon wrapped in black electrician's tape not only to protect it from damage in the manner of combat and documentary photographers but to lessen its value in the eyes of gonnifs on the prowl for an easy snatch. It was also a passport to ordinarily inaccessible places; the camera and his manner declaring him to be authorized to go anywhere.

He knew that most institutions prided themselves on security, but except for those buildings that housed or accommodated people who might be terrorist targets or repositories of great secrets, the average building or part of a building posted with warnings against unauthorized trespass or entry was easily penetrated. All you had to do was think black.

Rahab thought black and walked down the service alley alongside the Angeles Hospice. Walked through the door at the top of the ramp, where the canned and sealed medical waste was delivered to trucks once a week. Strode silently along the passageway behind the nurses' station to Kenny Gotch's room, arriving there swiftly and unerringly because he'd been there before.

Now he was back to gather up Kenny Gotch's pitiful belongings.

The room was empty, the body gone, the bed stripped down to the mattress with its browning stain of blood.

There were no cops. The room wasn't under surveillance and wasn't sealed off as a crime scene. The little finger blade, the valvulotome that had stuck in Gotch's throat and come away from his gloved finger, had apparently not yet been discovered. The concealing towel had done the job.

The closet door was open. He went through Kenny Gotch's pockets as quickly and efficiently as a master dip and found them cleaned. He saw the shopping bag on the floor against the wall, stooped and fingered through it, picked it up and used the window going out, thinking black.

"Was it good?" Mary Bucket asked.

"It was good," Whistler said.

"You mind if we go? I've got a ton of work piled up on my desk. You pay at the register."

Mary waited at the door, an old-fashioned girl out on a date, as he paid the bill and then held the door open for her. Whistler noticed that the dramatic-looking character in black, with the red cord securing his ponytail, was gone.

When they were outside, walking back to Angeles Hospice, her arm tucked back into the crook of his arm, matching him stride for stride, she said, "I feel like I'm drowning in paperwork sometimes. You?"

"I work out of my hat and there's no room for paperwork in my hat."

"On the subject," she said. "You happen to know your friend's address and telephone number?"

"You going to mention that he was in the room in your report? What has a visitor in a patient's room when the patient died have to do with a medical report or a death certificate?"

"Nothing. I just want to cover my ass just in case."

"In case of what?"

"In case I get hit in the face with a one-in-a-million chance somebody asks a one-in-a-million question."

"It's none of my business but it seems to me that Kenny Gotch hemorrhaged and died. There's a chance you could be making yourself a lot of unnecessary trouble if you write it up that an unannounced and unnoticed visitor got past you into the room."

"I'll think about it," she said, "but I'd better have the information just in case."

"Well, I don't know his address and telephone number offhand. I'll have him give you a call and you can sort it out between you."

She was grinning up at him.

"What?" he asked.

"My God, but you're a cautious man."

They'd broken stride, were walking along mismatched, bumping hips and elbows. She kept on grinning and did a little skip like the one Dopey made famous in *Snow White and the Seven Dwarfs,* the half-stride of a marching man getting back in step.

# 9

*Abe* Forstman, wearing a sweater and a jacket, brushing back the few strands left on his balding head, was standing at the reception desk when Whistler got back to the hospice with Mary Bucket. The volunteer at the reception desk, a sweet-faced, gray-haired woman, saw them coming and said something to Forstman who turned, smiling tentatively, as though wondering about how he should act in this place.

The volunteer frowned, showing her distress now that Forstman's back was turned, and beckoned Mary with her chin.

They conferred for a minute and Mary returned, sticking out her hand to shake.

"Are you Mr. Forstman?" she asked.

"Yes, I am. Are you the lady I talked to on the phone?"

"Yes, I'm nurse Mary Bucket."

"You wanted me to sign some papers and pick up Kenny's belongings."

"There's been a mix-up about Mr. Gotch's things," she said. "I'm afraid they've been temporarily misplaced."

Forstman smiled wryly, as though commenting that such things were no more than should be expected nowadays. "Temporarily?"

"Somebody could've put them someplace where patient belongings aren't usually put. We have a lot of part-time volunteers. Employees come and go."

"You don't think somebody could've come along and stolen his things?" Whistler asked.

"I don't think Mr. Gotch had much anyone would want to steal," Mary said.

Mary turned to the desk and murmured something to the gray-haired volunteer, who walked over to a filing cabinet. They all watched her as though they couldn't speak again until she returned. When she came back she handed Mary a sheet of paper.

"Here's a copy of the inventory," Mary said, offering it to Forstman.

He scanned it for a minute, then shrugged.

"Can I have a look?" Whistler said.

For a second it looked like Mary was about to protest, no doubt ready to claim the right of privacy for the dead Kenny Gotch, but Forstman handed it over before she had the chance.

Every item, no matter how insignificant, had been inventoried. Besides the clothing Kenny Gotch had worn when admitted to the hospice, they'd even counted the three handkerchiefs in his possession and a half-used book of matches. He'd also had a ring of three keys, thirty-two dollars in bills in a silver money clip and eighteen cents in change, a checkbook, an address book, a little twenty-five-cent notebook, a ballpoint pen and a wallet.

"Do you know if there were any credit cards in the wallet?" Whistler asked Mary.

"Credit cards? Do people go around stealing the credit cards of dead people?" Forstman asked.

"You heard the saying about people stealing the pennies off a dead man's eyes?"

"I never understood that."

"Well, it means what it says. There's people who'd steal anything they can get their hands on."

Mary looked at him without expression. "If there's no mention of credit cards, there probably weren't any credit cards. My personnel are trained to inventory everything," she said.

"Well, sure, but you have a lot of part-time volunteers. Employees come and go," Whistler said, trying not to make it sound too smart-alecky.

Mary gave him a sharp, almost angry glance.

"There's no mention of a driver's license either," Whistler

said, clearly meaning that nobody lives in California without a driver's license.

Mary took the list out of Whistler's hand and gave it back to Mr. Forstman. "Everything belonging to your cousin is listed here. As you can see, Mr. Forstman, your cousin didn't have much of value," Mary said.

"Well, thirty-two dollars and eighteen cents . . . ," he said, vaguely.

"I'll look into the possibility of reimbursement if you want to make a claim," she said.

"No, no," Forstman said. "I was just thinking out loud. Why would anybody want to steal thirty-two dollars and eighteen cents? My God, to think there are such people," Forstman said. He gave Whistler a look—suddenly very sharp, very perceptive—and said, "You don't mind my asking, who are you? You a security man here?"

"I'm a friend of the friend of yours who came to visit your cousin—"

"My wife's cousin—"

"—and happened to be here when Gotch died."

"—three times removed. So?" Forstman said.

"So my friend and your friend—"

"Mike Rialto," Forstman said.

"—was worried about the fact that some of Mr. Gotch's blood got on him."

"I can understand that," Forstman said, looking bewildered but afraid to ask how Mike Rialto had gotten any of Kenny's blood on him.

"That's why I happened to be here. Mike asked me to ask a few questions."

"Didn't he get any answers to his questions?" Forstman said.

"Mike told me your relative died before he had the chance."

They stood there, a feeling of awkwardness in the air, as though a conference had been called and now nobody had anything to say.

"Would you like me to go with you over to your cousin's place when you have a look around?" Whistler asked.

"I don't even know where he lives," Forstman said. "He wasn't my cousin. He was my wife's cousin by marriage three times removed. Something like that. You understand what I'm saying? Kenny and me was never really that well acquainted."

"His address is right there on the inventory. You're going to have to take a look."

"Oh, I suppose I'll take a look."

"So maybe I can give you a hand. Just like Mike would do if he was here."

"I can't pay for any of these services," Forstman said.

"I'm not asking for any pay, Mr. Forstman."

"A Good Samaritan?"

"Why not? Such things are not impossible," Whistler said.

"What do I call you?" Forstman asked.

"Everybody calls me Whistler."

"Whistler?" Forstman said. "You in show business?"

# 10

Kilroy allowed his mind to idle during the drive down to the coast, drifting from vague image to vague image, letting his brain rest. When he hit the Coast Highway he sat up straighter, put both hands on the wheel and sharpened his vision. As many times as he'd driven the road to Lucifer's he was still apt to miss the narrow, unmarked turnoff if his mind was elsewhere.

For one thing, from this side of the road, only the back of the small, weathered sign could be seen. It was coming up on the right; he might have passed it by again and would have had to make a U-turn along the highway, then cross the traffic once more to get to the dirt road cutting through the cliffs and dunes down to the ocean where the very exclusive members-only restaurant was hidden out of sight.

He slowed down when he spotted the restaurant's parking lot and the glass-enclosed terrace beside the sand, his view of Lucifer's itself obscured by a chaparral-covered hillside.

On his left another short road of decomposed granite climbed steeply to wrought-iron gates like those that guarded the entrance to Xanadu, the extravagant mansion in the film *Citizen Kane.* They were rusting and the top bolt of the gate on the right had torn out of the stone and stucco, giving the entrance to the great house beyond an eerie sense of abandon and decay.

But the left-hand gate, more than wide enough for any car, worked well enough. He was out of the car, the gate swung easily away, and back in the car within a minute.

The isolated mansion on the cliff had been built by the mother of a child guru from India—by way of Honolulu—who was the master of a cult devoted to Kali, the fierce and terrifying aspect of Devi, the supreme goddess in the Hindu pantheon. In some incarnations she is tranquil and loving, but Kali is depicted as a hag smeared with blood, wearing a garland of skulls and a girdle of severed hands, holding in her own four hands a sword, a shield, a strangling noose and the hand of a giant.

Myth claims that Kali developed a taste for blood when she was told to kill the demon Raktavija, who produced a thousand more like himself each time a drop of his blood fell on the earth. So Kali pierced him with a spear and, holding him above her head, drank his blood before it reached the ground.

In her temples, such as the well-known Kalighat in Calcutta, goats are sacrificed to her every day.

Hinduism is not an altogether gentle faith, but the worship of Kali as practiced by the boy guru was understood to be benign, freshly slaughtered lambs purchased from a local butcher serving instead of the more inconvenient live sacrifice of a goat ever since a man from Arkansas had been sent to jail and could no longer do the service.

At the same time there were whispers of a secret chamber,

cut into the side of the sandstone cliffs, on the side away from the restaurant and giving out onto a long stretch of barren, uninhabited and hidden beach, where other, less innocent and harmless rituals had been conducted and into which lost children and other derelicts had disappeared, killers and sophisticated perverts, it being said, needing as much solitude for their rituals and reflections as do poets and lovers.

So this patch of coast already had a reputation for evil by the time the child guru grew up, turned eighteen, and married an airline stewardess twice his age.

The mansion appeared empty now, the mother having moved to New York, where she managed a rock and roll group called Karma Sutra. The guru and his wife, it was sometimes mentioned around the table at celebrity dinner parties, had returned to Honolulu, where they apparently owned and ran a combination spiritual retreat and whorehouse.

The membership of Lucifer's had purchased the decaying mansion in the name of a blind corporation, these all being clever men who knew how to distance themselves from the ownership of any properties that might one day, by accident or intent, come under public scrutiny.

Kilroy had the key to the mansion; he was its custodian and this year's master of ceremonies for parties filled with rituals drawn from a dozen cultures. Designer cults for every taste.

He fitted the key into the well-oiled lock, which had been cunningly made to look like a rusted mess by a studio special-effects technician.

*11*

*Kenny* Gotch's apartment was over a garage at the back of a court on Sweetzer, three blocks down from the Sunset Strip. Walking behind Abe Forstman up the wooden stairs along the side, Whistler had no worry about how to get in. Even from downstairs he could see that the flimsy French doors leading out to a little side porch would give way if somebody just leaned a shoulder against them. It wasn't the kind of neighborhood or building or apartment that promised anything but slim pickings, even for some casual addict out cruising for a quick score, so there wasn't much need for heavy security even if the tenants could afford to install it.

It turned out there wasn't any need to put his shoulder to the doors; the front door was already a little ajar.

Forstman hesitated when he saw it wasn't shut, so Whistler got in front of him and went in first. Either somebody'd been there before them or Kenny Gotch'd been a messier house-keeper than Mary Bucket had accused Whistler of being.

It was one of the tiniest flats Whistler had ever seen, even in Hollywood, where closets rent for four hundred bucks a month. The living room was furnished with a ratty couch— no more than cushions dropped on a wooden frame—a torn and scarred leatherette ottoman, a kitchen chair and a low chest of drawers painted black and serving as a table, with a thirteen-inch color television set sitting on it. The room was heavy with the smell of candle wax; there were black candles bunched to one side of the TV and votive candles in red glass lined up on the windowsill.

There were two posters on the wall, one of a nude girl draped over a Honda motorcycle, the other with the jaggedly painted faces of some heavy metal rock group, faces painted with lightning flashes and evil grins, glaring threateningly at anyone who dared look them in the eye.

Somebody had tossed the room, not neatly but well.

Magazines and newspapers were scattered all over and the three drawers in the chest had been pulled out and dropped on the floor with their contents strewn everywhere.

A kitchen about the size of a mousehole, with one of those rigs that incorporated sink, fridge and stove top all in one unit, occupied two-thirds of the space. A counter and a cabinet above it filled the room out.

Forstman stood one step inside, looking sad and ashamed.

"Hey, Abe," Whistler said, "he was only a cousin by marriage three times removed. You don't have to take any blame for the way he lived."

"He was a human being with a lot of troubles and maybe, if I'd been told about him soon enough and if I cared enough, I could've done something."

"No, you couldn't, Abe. Believe me when I tell you that you couldn't."

Whistler went into the bedroom. There was a mattress on the floor. The sheets and pillowcases were soiled. There was a patch of stain on the pillowcase where a sleeper's mouth would have been. Whistler could practically see Kenny lying there in his drug-induced sleep drooling onto the pillow. A telephone squatted next to the rumpled bed like a giant bug.

Another chest of drawers was shoved up against the wall, the drawers and their contents tossed on the floor as well. No closet. Just a niche in the wall opposite the bed with a curtain hiding the clothes lined up haphazardly on a pole.

A tall man could stand in the middle of the floor with his arms outstretched and practically touch all four walls.

There was another poster on the wall of some satanic musical group out to tempt the adolescent taste for rebellion with references to the devil and evil ritual. Like kids dressed up for Halloween scaring themselves, powerful in the knowledge that they could intimidate other kids, half believing their own mumbo-jumbo.

The bathroom was twice as large as the kitchen and managed to contain a toilet, a sink and a shower stall. The person who'd searched the apartment had opened the medicine cabinet built into the wall and swept the shelves of their contents. A bottle of iodine, a can of Band-Aids, a rectal thermometer, cotton swabs, cough medicine, and half a dozen bottles of laxative for the relief of the constipation that grabbed the guts of drug addicts were smashed in the sink or broken and scattered on the worn linoleum.

Forstman had come as far as the archway between bedroom and living room. His pained expression had grown more pained.

"Well, at least he had a little porch," he said. "On a nice evening Kenny could've sat out there and read his newspaper."

Whistler was about to say that reading his newspaper on a porch is what Forstman might've done living here, but Kenny would've been putting on his makeup about the time when night began to fall, ready to walk up to the stroll and peddle his ass for the price of a meal and a bag to snort, a spoon to shoot up or a rock to smoke. But he kept it to himself. Let the old man believe what he wanted to believe, that his wife's cousin three times removed had taken the time to enjoy the simple things life had to offer, even here in La-La Land.

"Mike told you what I told him?" Forstman asked.

"About Kenny knowing something about that little girl who was killed back in eighty-four?"

"Yes, that."

"He told me."

"So, I ain't seen Mike since I told him. Since he went to see Kenny. He find out anything?"

"He says they didn't have a chance to talk. I told you."

"I thought you didn't want the nurse to know. So, because Mike didn't find out anything was the reason you were over to the hospice?" Forstman asked.

"When you don't know anything, anything you happen to find out is something."

"So, coming here, what are you hoping to find?" Forstman asked.

"I don't know."

Forstman gestured at the wrecked apartment. "Shouldn't we call the police?"

"All they'll do is come and take down names," Whistler said. "So, if it's okay with you, I'll just have a look around. You never know what you'll find. You don't have to hang around, if you don't want to."

"How're you going to get back to your car?"

"That's no trouble."

Forstman started to leave, picking his way through the mess on the floor, Whistler right behind him, walking him to the door. Forstman stopped and turned back.

"Kenny's car?"

"I'll ask the manager what kind he owned and where he usually parked it. Don't worry about it."

"I'm going to have to come back and do something with all this junk, won't I?" Forstman said, as though hoping Whistler would tell him there was a way of avoiding it.

"Sooner or later."

"Gotcha," Forstman said and then looked embarrassed. "I just said that without thinking."

"Said what?"

"Gotcha. It sounds like I was making a joke with Kenny's name."

"I don't think he'd mind. I bet plenty of people made jokes about his name if they knew his name."

"Why wouldn't they know his name?"

"Because that's not what he always called himself on the street."

"What did he call himself?"

"Harriet LaRue."

Forstman just stood there, taking it in, the awfulness, the shame, the pity of the life his distant relative by marriage had lived.

"Harriet. That was his mother's name," he said. "But where'd he get the LaRue?"

They stood there thinking about it.

"So, what's in a name?" Forstman finally said, and went

on his way after Whistler assured him that he'd keep in touch.

Whistler watched him from the landing until the old man had made it safely down the stairs, then went back into the bedroom.

He swept the junk on the floor into a pile with his foot, then sat down on the mattress and started picking through it. It was a lousy thing to do, he thought, picking through a dead man's personal things. Even though there wasn't much to pick through, even dead people had rights.

Then he thought about Sarah Canaan and her father and mother, and her uncle, Isaac, who hardly ever took his hat off and was said hardly ever to sleep. And he thought about the days and nights, week after week, when he'd gone hunting the streets and alleys of La-La Land looking for the little girl . . . and finally finding her in Hollywood Cemetery. And he thought about what Kenny Gotch had confessed to Abe Forstman and how Mike Rialto had gone to see him to follow that up and got showered with blood, which scared him half to death.

"So Kenny Gotch has rights and Sarah Canaan's got rights," somebody said. It was a second before Whistler realized that it was himself who'd spoken.

He went on poking through the junk.

The kind of stuff people saved could make you wonder about the kind of life they lived.

Whistler came across half a dozen magazines featuring half-naked girls and women displaying their treasures. Then it came to him that he was looking at a bunch of transsexuals and transvestites, men with their peckers piked, concealed in the cracks of their asses, plump chests made to pout with tricky half bras or showing all the charms of silicon implants. They were all smiling broadly, yet there was a sadness in their eyes, wondering where nature or society had gone wrong, flaunting everything they had because they could think of no other way to declare their right to their own humanity. And along the way making a badly needed buck.

He looked through the books that had been swept off the shelves. There weren't many, popular novels most of them, but one book caught his attention. It was *Magick in Theory and Practice.* A familiar title.

Years before, when he'd been just another one of the innocents come to La-La Land by the thousands looking for a shot at fame and fortune, he'd known a woman, Franchesca Isis, who called herself a countess, a black-haired, black-eyed beauty—an aspiring actress—with an accent that might have been French but which she claimed was Egyptian.

She told everyone that she was a woman with occult powers derived from the ancient *Book of the Dead,* Crowley's *Magick in Theory and Practice* and other esoteric sources. He wouldn't have given a damn if she'd advertised herself as the Wicked Witch of the West. He was intent on getting into her panties and was willing—as young men are apt to be—to listen to all kinds of nonsense in order to get there.

He'd spent more than one evening listening with apparent attention and respect as she went on about the spells she could cast on all the fools and assholes she had to meet while making the rounds. The small-time producers, half-assed directors, big-time agents and other assorted seducers and rapists who lusted after her and made promises they had no intention of ever keeping.

She had a lot of the language down pat and spoke familiarly of Beelzebub, the prince of devils; Belial, the vicious demon who drove a fiery chariot and was named the Beast in the Book of Revelation; Sir Francis Dashwood, the English satanist who'd turned the ruins of a Cistercian abbey into a brothel and with whom Benjamin Franklin had lifted a glass and a pretty ass or two; Hecate, the triple goddess of mythology; and other demons, devils and practitioners of the black arts including this Crowley, whose books were jammed onto her bookshelves with a dozen others.

When he once asked her why she didn't go ahead and do what she said she could do, turning those sons of bitches into cats or frogs, making their balls shrivel up and turn to stone, turning their eyes into prune pits, she'd looked at him with disdain.

"You'd really want me to do such terrible things to other human beings?" she asked.

"What we're talking about are a bunch of dick heads trying to get you to spread your thighs, cop their joints or do other nasty things just to get an audition or a one-liner in a B flick. Not even a guaranteed featured role," he said. "Not even a cameo. Not even an 'introducing Franchesca Isis.'" (Which he'd looked up to discover was the most important of the Egyptian goddesses, the name she'd picked to try to make herself different, give herself an edge, lift herself above the crowd of black-haired, red-haired, yellow-haired girls and women ready to spread thighs, suck joints, swing from chandeliers, do anything anywhere, anyhow, anytime, for just a shot—a little shot—at the holy grail of fame and fortune, all the time cursing the men who tried to exact that price for favors done or merely promised.) "So, I'd like to see you lay a spell on one of these pricks," he said.

"Tell me you're not like those sonsofbitches," she said. "Tell me you don't want to fuck me too."

"So put a spell on me."

"You don't believe I can really do it, do you?"

He shook his head and shrugged his shoulders, holding out his arms with hands palms up in what he thought was a very eloquent, though unchallenging manner. Because even though he was fed up with listening to her crap, he had not lost all hope of getting to her treasure, and he wanted to express his doubts and reservations in the nicest way possible.

She took a big volume from the shelf and placed it on the table between them, there in her kitchen.

"Do you know what this is?" she asked.

"A black book. A grimoire," he said. "Don't you think I've been listening?"

"Sure you've been listening . . . with one ear," she said. "Well, this is *Magick in Theory and Practice,* taken from *The Book of Raziel,* which has been derived from *The Book of Signs,* the great book of magic written by Adam. There are spells in here for all occasions."

"So, pick a good one."

He was challenging her now. He knew he could lose it.

After all these weeks of listening to the drivel she spouted, trying to make herself different and special even in his lowly eyes, he could lose it now. She was staring at him, one hand on the book.

"I could easily call up Satan himself," she said.

"I'd like to meet him," he said.

She stared some more and then she said, "You want to smoke a little grass?"

"Is that to get us into the proper mood?"

"Well, yes, the proper mood," she said.

While they lit up a couple of joints taken from a black lacquered box, she had a little smile on her face.

"You think you're smart," she said.

"No, I don't."

"Yes, you think you're smart. You don't believe a word I've ever told you."

"For God's sake, sure I do."

"You don't know what terrible things I could do to you."

"Well, I'm willing to take the chance. I'm willing to find out," he said, smiling, staring into her eyes. "You mind telling me something?"

"If I can."

"You said I only listened to you with one ear. What about the other ear? What's that listening to?"

"My crotch. You're always trying to hear if my pussy's purring yet."

"Well, is it?"

She'd placed the curl of her tongue between her teeth and made the sound of a satisfied cat.

Afterward, he'd told her that she'd made him a believer, no longer having any doubts that she was a witch and able to cast powerful spells.

He came back from his memory sitting on the ratty couch, the book in his lap. The room was golden with the light of late afternoon. He was growing old, Kenny Gotch was dead, and maybe it would be better to leave it that way.

An hour later it was almost dark. He'd made piles of magazines and papers, insurance offers, advertisements, catalogs, this and that. He'd piled up the scattered shirts and socks and underwear in separate piles, thinking wryly that here he was doing household chores for a dead man.

Having neatly stacked the clothing, he suddenly felt that he should complete the task and at least put them back into the little chest.

He picked up one of the drawers, which had landed upside down on the floor and turned it over. There was something stuck in the back of the drawer between the bottom and back where the old wood had shrunk away. He plucked it out with the blade of his penknife.

It looked like a small piece of buff-colored plastic, the finger broken off the hand of a doll, smaller than his pinkie.

A chill passed across his back; a ripple of fear, a premonition.

For a moment he thought someone had come into the apartment through the French doors, but there was no one there when he went to the archway between the bedroom and living room. He wrapped the finger in one of Gotch's clean handkerchiefs and carefully put it into his jacket pocket. Unless he was much mistaken, what he'd found was the mummified finger of a child. Among other mutilations inflicted on the body of Canaan's niece, Sarah, one of her index fingers had been removed.

# 12

In the year 273 the birthday of Jesus Christ was fixed at midwinter—December twenty-fifth according to the Julian calendar—to coincide with Saturnalia and the birthdays of the ancient gods, the Greek Dionysus, the Persian Mithras and the Greek Apollo.

Upon August fifteenth, formerly the feast day of the mother

goddess Diana, the Assumption of the Virgin Mary was celebrated.

All Souls' Day, the feast of the dead, had been celebrated on the first of May for over a thousand years. Flowers had been strewn on graves, for according to the earliest teachings of the earliest religions the dead and the seeds of flowers held the same promise of rebirth.

But the early Catholic church wanted the faithful to suffer the terror of hellfire, so they moved All Souls' Day to November, when flowers were not in bloom.

That's how we ended up with Halloween, when kids dress up as ghosts and goblins, the dead are said to rise from their graves and crypts, witches go around on broomsticks in company with familiars—goats and owls and black cats—and satanists, Wiccan witches (which are not to be confused with one another), Druids and other cults and fringe religions throw the most solemn, rip-roaring rites, masses, ceremonies and orgies of the year.

Fueled on booze and drugs and naked flesh they often get out of hand. Ask any cop what goes down on Halloween.

Kilroy had been elected master of ceremonies for this year's Halloween do, only days off, by the members of the Inner Circle, the governing board of Lucifer's, the private club and restaurant listed with the office of the secretary of state of California as a public benefit corporation, a designation usually used to define a church or charitable organization.

A place like La-La Land has a restaurant, a club or a bar for every appetite and inclination. There are lesbian bars where waitresses with tattooed arms snap change for twenty from the singles folded like rings around each finger of the left hand. There are homosexual theme clubs; one devoted to motorcycles and black leather, another to aficionados of war wearing antique uniforms, and still another where entertainers in spangles swing on trapezes above the heads of customers dressed in spangles, too.

Some are obvious and some discreet. The names sometimes give them away if you know the code. The Queen's Inn, The Flaming Faggot, Sappho's, and Lucifer's.

Lucifer's had all the subdued ambiance of a posh and very exclusive New York supper club, the walls covered in green pool table felt and the ceilings in red, polished dark wood and copper everywhere, votive candles on the tables. A customer walking in by chance might think himself or herself in Manhattan except for the long row of windows looking out toward the sands and the Pacific beyond.

There were poster-size photographs of young men dressed as devils, tights bulging at the crotch, decorating the ladies' room, which was not much used except on special evenings when women were welcome by invitation only. Much the same photographs were in the men's toilet.

The clientele of Lucifer's was exclusively male, and among them were many who had a special interest in young boys and girls. Photographs of naked children engaged in sexual acts with one another or with adults were passed around the way fathers might pass around pictures of their kids at a business luncheon. Conversations often dealt with satanism and drugs because both figured prominently in the seduction and capture of children. They were also profitable enterprises by which many of Lucifer's customers made their livings.

Lucifer's also boasted among its members many lawyers, businessmen, artists and executives from the film world, doctors, a clergyman or two—sophisticates who were in it for the contacts and who pretended to be amused by the childish rigmarole, the camp worship of Satan—some pimps and thieves, and even a couple of murderers for hire unknown to all but a few. Pedophilia and erotomania are aberrations that cut across education, wealth and class.

The greatest difference between the members of Lucifer's and run-of-the-mill sexual omnivores and fantasizers was the lavishness with which they surrounded their perversions with show and ritual, elevating, as believers have always done, their personal taste and prejudice to the level of religion.

One thing you could certainly say for La-La Land, even evil was reduced to the level of spicy, naughty show business.

Kilroy intended to give them more than they'd ever bargained for; to give them a Halloween to surpass all Halloweens in living memory. He, the expert, the technical advisor to the faithful, the priest of Belial.

He walked around the representation of hell that workmen hired from the Motion Picture Craft Guilds had been constructing on and off for the last six months according to carefully researched plans and drawings.

Naked store mannequins, retrofitted with anatomically correct genitals, writhed on spears and curled up in synthetic flames that snapped and flickered at the turn of a wheel. Papier-mâché children, split and gutted, rolled down an endless waterfall of fire that moved at the punch of a button. Women in effigy copulated with dogs and goats, and monsters borrowed or stolen from studios that constructed the special effects for all the science fiction and horror films that come tumbling off the Hollywood assembly line ravaged men and women, and devoured children.

There would be living nudes engaged in fornication, fellatio and cunnilingus, frottage and buggery; homosexual pairs, lesbian triads and heterosexual quartets performing at showtime.

Except for the theme and subject matter, the entire effect was designed to be something any Disneyland would have been proud of.

He stood for a moment staring at the sunset out of the picture window, all but obscured from watchers on the beach by a tangle of trees and undergrowth. The sun sank like a bloody grapefruit, sliding down the tissue paper sky into the painted cardboard sea.

# 13

**Kenny** Gotch was delivered to the County Morgue about five o'clock in the evening.

The sky was a pastel American flag, bands of white mare's tails alternating with the glowing pink of the reflected sun on their undersides, a patch of blue up in the southwest, the north star promising larger constellations. A sky out of *Fantasia* or some other Disney film produced back in the forties and fifties.

The morgue at Angeles Hospice was scarcely ever crowded, even though it was a facility that dealt exclusively in death.

The county morgue was always crowded because it may be an axiom of civilization that when metropolises grow beyond human scale certain facilities like public toilets, morgues and free clinics become inadequate and certain people like children, old folks and the dead receive less care.

His body was placed on a gurney in the corridors leading to the necropsy rooms, where masked white-coated priests sliced corpses open and read their pasts in the entrails, everyone having no doubt at all about their futures which were, of course, no longer of any concern.

Kenny had never been one to grow impatient when waiting in line for a shower in the bathhouses or a seat in the motion picture palaces; the act of waiting had been itself a comfort to him, presenting the illusion that he was among friends.

He made no complaint now, waiting his turn with the medical butchers, lying there draped in a blood-stained sheet, a steel device protruding from his throat.

# 14

*Whistler* stood up, flicked on the lights and walked into the bedroom for a last look around. The devilish musicians in their fright wigs, with their scarlet eye wells and green mouths, leered at him, daring him to taunt them as he'd once taunted Franchesca Isis, ready to go through all sorts of mumbo-jumbo just for a shot at her treasure.

The feeling that he was missing something, like the pitiful little withered finger, stuck in some other crack or cranny in the rat's nest of a room, nagged at Whistler. Something he'd seen and then forgotten the next second. You could waste a lot of time on such vague auras of unease, but when all was said and done, what else was there to go on except emotions, impressions and a sensitive sense of disquiet.

He went back into the bedroom. The light from a wall sconce outside the window shed a harsh light into the room. It fell on the floor and telephone like blue rain, and he saw what he'd looked at but hadn't seen before. The telephone wasn't your everyday standard telephone; it was an upmarket specialty with redial, speed dial and LED readout.

He sat down on the mattress and put the phone in his lap. It was a Panasonic with a twenty-eight-number capacity. An item like this cost a hundred twenty-nine bucks, maybe ninety-nine bucks discounted. It was the sort of gadget a junkie without the price of a haircut might like to have but couldn't afford unless he bought it from another junkie thief for ten bucks or lifted it himself while prowling some john's house or apartment for the price of a fix. A little something extra, besides the silverware or the television set or the hi-fi rig. A little something for himself because it wouldn't have been worth carrying away for the buck or two a fence would've given him.

So a little gadget to feed a fantasy. Whistler could imagine Kenny Gotch lying on the sour-smelling sheets, a shot of smack, a snort of coke, singing in his veins and in his head, picking up the Panasonic and hitting one of the many buttons to summon up a beautiful hooker who loved him madly, a heavy dealer who was in his debt and supplied him for nothing more than his good favor, a faithful bone breaker just waiting for the order to go out there and waste this one, that one, mother, father, sibling, untrustworthy friend who'd abandoned him. Punching up the numbers and watching them appear on the little LED readout. Mumbling into the mouthpiece to whatever loser like himself picked up, any merchant, any voice out there that would talk to him for five minutes.

The cardboard directory on the face above the dialing pad was only partially filled out. Numbers had been entered on more than one occasion judging from the different colored pens with which Gotch'd jotted down the names. Bookstore, Jane T, Mike, Pooch, Jet, Bobby D, Bobby L, Chick, G.G., Pizza, Flick, Chink and half a dozen others, eighteen in all, eight of them double entered, making twenty-six entries, the second reference with a $W$ in brackets next to it. $W$ for work, no doubt.

The repeated names were printed one below the other in the spaces provided next to the memory buttons. In order to double the capacity of the directory there was a button that activated the lower tier of names and numbers.

Whistler took out the three-by-five cards, held with a rubber band, which served as his diary, day book, weekly organizer and personal directory. He found a clean card and noted down the names and button locations.

He started punching the memory buttons, calling up each number on the display and then hanging up on the first ring after memorizing the number, which he then wrote down. It took him ten minutes to go through the numbers on the top tier and five to hit all the numbers on the lower tier.

He checked his notations against the telephone's directory.

Thirteen names in the upper tier. Thirteen in the lower. Which left just one button without an entry, top or bottom. He hit the button for the upper number. It came up 213-(0000). The lower directory gave him the same readout. The Hollywood prefix was 213, so the telephone was probably displaying its own prefix and an empty memory.

Why were two stations out of twenty-eight left blank? It could happen. Not everybody, especially a twangy boy with habits, had twenty-eight numbers they called so often they'd put them into an automatic dialer, but if you filled up twenty-six, why not twenty-eight just to make it neat, even if the last two numbers were POP-CORN for the time and the number of the weather bureau?

He bent over and raised the telephone closer to his eyes, trying to read some of the small print. A shuffling step in the living room brought his head up fast. He sat there, hefting the phone in case he needed to use it for a weapon. Mary Bucket appeared in the doorway.

"What's wrong?" she asked.

"You scared the liver out of me creeping in like that."

"I wasn't sure it was you and not somebody else who might be in here," she said.

"What are you doing here?" he asked.

"I came to see if you needed a ride back to your car," she said. "It's the end of the day for me. So, are you finished?"

"I've seen about all I'm going to see," he said.

"Are you the one who's making these neat piles?" she asked.

"It was a mess when Forstman and I got here. Somebody'd been here before we arrived. Maybe the same gazooney who clipped Kenny's stuff out of the hospice."

"His things have just been misplaced," she said, snappishly.

He nodded, not about to argue the point. He put the phone on the floor and started to stand up, wanting to do it in one long, fluid motion, but the effort was too much for him and he staggered sideways. Mary reached out and steadied him.

"When I was one and twenty," he said.

"What?"

He smiled, never knowing that his smile had a wistful quality to it that made the hearts of many women flip over. "It's a line of a poem a friend of mine likes to recite to remind us that we're all growing old.

" 'When I was one and twenty I heard a wise man say, "Give crowns and pounds and guineas but not your heart away; give pearls away and rubies but keep your fancy free." But I was one and twenty, no use to talk to me.

" 'When I was one and twenty I heard him say again, "The heart out of the bosom was never given in vain; 'tis paid with sighs a plenty and sold for endless rue." Now I am two and forty, and oh, 'tis true, 'tis true.' " He smiled again. "I changed the last part. It's really 'two and twenty.' "

"So, you're forty-two?" she said.

"Give or take."

"Someday I'd like to meet this friend who recites poetry," she said.

"If you feel like a cup of coffee, you can meet him right now."

He turned out the lights, standing in the doorway one last time, as though expecting the room to speak to him.

"Hey, what's going on up there?" a voice called out from the dark at the bottom of the stairs.

Whistler closed the door and went down after Mary.

An old woman in a housecoat, her hair held flat to her head under a net, looked them over as though suspecting them of dirty doings.

"Who are you?" she asked.

"I came with Mr. Gotch's relative," Whistler said.

"You a relative, too?" the old woman asked, glaring at Mary.

"No, she's with me," Whistler said. "Mr. Gotch's relative left already."

"The old man who was with you? I saw that. How about the man in black, was he related, too?"

"What man in black?"

"The one what was the first marcher in the goddamn parade."

"What did he look like, this man in black?"

"About thirty, I think. Black shirt and black pants. Black hair, parted in the middle and combed straight back in a ponytail wrapped with a red cord or elastic band."

"You'd make a good witness."

Whistler glanced at Mary. The vague look of recall she'd had in the lunchroom drifted across her eyes, but the old woman said, "I been a witness more than once," and the look went away. "Well, I don't know any man in black," Whistler said. "I was with the old man. He asked me to stay and have a look around."

"Why's that?"

"Just to see if everything was all right."

"Like what?"

"I don't know."

"You don't know a lot, do you?" she said.

"There's nothing for you to worry about," Whistler said. "Can you tell me—"

"I ain't worried," she said. "Do I look worried?"

"—where the manager's apartment is?"

"I'm the manager. What the hell do you think I'm doing out here in my housecoat, baying at the moon? Have you got a name?"

"Whistler. My name's Whistler and this is Mary Bucket."

"A couple names like that could lead a person to think they was being lied to."

"We're not trying to lie to you," Mary said. "Mrs. . . . ?"

"Prager."

"Have you heard that Mr. Gotch died this afternoon, Mrs. Prager?" Mary asked.

Tough as she tried to seem, Mrs. Prager's eyes filled up with tears.

"Poor little bastard," she said. "It's no surprise."

"Why's that?"

"He was a junkie and a sniffer and he did unnatural things with his body. He had funny friends and he sold hisself to all comers on the boulevard. He came here looking for heaven but he surely didn't find it. Who the hell are you?"

"I'm the head nurse at the Angeles Hospice, Mrs. Prager," Mary said.

"That where he died?"

"Haven't you noticed that he was gone?" Whistler asked.

"My tenants come and go. They rent a roof over their heads and a place to call home. They don't appreciate intrusions. But, sure, I knew he was sick. I didn't know where he was hospitalized. Angeles, huh? Last stop on the subway." She looked at Whistler. "You a doctor?"

"No, I'm a private investigator."

"An eye? You don't look like an eye."

"You met a lot of eyes?"

"I watch the television."

The movies and television made everybody experts on how other people are supposed to look, Whistler thought.

"Can you tell me, Mrs. Prager, where Mr. Gotch kept his car?" he asked.

"What car? Kenny couldn't afford a car. Everything he got went into his arm or up his nose or he spent it on crazy charms and spells, things like that."

"Charms and spells?"

"Sure, you know, all that crap. Cat's eyes, fetishes, rags and tags and bobtails."

"How'd you know about things like that?"

"He showed them to me. Junk, all junk."

"You know much about junk?"

"I read the tarot. I know a little something."

"You ever tell Kenny Gotch's fortune?"

"I didn't have to read the tarot to know Kenny's future. His fate was written in his eyes."

"Well, good night, Mrs. Prager," Whistler said, "I hope you won't be bothered anymore tonight."

"Take care of yourselves." She turned her head at the sound of approaching footsteps.

"Well, here they come."

Whistler saw two uniformed cops walking toward them.

"I called them an hour ago, after I seen that first gazooney creeping up the stairs. Oh, don't worry," she said, reading Whistler's eyes, "I ain't going to say anything about you two."

"How do you really know we are who we say we are, Mrs. Prager?" Mary said.

"You got to take people on trust every now and then," the old woman said, giving them the wrinkled landscape of her smile once more.

Whistler and Mary passed the two young cops as they walked out.

"You the people called in a prowler?" one of the cops asked, adjusting the nightstick in its harness.

"The old woman in the bathrobe back there," Whistler said.

# *15*

*There* was a room like the command center of a spacecraft on a science fiction television series in Walter Cape's mansion on the hill. A great arc of windows, cantilevered out over the bulk of the building, gave the impression to anyone sitting in the leather chairs facing them that they were suspended in space with the lights of an alien underwater city glittering far below.

As they talked, Walter Cape, sitting there in black trousers, white silk shirt and elegant maroon sweater with black piping, looking like a man enjoying a lucid hour—which was the case—and Bennu Rahab, still all in black, watched the fairy lights beneath the sea grow more numerous and intense as La-La Land thrust itself up out of the gloom into the clear sky of the growing dark.

Rahab studied his transparent reflection in the window, the pinpoints of light beyond, pleased with the magic of it, the way the black glass gave back the image of a man twenty-five years younger, all the blemishes smoothed away.

Cape studied Rahab studying himself. He understood exactly what he was doing and it bitterly amused him because it was the same sort of thing he'd done and often still did when the need for self-delusion was upon him.

"Will you have something to eat with me?" he asked.

"All right."

"What will you have?" Cape asked.

"Whatever you'll be having," Rahab replied, unaccountably pleased that this rich man who paid him so well for errands run was actually inviting him to dine.

A servant who looked like a trainer or a keeper in a psychiatric ward came into the room and stopped six paces behind them. Rahab hadn't caught the movement of foot or hand that had summoned him.

"A Chateaubriand for two, Malcolm. Fresh asparagus. Creamed potatoes. A dozen escargot to start. Hearts of palm salad dressed with raspberry vinaigrette. You choose the wine. Two perfect martinis now. Thank you, Malcolm."

The manservant went away.

Cape cleared his throat and kicked the shopping bag on the floor between them with his foot.

"These are the dead man's things?" he asked in a voice that resembled the squawking of one of the large black birds that nested in the pines beyond the security fence.

Rahab set the bag on his lap and one by one removed and placed on the table a half-used book of matches, three handkerchiefs, a ring of three keys, a notebook, an address book, a checkbook, a ballpoint pen, a wallet, thirty-two dollars in bills in a silver money clip and eighteen cents in change.

Cape stared at the accumulation and then leaned forward, his hands in his lap, looking closer, as though expecting one of the items to move of its own accord. He placed his hands on the tabletop. They were encased in rubber surgical gloves.

A little smile touched Rahab's lips. It amused him to think that the old man was afraid of contamination, terrified of even the thought and mention of AIDS. At his age when the virus would probably not even have the time to gestate before the old man died.

"There's none of the dead man's blood on that stuff," he said.

Cape didn't answer. He extended one finger and poked around, pushing the coins and the bills in the money clip toward Rahab.

"Put that away," he said.

Rahab picked up the money clip and removed the bills, tossing them to one side along with the change, refusing the implication that he was being given a tip with a dead man's money.

Cape picked up each handkerchief in turn by one corner and lifted it so that it fell out unfolded, then dropped each one back into the shopping bag, which Rahab had replaced on the floor between them.

The servant came back with the two perfect martinis in double-size glasses. There was a rim of frost on them. Rahab waited until Cape tasted his, smiling and nodding.

He tasted his own. It was ice water with a little lemon juice. He said nothing about it. It was all about tricks and ruses, giving offense and withholding satisfaction.

Cape picked up the ballpoint pen.

"Do you need a pen?" Cape asked.

"No, thank you," Rahab said.

Cape dropped it into the bag. He quickly flipped through the pages of the five and dime notebook. "Poetry," he said. "It seems that our Kenny was a poet. I never knew that." He held the notebook out above the bag, about to drop it, then thought better of it. "Not contaminated? You say these items are not contaminated?"

"You can't get AIDS by casual contact."

"So they say, so they say, but they're finding out new things every day. At first they announced a gestation period of a year, for instance. Do you recall? Then it was three to five. Then ten. For all we know we could all be ready to break out in the plague."

Rahab shrugged his shoulders.

"You have the courage of youth," Cape said, but there was irony underlying the remark.

Cape put the notebook into the pocket of his sweater and

went on to the checkbook. "He scarcely ever used it," he remarked.

"His business was mostly cash," Rahab said.

The checkbook went into the shopping bag. Cape placed the address book into his pocket without looking into it. He looked the matchbook over, then tore one off and struck it alight, placing the matches in the ashtray on the table and setting them all afire.

Only the money and the wallet and the ring of three keys were left on the table.

"Do you happen to know what locks these keys fit?" Cape asked.

Rahab reached out and touched a brass Yale. "That's the key to his front door." He touched another. "That's a key to a padlock. You'll see in his wallet, he didn't have a car registration, so I imagine he had a bike to get around on and that would be the key to the lock for the chain. I don't know about the other key."

"It's worn. It's the oldest of the three."

"So, it could be the key to the house where he lived somewhere before he ran away."

"I remember this key," Cape said. "He was wearing it around his neck when I first met him. He was wearing it around his skinny little neck on a piece of string." There was something crawlingly tender in the way he said it.

He picked up the wallet and unfolded it, plucked an identification card from its place behind a cracked glassine window. The other flap had pockets for cards. Cape tossed two membership cards to movie cassette stores and three squares of paper torn off an advertising flier on the table.

The interior of the wallet was empty. Cape folded it and put it into the side pocket of his jacket.

"That's all, nothing in his apartment?"

"Nothing that would incriminate anybody that I could see. Nothing in that stuff either." He didn't have to speak the subtext, which remarked that gathering up such junk was a waste of his time and skills.

Cape nodded as though praising Rahab.

"If he'd left any last words, it would be natural to assume

he'd have them close by. We could expect any such corre-
spondence to whom it may concern to be right here."

Cape removed the gloves and smiled at the sound of the
serving cart being wheeled along the floor behind him.

His manservant or guardian laid down the dishes: two
bowls of some thin gruel, a tray of thin dry toast, two plates
upon each of which resided a sliver of boiled chicken and a
puree of carrots.

*"Bon appétit,"* Cape said, grinning a wicked grin, like a
child who has fooled a grown-up by inviting him to a tea
party and serving him nothing but stones and mud.

Gentry's was half-filled with customers, mostly coffees.
Bosco was sitting on his stool behind the register reading
*The Faiths Men Live By* when Whistler and Mary Bucket
walked in. He looked at Mary and smiled broadly. Bosco
fancied himself a judge of character, able in an instant to
evaluate anybody who walked through the door; especially
anybody with one of the regulars; especially anyone with one
of his friends; especially if the person with the friend was of
the opposite gender.

The expression on Bosco's face told Whistler that the one-
armed counterman approved of the lady. Bosco liked pretty
women but was instantly suspicious of any woman likely
to be called beautiful. Heart stoppers were accepted under
advisement only after long acquaintance.

Whistler made the introductions. Mary looked at Bosco's
empty sleeve.

"How long you been without your arm?" she asked.

"Nine, ten years."

"Used to it?"

"The hand gives me hell every now and then."

"There are ways to think your way past the pain."

Bosco nodded. "I know a couple."

"Whenever you want to talk about it, maybe I know a couple you don't know."

"Is that your business?"

"I'm a nurse at Angeles Hospice."

That information seemed to please Bosco even more than her appearance.

"You want me to ask those customers to clear your booth, Whistler?"

"I wouldn't want you to do that. We'll just sit up at the counter until they go away."

Bosco got off the stool and went to the back counter, marking the book he was reading with a leather bookmark and tucking it into the armpit of his empty sleeve.

He laid out two setups and two coffee mugs, then reached for the pot. "This a dinner date or are you just killing time?"

Whistler looked at Mary.

"All you invited me for was coffee," she said. "Maybe you've got things to do with your evening."

"He's got nothing to do with his evening," Bosco said. "Your booth'll be ready for you in two minutes."

He piled the cutlery and china on a small tray and went over to put the setups on the table in the booth that was just being vacated, first clearing the used plates and cups off the Formica top and wiping it down with a clean damp towel. He did it all with the easy grace of a man who'd learned to live with his handicap.

"Battle wound?" Mary asked Whistler.

Whistler made a thumbing gesture over his shoulder. "Out there. He faced off a pimp who was abusing a baby hooker. The pimp blew his arm away. Bosco broke his neck with a punch."

"Was he tried?"

"It never came to that. What'd happened was very plain. There were plenty of witnesses. Nobody tried to make a case."

"What happened to the baby hooker?"

"She found another pimp."

"Your table's ready, sir," Bosco said at their backs.

He'd conjured up a candle from somewhere. It was lit and stuck in a beer bottle. He had a towel draped over his good arm. He was making a little fuss meant to amuse Whistler's new friend.

Mary played along, seating herself as though Bosco were

the maître d' in the best restaurant in Beverly Hills and she a valued patron who'd have her quail and lobster nowhere else.

"The next thing you know you'll be giving us linen napkins," Whistler said, vaguely embarrassed by what Bosco's attentiveness implied.

"I can do that," Bosco said. "May I suggest a beef filet with baked potato, asparagus and a vinaigrette salad?"

Before they could say yes or no—before Whistler could say he'd rather have fries with his steak—Bosco was gone.

There was a certain magic to it, the candlelight making a pool of soft light just where they sat, the dusk falling outside the window. It was an hour of the night when the hookers' stroll took on the hard-edged clarity of a movie set and the hookers, thieves, twangy boys, cops and bone breakers strolling here and there in purple slacks, pink hot pants, electric toreadors, black leather minis, feather boas and tinselly scarves, the men strutting about with small hand towels enhancing the bulge at the crotch, the ladies showing shelves of powdered tit, looking clean and freshly painted, extras in a musical extravaganza waiting for the call to action.

Mary had unbuttoned a button at the top of her white blouse—no Popeye tee shirt underneath—and adjusted the collar, the soft swell of her breasts revealed now, a rosy sheen to her skin, the color in her cheeks high, her eyes lustrous, the wells tinted with violet shadows, her hair looser than it had been, framing her face.

The sounds in the coffee shop were hushed as though all the other customers understood that an event of some tenderness and importance was taking place. Bosco had found a station on his radio beside the register that played chamber music rich with strings.

Yondro, the short-order cook working the kitchen, had outdone himself and prepared steaks of a flavor and quality Whistler had never experienced in Gentry's before. Bosco had produced a bottle of red wine and a wineglass from the same bag of tricks from which the candle had appeared. Mary noticed that Whistler didn't have a glass but didn't comment.

The coffee was strong and hot.

They talked. After a while they began to believe they knew all there was to know about each other. At least everything that mattered.

Memories of other dinners, other companions, flooded back, creating a background that filled Whistler's mind, making this dinner and this companion all the more vivid. He reached out for the afterdinner drink that wasn't there, the cigarette he wouldn't have smoked even if it had been there, all the old habits reasserting themselves, the little rituals that had once accompanied the hours of pleasure.

"You want to check out that bet?" Whistler asked.

"What bet?"

"You know, who's got the messiest house."

She studied his face for a moment, then she touched the collar of her blouse, making some unspoken feminine comment in the gesture about not being dressed for a first encounter and shook her head.

"Why don't we let the band play a few more tunes before we start dancing," she said.


"Why did you want that junk?" Rahab asked, taking a small bite of chicken, his expression showing that he found it nearly tasteless.

"There are a thousand ways for a dead man to give away secrets. But I give away no secrets of mine," Cape said, showing his false teeth in a wolfish grin. "What I commissioned you to do was a favor for a friend. I won't tell you more."

"Oh?" Rahab remarked, the single sound an editorial comment, an essay in skepticism.

"Haven't you heard that I do favors? I trade in favors. That's how I made my living, made my fortune. Just trading favors. Nothing but trading favors," Cape murmured on, listening to himself repeat the mantra in a dozen different constructs, the way old men search around in the repetition of words seeking the truth at the heart of what they mean to say. "Is there a favor you'd like me to do for you?"

"I don't need favors," Rahab said. "The usual cash will do me fine."

Cape reached into his shirt pocket and withdrew a folded check.

"I thought your charges were a little excessive this time, Ray," he said.

Rahab unfolded the check and glanced at the spidery letters, numbers and signature.

"Killing a dead man or a nearly dead man comes high. It's much harder to take a man down who's fixed in place and surrounded by caretakers than one who is moving around, risking himself in public places. You should know that."

"Even so, we've been partners in various enterprises for some time now," Cape said. "Does everything have to be measured in dollars and cents?"

Rahab looked at the old man with some astonishment, this man who would take a profit out of every breath you breathed if he could, who weighed the value of a favor done to the nearest milligram. Was he trying to make a claim on imagined friendship in his old age?

"Believe me," Rahab said, folding the check in two, "I made you a bargain price."

"Well, make me another," Cape said, slipping a folded piece of paper into Rahab's hand. "Make me a real bargain price on this one."

Rahab's eyelids flickered as he read the name on the slip of paper. How many favors would Cape do for this friend of his who ordered so much killing? He placed the attaché case on his knees and snapped the locks.

"Have you finished your dinner?" Cape asked, his eyes flickering down to the contents of the attaché case; to the camera body and telephone, lenses and filters, the neat array of miniature tools and instruments.

Rahab placed the folded check in a side pocket of the case and closed the lid.

"Yes, I've finished. Thank you. Now I have to go. I have things to attend to," he said, tucking the slip of paper into the case beside the check.

He looked into Cape's eyes. They stared at each other for a long moment, the dispassionate killer and the man who ordered murder, and he understood that the favors Cape was doing for this friend were no favors. He was enjoying every violent death vicariously, triumphant in the knowledge that his withered hand was still able to deliver destruction.

Rahab was at the archway, about to leave the room, when Cape called his name.

"Yes?" Rahab said.

"Too bad you have to leave in such a hurry," Cape said, "we're having strawberry shortcake with ice cream for dessert."

# *16*

*Whistler* sat in his Eames chair, the one really fine piece of furniture he owned, facing the sliding glass doors and the deck, the sound of the commuter traffic rising from the freeway like the roar of distant air armadas coming to bomb the city into extinction.

The list of twenty-six numbers taken from Gotch's phone lay upon the slice of polished oak he used for an end table.

He'd been sitting there half-regretting his ten—going on eleven—years sobriety in AA. If he were still a practicing drunk, he could forget about his friend Isaac Canaan, haunting the Hollywood stroll like a dybbuk. He could drown the memory of little Sarah's broken body draped across the tombstone in the cemetery. He could put the unexpected feelings he was discovering for this Mary with the ridiculous last name into a drunk's perspective and while away the hours, the days, the weeks and years without commitment to anything but the bottle and the wet grave waiting at the end of it. He could let somebody else bury the dead and seek a suitable revenge.

It was around the dinner hour, commuters were still fight-

ing the traffic on their way home from work, some already
at home, kicking off their shoes and lying back for a couple
of breaths, watching the news, ready for a little reward at the
cocktail hour. Some already sitting down to dinner.

He looked at the top three-by-five in the little packet,
wrapped in a rubber band, he carried with him.

He punched in one of the numbers. The phone rang on the
other end four times and then was picked up; first time
lucky.

"Yeah?" a man's voice said in his ear. It had the flat
abruptness that young males liked to effect, as though there
was nothing the caller—whoever they might be—had to say
that was of any interest.

"Hello?" Whistler said.

"Yeah?"

"You don't sound like Kenny."

"Maybe that's because I ain't Kenny."

"Well, is Kenny there?"

"There's no Kenny here."

"Wait a minute. Isn't this Kenny's number?"

"No, it ain't. It's my number."

"Well, that's what I'm trying to find out here. Who is this?"

"Gambler."

"What's that?"

"My name."

"Okay, that's your street name. What did your mother
call you?"

"George," he said, like an obedient child and then, realizing what he'd done, said, "Who the hell is this?"—a little
edge creeping into the uninflected anonymity of his voice.

"This is a friend of Kenny's?" Whistler said, lifting his
voice, as though asking if that was sufficient identification.

"Kenny who?"

"Kenny Gotch."

"Oh, that Kenny," the voice said, changing timbre slightly,
suspicion and doubt stirring around like thin shadows.

"So, you know Kenny?"

"Yeah, I know Kenny."

"So, is he there?"

"No, he ain't here. Why would he be here?"

"Because maybe he lives there?"

"He don't live here. He never lived here."

"Well, how about Harriet LaRue? She live there?"

There was a silence that seemed longer than it probably was.

"What the fuck you talking about? Who the fuck are you?"

"So, does she?"

"No Harriet Somebody ever lived here. I don't know any Harriet Somebody."

"She gave me this number. She told me to give her a call and ask whoever answered for Kenny Gotch. I figured it was like a password. You understand my meaning?"

"You a customer of this Harriet Somebody's?"

"If you don't know this Harriet LaRue—the name's LaRue—how come you know she's selling something?"

"I can't talk anymore. I don't know why the fuck Kenny gave you my number except he wanted to play a joke. Well, you tell Kenny or this Harriet whatever—"

"LaRue, George. Fachrissake, can't you remember a name like that?"

"—that I don't think it's very funny. You tell him I don't want anything to do with him anymore and he bothers me again I'll see to it he quits," Gambler said, the fear polishing his words to the brightness of a bell. Then he hung up.

"So, okay, George Gambler," Whistler murmured to himself, making a check mark next to the name and number, "maybe we'll have a face-to-face, find out how come you know Kenny Gotch but claim you don't know Harriet LaRue."

The number for Chick was a fast-food takeout. Somebody's broasted chicken.

It was a matter of overtime. Official policy denied the junior medical examiners overtime because if they got paid for overtime in order to clear up the body jams that sometimes clogged the corridors of the morgue and tested the capacity of the necropsy labs the juniors would be making more than the chief medical examiner himself, and that would never do.

On the other hand the executive deputy medical examiner sometimes had reason to want a little overtime for himself—his wife wanting a new car, one of his daughters needing a graduation dress, something, all the time something—so he stayed late and cut a few extra.

That was also prohibited by regulation but that reg could be superseded and circumvented under the power vested in him by another reg that said the executive deputy medical examiner, as part of his administrative duties, had the right to declare an emergency and authorize overtime when too many corpses started piling up and began to constitute a danger to the general health and well-being of members of the maintenance workers union and the drivers of linen service trucks, represented by Teamsters Local 386, everybody being aware that it was never a good idea to fart around with the Teamsters because they could make life miserable.

So the need to buy his daughter a new dress or his wife a new car or himself a new set of golf clubs worked right in there with a commendable response to a clear and present civic and social danger.

His name was Bolivar Boltiseri, a short, wide, thickset little Brazilian, known to friends as Bull and to colleagues and employees as Bull's Balls or Geenuts for his habit of saying "Gee" whenever surprised, pleased or dismayed, this being one of the first English words he learned to speak. He was well liked by his subordinates and widely respected for the considerable skill he brought to his work.

Gloved, masked and gowned like an astronaut, sharply aware of Gotch's red toe tag printed with the large black letters of the disease that had killed him, scientifically intrigued and fascinated by what organic damage he would find, he was ready to make the first incision, opening Gotch from throat to groin, when he spotted the little open-work cage of steel.

"Gee," he said.

Moments later, having removed the small curved blade that had severed Gotch's carotid artery and rendered him a corpse at least a few days before his time, he said, "What the fuck is a valvulotome doing in the throat of an AIDS patient who was going to die any day, any hour?"

Whistler dialed the number of the bookstore on Hollywood Boulevard where the hookers did their browsing when the weather outside was too bitchy for business.

If somebody had the number of a bookstore programmed into a telephone, it figured that person either knew somebody who worked there or that person bought a lot of books.

"This is Kenny Gotch. I was wondering if you'd check my account," Whistler said.

"How do you spell that last name?"

Whistler spelled it out.

"Here it is. Yes, Mr. Gotch, what would you like to know?"

"Have I got a credit balance with you or do I owe you some money?"

"The account balances. You don't owe us and we don't owe you. I notice there's been no activity in your account for more than six months. Have you been out of town?"

"No, I just haven't been reading as much as I used to."

"I see. Do you want us to go on with the search for the last three titles you requested?"

"Which three titles would that be?"

*"The Key of Solomon, The Book of Signs,* and *The Constitution of Honorius."*

"Yeah, keep on searching. If you come across any of them give me a call at this new number. I'm minding a friend's house for a while."

"Yes, sir."

Whistler gave the clerk his own number.

"You still understand that the chances of finding good copies of the three books you requested are pretty slim," the clerk said. "This being the Age of Aquarius and all that."

"Yes, I know."

"I just wanted to remind you so you wouldn't think we weren't searching the market as thoroughly as we could be."

Whistler hung up and went on punching numbers.

He got two disconnects and a no answer, from "Jane (Home)," in a row.

The disconnects were expected in a town full of nomads and snowbirds, the no answer a surprise in these times when every hooker and bookie had an answering machine, every crack dealer a beeper and nearly every thief a cellular phone.

The next call was answered by the voice of a woman identifying herself as the housekeeper of the rectory at St. Jude's Roman Catholic Church.

"Is this the St. Jude's in Pomona?" Whistler asked.

"No, this is St. Jude's in Van Nuys," she said.

"Father Patrick's parish?"

"No, Father Charles Mitchum's parish."

"I must've got the wrong number."

"Not necessarily," she said.

"Pardon?" he said.

"If you were trying to call a priest because you're in spiritual difficulty, it may be that you were led to get what you'd call a wrong number because Father Mitchum, not Father Patrick, might be the priest who can give you the counsel you're seeking."

"Well, I don't think so," Whistler said. "I'm supposed to call Father Patrick about the air-conditioning in the rectory. You got trouble with the air-conditioning in your rectory?"

"We don't have air-conditioning in our rectory."

"Well, there you go. Maybe, like you say, something led me to read the wrong number for the wrong church out of the book. I mean maybe I *was* meant to call St. Jude's in Van Nuys because you need air-conditioning in the rectory."

"It would be nice," the housekeeper said, "but I don't think St. Jude's—this St. Jude's—could afford it. Are you sure you're not having any spiritual difficulty?"

"The only difficulty I'm having is getting enough work, these hard times."

"They get nice breezes in Pomona," the housekeeper said. "I don't know why they'd need air-conditioning in Pomona."

"Well, the Lord giveth and the Lord taketh away," Whistler said.

"You're sure you couldn't use a little spiritual counseling?"

"Well, maybe I could," he said, "and maybe we could talk

about a little air-conditioning. You never know. When do you think Father Mitchum can see me?"

She got all flustered for a moment, explaining that Father's calendar—which he took care of himself—was in the office, so if he'd just wait a moment, she'd pick up the phone in Father's office and check his desk calendar from there.

She was back in about two minutes. "How about tomorrow at three o'clock in the afternoon?"

"There's no charge for this, is there?" he asked.

"Of course not," she replied, much offended but being careful not to show it.

"Because I was going to say maybe I could make Father a deal on some air-conditioning in partial trade for the counseling."

"That's very kind of you," she said, "but I think not. It gets very hot out here in the valley as you can well imagine, but we don't coddle ourselves the way they apparently do over in Pomona. What name?"

"Whistler," he said.

She repeated it, calling him "Mister Whistler" with a lisp and then hung up.

He sat there with the dial tone buzzing, thinking of how silly the name he'd taken for himself sounded when combined with mister, thinking about Kenny Gotch, religiously betwixt and between, reaching out for comfort in his time of trial to a priest in a church that couldn't afford air-conditioning.

# 17

*When* somebody rang her bell Mary peered through the peephole in the door of the little house on Pinehurst midway up the hill from Franklin.

She frowned at the distorted fish-eye images of two bulky men in sport jackets and double-knit slacks.

"Yes?" she asked, without opening the door even though the security chain was engaged.

"Does a Mary Bucket live here?" the man closest to the door asked, raising his voice louder than it really had to be for him to be heard.

"Yes?" she said again, no more than that, giving nothing away, like a cautious farmer to whom words were nuggets of gold.

"We're the police."

"Yes?" she said yet another time.

He reached into his back pocket and took out his shield case, thumbing the flap back and holding the badge up to the peephole.

"Let me see the ID," she said.

He turned the case around and held up the ID behind the celluloid window.

She read the name, "Ernest Lubbock. What station?" she asked.

"Hollywood."

"What's the other man's name?"

"Jackson. Martin Jackson."

"Just a second."

She went to the phone and called Hollywood station, verifying that they did indeed have two detectives, assigned to homicide, by the names of Ernest Lubbock and Martin Jackson, and that they had indeed been sent out on a case involving the unlawful death of one Kenneth Gotch.

She went back to the door and opened it.

"You satisfied?" Lubbock asked.

"Take it easy, Ernie, for God's sake," Jackson said. "The lady done the right thing what with all kinds of freaks and funny faces running around breaking in here and there. Thank you, Ms. Bucket. Now, if we could have a few words."

Mary acted reluctant, even after getting the verification, about letting them in. Lubbock sighed and turned his head away, as though losing patience with her.

"Are you the head nurse at the Angeles Hospice?" Jackson asked.

"One of them. We've got six on regular shift and a seventh to fill in."

"So, all right, were you the supervising nurse on last out last night and this morning?" Lubbock asked, shifting his considerable weight from foot to foot.

"Last out?"

"Graveyard."

"Yes, I was."

"So you were on duty this morning when one Kenneth Gotch was found dead?"

"I was. It was no surprise. He had AIDS. He died of Kaposi's sarcoma."

"Not exactly," Lubbock said, rocking from side to side.

"Something wrong, detective?" she asked. "You got a nervous disorder?"

"Well, lady, what I got is a full bladder and I also got to move my bowels. Seeing as how you're a nurse, I don't mind telling you that I had my gall bladder out and ever since then, if I don't watch what I eat—like I have too much grease?—well, it just goes through me like the old you know what through a goose."

"You want to use my bathroom?"

"I'd appreciate it."

She finally relented and let them in, telling Lubbock to go down the corridor off the living room and take the second door on the right, asking Jackson to sit down on the couch, sitting down on the arm of the easy chair herself, letting him know that they weren't going to be staying any longer than necessary.

"What are two homicide detectives doing coming around asking about the death of an AIDS patient and what did your partner mean about not exactly?"

"Kenneth Gotch didn't die of whatever it was you said. He was *going* to die of Kaposi's . . . whatever . . . any day—the ME said so—but that's not what he died of."

"What did he die of?"

"Don't you know?"

"Are we going to be cute?" she said. "Are we going to ask silly questions and see if somebody drops their drawers?"

"What are you talking about, lady?"

"What I'm talking about is, if I knew that Mr. Gotch died of something other than Kaposi's sarcoma I would've put it into my report."

"You didn't see anything unusual about the dead man?"

"Tell me what it was I should've seen."

He reached into his pocket and took out a small brown envelope, opened the flap and upended the mouth of it over the coffee table. A little curved scalpel attached to a cagelike device no bigger than a thumb fell onto the glass.

She leaned over her crossed legs, her hands clasped in her lap.

"That was found in Gotch's throat," Jackson said.

She made a noise as though someone had punched her in the belly.

"You know what that is?" he asked.

"A valvulotome," Mary said. "A finger blade for cracking heart valves. When the operating field is full of blood so the surgeon can't see and has to feel his or her way. This little cage part fits over the fingertip so you can hook and cut. You understand?"

"We've been told."

"Since the heart-lung machine was invented, it's hardly ever used anymore," she said.

"So how did it get in Gotch's throat?" he asked.

"I've got no idea."

"When you saw the blood all over him, didn't you wonder?"

"Throat and lung hemorrhage is common with Kaposi's. I had no reason to suspect that the patient hadn't finally succumbed to his illness," she said. "Where's your partner? He's taking a long time for a shit."

"Huh," Jackson said, as though startled and dismayed by her mouth.

"I'm a nurse, remember? No reason to be shy around me. You say what you please and I'll say what I please. So what's taking him so long?" She started to rise off the arm of the chair as though she intended to find out.

"Lady," Jackson said. "Why're you getting mad?"

"I'm not getting angry. I'm just . . . well, my God, you come in here and tell me that a patient of mine got . . ."

"Murdered?"

"Whatever you say . . . right under my nose. I'm supposed to be responsible for patients in my care and—"

"That's why we're here," Lubbock said from the doorway. He walked very softly for such a big man. "You know anybody still keeps knives like that?"

"I suppose any number of surgeons might keep a valvulotome as a curiosity if nothing else," she said.

Lubbock walked across the room.

"But you don't happen to know if any surgeon was in Kenneth Gotch's room this morning?"

"Not that I know of."

"Any nurses, any orderlies, any volunteers go in there around six, seven, seven-thirty?"

"I'll have to ask."

"Oh, that's all right, we'll be doing that," Lubbock said. "It okay if I take a load off my feet?"

Mary waved her permission, then slid off the arm of the chair and settled herself on the cushion, ready now to have them stay as long as they had to stay.

"Who found Gotch dead?"

"I did."

"So, who was the last person to see him alive if you was the first person to find him dead?"

"Probably the visitor who was in the room with him."

"The visitor? There was no mention of a visitor on your report."

"There's nothing that requests that information on the form."

"So, at seven o'clock in the morning you allow visitors?"

"No. Visiting hours don't start until after ten except under special circumstances, but people come early. Before they go to work."

"Nobody stopped him getting in there before visiting hours?"

"Nobody saw him go into the room."

Lubbock and Jackson exchanged glances, as though commenting on the miserable security the Angeles Hospice had in place, even though what a facility full of dying people would need elaborate security for apparently didn't figure into their reasoning.

"This visitor was a relative?"

"A friend of a relative."

"He told you that?"

"Yes."

"What else did he tell you?"

"Nothing much. He was spattered with blood when the patient threw up and expired—"

"Wait a minute, wait a minute," Lubbock said.

"—and I was too concerned about washing him off to hold much of a conversation with him," Mary went on, insisting on finishing her statement.

"Didn't it ever enter your head something was funny? This visitor being close enough to get spattered with Gotch's blood?"

"I was taking care of an emergency."

"So, are you thinking about it now?"

Mary stared at him for a moment, then hugged herself and shuddered, looking away as though there was danger in Lubbock's eyes. "Jesus Christ."

"You could say that, lady. You was probably standing there in the same room—"

"Washing his face and neck," she said.

"—with the man what'd just finished slitting Gotch's throat," Lubbock finished.

"On the other hand . . . ," Jackson said.

"On the other hand what, Marty?" Lubbock said.

"Never mind, Ernie, just a thought."

You didn't have to be a mind reader to know what he meant. On the other hand Mary had been in the room. There were stories in the papers all the time about nurses flipping out and killing terminal patients, believing God had given them a mission to relieve them of their suffering.

Whistler kept on moving down the list, punching in the numbers, listening to the busy signals, the distant ringing in empty offices and houses, the clicks and beeps of machines. A Chinese takeout, a liquor store, a disconnect, somebody by the name of Kilroy who this time wasn't there.

He tried to figure out a pattern of preference, the most used or most needed numbers first, home and work numbers paired, but it soon became clear that no matter how organized the telephone directory had been at the beginning, time had left it in disarray.

The next entry after Kilroy was a photo studio called Rahab; a silky voice on a machine told him so.

The next was somebody by the name of Bobby L whose machine informed him in the sexiest voice imaginable that she was only *temporarily* unavailable.

The one after that was Abe Forstman's, marked on the directory as "cousin" with a question mark after it. Did that mean Kenny Gotch was as unclear as Abe seemed to be about their relationship or was it an idle notation giving away his reluctance to have much to do with anyone who might report back to his mother and father in Chicago?

Abe Forstman's wife picked up and identified herself instead of just saying hello or yes the way people usually do.

"I'm a friend of your husband's, Mrs. Forstman," Whistler said. "I was over at the hospice when your nephew—"

"Cousin by marriage—"

"—passed away. Cousin. Yes—"

"—three times removed."

"—okay," he said. "I went with your husband—with Abe—over to Kenny's apartment and I told him I'd call when and if I found out anything."

"So, you want to speak to Abe?"

"Yes, I think that would be a good idea. And Mrs. Forstman? I'm very sorry to hear about Kenny."

"My cousin by marriage three times removed."

"That's right."

"I'll get Abe," she said.

It took a minute that seemed about fifteen minutes long, Whistler sitting there waiting with the characteristic stare of someone trapped in a cage of time.

Abe Forstman cleared his throat before saying hello. It made Whistler acutely aware of the old man's mortality and what he must be feeling losing a young relative, no matter how distant, to this new plague that God, Satan or somebody had visited on the earth.

"This is Whistler, Mr. Forstman," Whistler said. "I just wanted to tell you I checked and found out that Kenny didn't have a car."

"Okay," Forstman said. "That's one thing less I got to worry about."

"Is there anything else you can tell me about Kenny?" Whistler asked.

"Like what?"

"Like did he go to shul or church or practice any faith?"

"I told you, I hardly knew the boy. I went over because he's my wife's—"

"I know, Mr. Forstman. I just thought you may have had a conversation with his mother and father back in . . . ?"

"Chicago. They're still in Chicago. Yes, we talked to the mother and father. We figured it would be better coming from one of the family. Even a cousin three times removed."

"I think that was the right thing to do."

"Kenny's mother took it very hard. She broke down right

there on the phone and her husband had to take the rest of the message. Get the details."

"You told him how Kenny died?"

"What could I do? It's not the kind of thing Manny wanted to hear, but how could I not tell him the truth? Everybody deserves the truth, no matter how hard it might be."

There was a lift to his voice as though he were asking for confirmation, and Whistler gave it to him by saying, "You did the right thing," again.

"Manny's coming to get the body."

"He could've paid the mortuary here for an escort."

"I told him that but he wanted to come take his boy home hisself."

"I can understand that," Whistler said.

"The wife's not coming with him. Harriet's not coming."

"I can understand that, too."

"Manny said they want us to come visit in Chicago if we ever decide to take a trip east. We hardly know the people. I maybe met them once or twice. At the wedding where I met Kenny. Wherever. I don't think we talked on the phone three times altogether, including this last phone call I had to make. Why should Manny invite us to come visit them in Chicago?"

"I don't know. Did you offer him a place to stay when he comes to get Kenny?"

"I told him if he didn't mind the couch. We got a small apartment, my wife and me."

"Well, that's why he invited you."

"What do we need with a big flat, just the two of us, my wife and me?"

"That was a nice thing to do," Whistler said.

"What's that?"

"Offering Manny a place to sleep when he comes to get his boy. Offering him the couch and the comfort of relatives."

"Yes, it's a comfortable couch," Forstman said. "It opens up into a bed."

"So, anyway," Whistler said, "there was nothing else said?"

"No, nothing else. You have anything in mind?"

"I'm just hoping for whatever I can get."

"What's your real interest in this, Mr. Whistler?"

"You mean because everybody deserves the truth no matter how hard it may be?"

"That's right."

"Well, I don't really agree with that, Mr. Forstman. It's nothing I think you'd want to know about that you don't already know about and I'm not sure about anything anyway."

"So, we'll leave it at that," Forstman said, clearing his throat again.

Whistler hung up. His hand was starting to cramp up from holding the receiver so long. But he shifted hands and went on punching in numbers until he'd run the string all the way to the bottom.

He took a break, opening the sliding doors onto the deck that looked out over the canyon and the freeway. It was bumper to bumper both ways. The arteries of the city were clogged. The commuters sat silently in their cars, nobody leaning on a horn, somebody getting out every now and then to stand tiptoe in the roadway, trying to see what the obstruction was up ahead. Patient as sheep until one day some mild accountant or salesman would go nuts and either abandon his car where it stood, walking off the freeway toward an off ramp and home, or pulling a hunting rifle from the trunk and shooting people down at random.

"You didn't see the knife?" Lubbock asked.

"Look at it. It'd be easy to miss buried in somebody's throat," she said, resentful that they should be playing the game on her, switching subjects, asking about this and that and then this again, the same questions from different angles, hoping she would expose herself—drop her drawers—in confusion.

Lubbock nodded, as though giving her the point.

"When was the last time any of your staff saw him alive?"

"Early this morning, when a nurse's aide went in to give him a bed pan and later on when she went back to give him a sponge bath."

"What time?"

"It's down on the schedule. Six o'clock."

"You didn't remember who was in there when we asked before."

"Fear sharpens the memory," she said, trying to make a joke.

"So, when you walked into the room you saw this visitor—"

"A fat man in a loud sport jacket who looked—"

"—standing there spattered with Gotch's blood—"

"—a little like that old-time actor—you know, what's his name?—Wally—"

"—and you told him to take off his jacket and his shirt and anything else—"

"—Beery. Yes, Wallace Beery. And he had—"

"—that could've got blood on it and—"

"—a glass eye."

"—you washed him off and then what?"

"I was thinking about his glass eye when a candy striper walked in."

"Hey!" Jackson said, tapping Lubbock on the arm. "You hear that? A glass eye, looks like Wally Beery in a loud sport coat."

"Is this what they call serendipity?" Lubbock said. "Is this luck giving us a kiss?"

"We should go to the track," Jackson said.

Whistler went back inside, closing the doors behind him, closing out the surf sound of idling engines, and finished off the list. When he was finished he toted up the score.

Twenty-eight numbers available on the speed dial.

Two empty. Down to twenty-six.

Five disconnects. Down to twenty-one.

Eight businesses. Three fast-food takeout restaurants, a movie house, a drugstore, a photographer's studio, a liquor store and a bookstore, every one a pickup except the photo shop. Thirteen numbers left.

The church was one.

Abe Forstman was one.

George Gambler was one. That left ten.

Two numbers for "Mike"; two for "Jane"; one each for Bobby L and Bobby D, one voice as sexy as the other; one for Diana, sounding worn-out and world weary on her machine; Pooch, who was not at home and not at work at this time of night; Jet, a black dude, five would get you ten; and Kilroy, who still wasn't there.

He ran the string a second time, with nothing added to what he already had. He waited an hour and then started down the list again.

"This candy striper?" Lubbock said.

"Diana Corday." Mary glared at him, shifting her weight in the chair as though imprisoned in it. They were going around again. Her irritation was turning to anger. That's what they wanted and she knew it, playing the goddamn game on her. Good cop, bad cop. The one called Lubbock, the one who'd used her toilet, making veiled suggestions that were frightening, almost insulting, the other one stepping in and smoothing things over, being sweet and kind. "She knew the patient. I let her go home right away. She's a volunteer, not a professional and it shook her up."

"She knew him?" Lubbock said, leaping on that fact like a cat on a rat.

"Slightly. They didn't have a relationship or anything like that."

"You know that for a fact, do you?" Lubbock asked.

"Well, that's what she told me."

"Well, she would, wouldn't she?"

"What do you mean by that?"

"You heard about people helping patients over the line?" Lubbock said.

There it was, Mary thought, he'd come right out with it, watching her with his piggy eyes.

"Well, anybody works in a hospital—a friend—could do the same. I mean anybody," Lubbock went on.

He said anybody but he meant her, Mary thought.

"Oh, no, oh, no," Mary said, shaking her head, "it was nothing like that."

"You know that for a fact, do you?" Jackson said, sweetly and kindly, making a mockery of his repetition of his partner's remark.

"When you saw someone in the room with Gotch and when you saw that Gotch was dead and when you found out that the visitor, this Wally Beery look-alike, wasn't even a relative, why didn't you call the police right then and there?" Lubbock asked.

"I didn't know how Mr. Gotch had died. It looked like he'd hemorrhaged into his lungs and vomited up his blood. I didn't know there was a knife in his throat."

"But this visitor in the room with his blood on him—"

"He was terrified. He said that he'd leaned over to hear something Kenny Gotch was trying to say—or he thought he was trying to say—and Mr. Gotch threw up and splashed him. It was on his cheek and neck. I cleaned him up."

"Why didn't you tell him to stay?"

"I didn't think I had reason to do that," Mary said. "Even if I thought I had reason, how could I have stopped him from going if he wanted to go?"

"You could've called security."

"We've got an elderly man and a boy who carry guns they shouldn't be allowed to carry. The job doesn't pay a hell of a lot."

Jackson slapped his knees with his hands and stood up. Lubbock stared at her a moment longer, then stood up too.

"I think that's all for the present," Jackson said. "Please don't take any trips out of town. We may want to interview you again."

She stood up, ready to show them to the door, wanting them out of her house.

"One more thing," Lubbock said at the door, handing over his card. "Anybody comes around to visit Gotch or somebody comes around asking about Gotch, you call this number and tell them I want you patched through to wherever my partner and me happen to be."

She nodded again, thinking about Whistler, deciding to say nothing about him to these cops.

"Do you think the man who was in there with Kenny Gotch was the one who killed him?" she asked.

"What do you think?" Jackson said.

On the third go-round Whistler listened to the messages of Bobby L and Bobby D and the tired Diana yet again, figuring them for professional girls, fellow merchandisers along with Kenny on the stroll, available to him, as he was no doubt available to them, for conversation and comfort in the long dark hours of the night.

Pooch answered this third time around. He gave his name as William Mandell when Whistler asked, sounding like a young boy. He didn't hesitate to say that he'd known Kenny but that they'd had a falling out. He hadn't heard from him in maybe eight or nine months he said, as though hoping that Whistler was a peacemaker asked by Kenny to make the call and patch things up between them. When Whistler told him about Kenny's death, he hung up before Whistler could question him any further.

Whistler reached Jet too.

Jet sounded wary and suspicious. Whistler couldn't con or work an address out of him.

"Kenny said you were his connection," Whistler said.

"Connection for what?" Jet asked.

"You know, a little of this, a little of that."

"Can't you say what you mean, bro?"

"Well, you know how it is."

"No, I don't. I don't know how it is. I know how it is with anybody who don't want to speak out, say what they mean. You heard of en-trap-ment? You heard of un-der cov-er po-lice os-si-fer?"

He'd hung up then, just like that, no more screwing around.

Whistler wondered if doing what he did, working with cops so much, taking an attitude when hassling and hustling hookers and pimps, grifters and gonnifs, marked the way he spoke. Warned the wary that he was cop, even if all he carried was a private license.

That was it, Kenny's handful of numbers, maybe everybody

he knew and had ever known since coming to La-La Land. Hell, if they'd all been true-blue, that would be more friends than most movie stars could brag about, but chances were that they were a lot less than friends, some even enemies.

Whistler picked out two clean file cards and made a list of the people he hadn't been able to reach after three tries; machine pickups or no pickup at all.

The two Bobbys, Diana, Jane still not available at home or at work, Mike and Kilroy.

Kilroy's machine had at last kicked in to inform Whistler that he had reached John Kilroy, associate professor of comparative religion, department of the humanities at UCLA.

On the second card he wrote down the names of those he wanted to talk to face-to-face, George Gambler, Father Mitchum, Jet—if he could ever run him down—and the weary Diana. Working on instinct, on the nuances of voice and position on Kenny Gotch's directory. Hell, maybe he'd be talking to all of them sooner or later. There weren't that many, after all.

"You have a profitable crap?" Jackson asked.

"I tossed the bathroom and managed three minutes in the bedroom. All of the usual stuff a woman's got and some not so usual."

"What's that?"

"A lot of herbs and ointments with funny names. Some twisted pieces of root. Crystals, charms and amulets."

"There's a lot of that. Christ, you can buy some of that stuff at the five-and-dime."

"She's a nurse, for God's sake," Lubbock said. "What's she doing with all that mumbo-jumbo?"

"For one thing, she could be a witch," Jackson said, looking at his partner sideways, pulling his leg a little.

But Lubbock wasn't taking it as a joke. "There was some books with some very funny drawings and symbols in them," he said, nodding his head in agreement. "You think we ought to get Essex in on this?"

"What I think is that Essex's the Satan maven in the police department, and spending all your time with a specialty like that makes a man narrow-minded. I think he'll go running around looking for a cult and a conspiracy when all I think we got here is a plain homicide," Jackson said.

"What makes you say that?"

"Somebody's dead, fachrissake. Let's worry about first things first."

"So, okay, we don't mention it to Essex yet," Lubbock agreed, "but I still don't get it. The woman's a nurse."

"Don't you know nothing? Who do you think witches were in the first place? They was women who cured people with herbs and charms."

"And rode around with broomsticks up their snatches," Lubbock said. "You think nurse Bucket rides around with a broomstick up her snatch?"

"I don't think so."

"Well, she sure rides around with a wild hair up her ass."

# 18

*Mike* Rialto had always been afraid of the dark. That's not to say he was afraid of the night, as long as there was a sufficiency of lights around. A city as big as Los Angeles, with all the shine bouncing off the sky, was a perfect place for him. It was the confines of a closed space—even his own apartment—that made him nervous after the sun went down. Even the late television movies didn't offer enough companionship to keep the fear at bay.

When he wasn't arranging the exchange of ass for cash, checking out the strolls for new talent fresh in from Des Moines or prowling around all night after some husband's or wife's straying tail, he could be found sitting on a bench by a bus stop on Sunset, Hollywood, Melrose or Santa Monica, waving to the night crawlers and kitty cruisers, building his reputation for eccentricity, polishing his image as one of La-La Land's prime characters.

They told the story of one evening when Richard Nixon, out there on the campaign trail that first time around, riding in his limo with a security car in front and one behind—a regular caravan driving west along the Sunset Strip on the way to a rubber chicken dinner—spotted the man sitting on the bench and asked about him; was told who and what Rialto was, this famous character in La-La Land.

Nixon told the driver to pull up to the curb right in front of the bench, lowered the window and said, "How's it going, Mike?"

Rialto peered one-eyed at the stranger with the familiar face, got up off the bench, stepped down into the gutter and stuck his head in the window.

"Everything all right, Mike?" Nixon asked, getting a kick out of what he read as the man's confusion at being confronted so unexpectedly with a figure of such overpowering celebrity; waiting for the gushing, fawning, flattering response he was sure would follow.

"Well, I'll tell you, Dick," Rialto said, as though it was an everyday affair for a presidential candidate to stop by and ask about his well-being, "I've been wondering. How come you don't call me anymore?"

Nixon, they say, went off laughing fit to beat the band.

Which is all by way of illustrating the quickness of Rialto's wit but says nothing about his childish fear of the dark. It was there like an imp gibbering in his ear.

But after all the pain and panic occasioned by his bloody confrontation with Abe Forstman's nephew, Kenny Gotch, he was smoked down to the short end of a roach, and the hope of sleep, even in the dark of his bedroom, beckoned. Besides, his glass eye was giving him hell, the angry tear duct giving out a steady stream of yellowish exudant, which he wiped away with his handkerchief now and then. He had to take it out and give the socket a rest. It was the only cure.

He hurried to his Cadillac and drove home . . . such as it was.

*       *       *

You didn't have to be a cat to smell a rat.

Canaan sat in his BarcaLounger, staring at *The Man of a Thousand Faces* with Jimmy Cagney as Lon Chaney, on some local independent channel. Not really seeing it.

Seeing little Sarah's broken body. Seeing the fragment of a glance that had passed between Bosco and Whistler when they'd lied to him about what it was he wasn't to be told, his cop's intuition kicking in, not really hearing the conversation after that.

Hearing the screams and lamentations of his brother and sister-in-law while Whistler talked about Mike Rialto bringing him some news about Kenny Gotch, the kid who had sometimes worn purple dresses and rhinestone shoes and called himself Harriet LaRue.

There was nothing Whistler would try to hide from him, nothing except news about the murdered child who had been his niece. Whistler would take care not to rake open that old wound. So he knew the truth, even though he hadn't been told the truth. All he needed was confirmation. All he needed was to get the story from the horse's mouth.

He'd rest another hour and then go out searching for Rialto in the all-night coffee shops and on the benches at the bus stops along the boulevards. He would find out what evil Rialto had stumbled upon in the bloody vomit of a dead man.

He knew what even a lot of the cops who saw all that he saw didn't seem to know. There was such a thing as evil in the world and it lived in the world under a hundred names, the best known of which was Satan, and there were millions of demons and devils in Satan's legions, not the least of whom was the one who'd destroyed his brother's child.

He coughed once and then went into a spasm, coughing violently into his hand. He got up and went into the kitchen without turning off the television. He took the *t'filin* from the kitchen drawer, placed the block upon his forehead and secured it with the black ribbons. Then he tied the other one to his forearm, crossing the tapes in the form of a pictograph, choosing *daleth* from the three, *daleth, shin* and *yod* (door, row of teeth and hand), available to him by tradition.

He touched his temples with the fingers of each hand and began to rock, imagining himself in Jerusalem at the wall.

When Rialto climbed the stairs to the second floor, turning at the landing to walk down to his own front door, he was not quick enough to turn around and run away.

Ernie Lubbock and Marty Jackson stepped out of the shadows.

"Lookee, lookee, lookee," Lubbock said. "Old piss-eye's home. You come to use the john? It's running out of your eye."

"Com'ere and let me wipe it off on your tie," Rialto said.

"We got no time for pleasantries," Lubbock said. "Open up and let's get inside out of the wind."

"There ain't any wind," Rialto said.

"There's going to be some wind when we start blowing in your ear," Jackson said.

Frick and Frack, Amos and Andy, Abbott and Costello, the clown act of Hollywood station, Rialto thought as he inserted the key into the lock.

Lubbock and Jackson shouldered Rialto aside and walked into the apartment like a couple of elephants, Lubbock standing astride in the middle of the living room, Jackson going on through, poking his nose into the bathroom on one side and the kitchen on the other.

"So this is how the other half lives," he said.

Rialto stood there watching them, the key in his hand, wishing it were a knife or gun. How he would have liked to get these bastards off his back before they started in on him.

"Take a load off your feet, Mike," Jackson said, sitting down on the couch, spreading himself out, Lubbock already in the recliner, leaving Rialto nothing but one of the straight-backed chairs that went with the chrome and Formica table beside the picture window. It was covered now with his typewriter and a scattering of reports he was making up.

"You working on anything besides selling teenage ass at the moment?" Jackson asked in the same tone of voice he would have used inquiring after Rialto's mother's health.

"I don't do pimping anymore," Rialto said, like a restaurateur saying he didn't do omelettes with truffles.

"Butter wouldn't melt in your mouth, would it?" Lubbock

said. "You are such an ice man. Look at you sitting there so cool, lying to us without a tremor."

Jackson picked it up. "We know that you are a procurer, a panderer and a pimp—"

"All of which is much the same," Lubbock threw in.

"—but what we don't know is when you grew the balls to become a contract man."

"Ho," Rialto said, a mild exclamation of surprise and forced amusement.

"Did you not hear me right?" Jackson asked.

"I thought you said something about a contract but I guess I got it wrong."

"I can understand your dismay to be so accused—" Jackson said.

"Especially since a creep like you, working in the flesh trade—"

"—thinking yourself beyond suspicion in the commission of an act of violence—" Jackson went on.

"—might consider changing professions," Lubbock said, finishing Jackson's sentence and his own.

"Might consider becoming a contract killer," Jackson said like a drumbeat.

Rialto jerked violently, a sickness rising up sour from his stomach into his throat, threatening to choke him or rush up through his sinuses to his eyes and spill out of the empty socket in a flood of acid. He coughed and made much ado about clearing his throat. "You caught me with one foot in the air," he said. "I was trying to follow you, but that last step was too much for me. Me, a contract killer? Give me some of that smoke or snort you're using."

"Do you know a Kenny Gotch?" Jackson asked.

"I wouldn't say that."

"Did you visit him at Angeles this morning?"

"I stopped by."

"Then you know Kenny Gotch."

"We never even got to say how do you do."

"For Christ's sake, the man threw up on you. I'd say you were pretty close."

"I thought he was trying to say something. I put my ear down."

"So what did he say?"

"He never got it out."

"Why were you there, Mike?" Lubbock asked, taking hold of the other handle of the interrogation.

"I told Kenny Gotch's uncle—cousin—by marriage, a couple of times removed, that I'd stop by. It was just an act of Christian charity."

"The man was dying of AIDS," Jackson said.

"Capriccio's socora," Lubbock added.

"I understand that's what done him in," Rialto said.

"No, what done him in, Rialto, was a blade—surgeons call it a valvulotome," Jackson said. He was holding up his forefinger and wiggling it. "Clamps on to the surgeon's finger so he can get into tight spots. Sharp as a whore's shinbone."

"Don't use them much anymore," Lubbock said. "A fucking antique. You collect antiques, Mike?"

"For God's sake, what'd I know about a thing called a valvulotome?" Rialto asked. He knew his voice had risen an octave, knew that he was giving off the stink of fear, the armpits and the back of his shirt wet with sweat underneath his colorful sport jacket. "I wouldn't even know how to use one to cut a man."

Jackson was up and off the couch in a flash. He moved around the room like a whirlwind, opening drawers, picking up objects off the shelves, going out into the kitchen, sweeping through it like an ill wind and coming back to dump a double handful of tools and cutlery on the table next to Rialto's elbow.

A pair of cuticle clippers, a nail clipper with a file, an assortment of paring knives, a pair of short-bladed scissors, an apple corer, a peeler and one or two other items.

"You wouldn't have to know much. All you'd have to do is practice with some of these items, available in anybody's house, walk into a hospital supply store, a pawn shop maybe, buy the blade, wrap it in your handkerchief, walk into the hospice, visit the room, bend over to say hello, unwrap the blade and put the point of it here . . ." He poked Rialto in the stomach up high and then poked again a little higher in the center of the chest where Rialto's heart was beating like a runaway clock, poked him at the base of the throat. ". . . Or here. Push down. Slice the carotid artery."

"Right here," Jackson said, poking again and again, Rialto wincing, the stink of his own sweat filling his nose, good eye smarting and glass eye weeping yellow.

"Hey," Rialto said, his only expression of complaint.

"Cuff the sonofabitch," Jackson said, straightening up and turning away.

"We better Mirandize him first," Lubbock said.


"I can't imagine why they did it," Rahab said, placing his black attaché case on his knees and snapping the locks.

"Did what?" Jeanne Millholme said, slapping at the curl of hair falling across her brow.

Her face was carefully made up, her lips painted with one color and outlined with a darker color, her eyes dressed with pale brown shadow and sketched with eye liner, creating what she no doubt believed was the face of a seductress, Rahab thought.

"Manufactured these pictures of you," he said, and carefully placed three eight-by-tens, one beside the other, on the table top between them.

She leaned forward, her elbows held close to her body, her clasped hands pressed against her belly underneath her breasts, lifting them out of the scooped neck of her peasant blouse somewhat, revealing that she wore no bra. She studied the photos carefully, without comment, her breath coming harder and faster, color rising from the neckline of her blouse and flooding her bosom, neck and cheeks.

"They're disgusting," she finally blurted out, as though spitting something foul from her mouth.

"Well," he said, as though they didn't deserve such severe condemnation as all that. "You were right. Somebody had retouched the portraits I took of you. And then they went a lot further."

"They've put my face on the bodies of old hags."

He bent over and twisted his head and shoulders, as though trying to see the photos right side up, seeing what she was seeing, as though he hadn't seen them before.

"Bodies of witches, do you think?" he said.

"I don't know about such things."

He looked around, at the painted skull, at the paintings filled with imps and demons and monstrous phalluses.

"But you've read about them. Witches. Warlocks. That sort of being?" he said.

"Oh, I've read about them. Who hasn't read about them? But I never made a *study* of them."

"Then you have amazing insight into what that world is all about."

She pushed the photographs away, frowning a little, not knowing if he was complimenting her again. Oblique, subtle, dangerous compliments.

"How did you manage to get these?"

"I can be very persuasive when I have to be. I simply demanded that the technician hand over everything and anything that had to do with you. I made it clear that it would be dangerous for him to do otherwise."

"Why would this person do such a thing? Does he know me?"

"He must have found something likely about you in the photos I took. Something in your paintings in the background perhaps."

He was enjoying himself. It was so easy to manipulate someone who already believed there were conspiracies against them. All you had to do was listen carefully and tailor your scenario as close to their construct as possible but not so close as to make them suspicious that you were simply going along with them, humoring them, making fun of them.

He wondered if she'd convinced herself that he had been the broker who had contracted for the children stolen from the villages around Chihuahua? She'd looked at him a certain way when she'd told him about her stolen son. If she was out to get him, once she'd identified him to her satisfaction, he wondered if she'd have the courage to carry out whatever plan of revenge she'd carried with her for ten years. And he wondered if her son was one of the children murdered and discarded by the stealers who had escaped the Indians or if her son had been one of the survivors dragged along to make the fractured enterprise show at least a small profit instead of ending up a total loss.

And he wondered if she was aware that she was on the edge, might have already fallen over. Already mental, her susceptible and fragile mind knocked permanently out of whack by the loss of her son.

"I still don't understand," she said.

"Well, why should you? I mean you have a certain amazing intuition. Are you sure you never had any experience with witchcraft? Down in Mexico, I mean."

"I'm sure I don't know what you're talking about," she said, cutting her eyes in such a way that he knew that he was meant to believe otherwise as she flirted with the ideas he was giving her to conjure with.

"The Espiritismo," he said.

"What?" She barked the word and retreated a little.

"Charms and curses. Master Gambling Oil for the armpits of gamblers. Essence of Bendover to control minds. Chango candles for evil deeds."

She laughed. It was like a hiccup.

"Perhaps you offended someone. It might have to do with one of your painted skulls. By taking it and painting it you would have offended some great taboo.

"The city's crawling with illegal Mexicans. Someone may have recognized you as the woman who received the skulls of the dead from their enemies. A relative may have gone to an Espiritismo priest and was told to get pictures of you. The technician at the photo lab was Latino. It all makes sense. Did you do what I suggested?"

"What?"

"Did you check to see if anyone was stealing your nail parings or hair from your brush?"

"You're frightening me," she said.

"I'm sorry. I'm just looking for explanations."

"I never offended anyone to my knowledge. I kept myself quite alone."

"Then perhaps they mean to blackmail you. Perhaps they know that you're a wealthy woman."

Her eyes narrowed and her lips thinned at the mention of money.

Rahab had discovered long ago that people born to money

or who had won, inherited or earned a great deal of money, were quick to throw up their defenses at the mention of it.

"Is it supposed to be a secret?" he asked, innocently.

"I don't take out advertisements."

"It's the easiest thing in the world to check on someone's financial history," he said.

"Did you?"

"No, but if we were partners in some enterprise that required a substantial investment for both of us, I'm sure I'd check up on you just as you would check up on me."

"Well, I'm not in any partnership."

"No, of course not. I was just saying that would be a reason for me to check on someone's financial health. Somebody else could have another reason or reasons."

She slapped at the lock of hair. "I hate these pictures," she said, throwing her hand in the air as though brushing them away.

"I don't blame you. I'm sure your body looks nothing like the one in those photos. I'm sure—"

"It doesn't."

"—you have a beautiful, strong, healthy body."

"I don't know how beautiful it is."

"You're an artist. You *should* know."

"Well."

"I'm an artist, too, and I can tell. Just from the turn of your ankle, the grace of your hands, the fullness of your breasts."

She slapped at the stray lock of hair, agitated and excited beyond any other expression.

"I hope I'm not distressing you," Rahab said. "I just thought that if anyone can discuss the human body, surely artists have that privilege." He was smooth as glass, as sweet as honey, the words just tumbling out like little gems, pinning her to her chair, seducing her.

"I don't know," she said.

"What would you say are the three most compelling subjects for a human being to study and discuss?"

"What?" she said, confused by his sudden apparent switch of theme.

"I've thought about it and I've decided there are three. Sex, because it's the fountainhead of all the body knows and feels in the bone. Death, because it's the one destination to which all are traveling. And reflection upon the nature of the higher power that guides and informs us."

"God," she murmured.

"Well, that's only a name a good many of us give to that mysterious higher power. There are other names."

"Oh?"

"Satan is a name some use to identify that being they worship, adore and obey."

He reached out and touched her with the tip of his forefinger at that spot just between her breasts where they began to swell.

"I can help defend you if anyone really is trying to cast a spell on you." He made his finger into a hook and dragged down at the front of her blouse. "I am a considerable magician myself."

She shrugged her shoulders slightly; the blouse slid off her shoulders and revealed her breasts.

"I think we should take some pictures of you as you truly are."

"No," she said, but stood up when he took her hands in his and allowed him to undress her, shivering and trembling all the while, until she stood there naked, wearing nothing but a necklace of carved ivory beads and a pair of sandals.

He took three dozen pictures, placing her first in the middle of the floor in the pool of light pouring through the French doors, later standing on a hassock and later still kneeling and lying on the couch.

He urged her to pose. He made her bend her knees slightly and spread her legs, thrusting her pelvis forward, framing her sex with her two hands. He probed and tested her reluctance, searching for the acts that her repressed nature thought most perverse, unnatural and shameful.

Her eyes glittered. She often wet her lips, running her tongue across them carefully as though they burned. The color that flooded her chest, neck and face, ebbed and flowed like the tides of the sea according to the workings of her mind and the abandon of the pose.

After a time he took off his own clothes. He stood up on

a small chest and demanded that she approach him shuffling backward, reaching behind her to fondle him, then turning to face him as he bent over and presented his ass to her which she was told to kiss.

He nearly burst out laughing as a moan of ecstasy escaped her lips. There was a lot to this satanism that was downright comedic.

She stopped him when he wanted to have intercourse, playing the mad woman skillfully, having seen what she wanted to see, the devil's mark imprinted on the bodies of witches and warlocks in the most secret places, in the folds of the labia in women, in men under the eyelids or in the pit of the arm. The mark told of by the servant of the child stealer, the one who waited while the others did the gathering, the mark of a spider the color of a dark raspberry concealed in the crack of his buttocks, reaching out four of its eight legs.

Lubbock and Jackson took Rialto to Hollywood station and put him in the holding tank in spite of his practically hysterical protests that he was no contract killer.

What would he be doing, he asked, tippytoeing into some death house crawling with the most dangerous kinds of germs and viruses, sticking a—sticking a what? . . . what had they called it? . . . a valvulotome—into a man's chest? Why would he risk getting splashed with blood? Contaminating himself with something the medical community said was sure death.

"Okay, let's say I *am* a contract killer," Rialto said, "which each and every person I know or ever knew will tell you ain't possibly the case, since I've been known to faint at the sight of my own blood when I cut myself shaving—"

"You should use an electric," Lubbock said.

"—but, okay, let's say I'm such a person. Wouldn't such a person, when confronted with the possibility of contamination and what amounts to suicide take precautions?"

"Like what?" Lubbock said, both of the dicks staring at him as though they were truly interested.

"Well, like the man would've been as weak as a kitten being as sick as he was. He probably couldn't've raised a hand to save hisself if somebody decided to put a pillow over his face and smother him to death.''

Lubbock looked at Jackson with comic dismay. ''You hear that? I never would've thought of that.''

''Only a contract killer would've thought of such a thing,'' Jackson said.

''Well, it's too much for this old brain to figure out,'' Lubbock said. ''A man's dead. He had a blade in his throat. This man was all alone with him and said he had a conversation with him just before he died.''

''I never said I had a conversation,'' Rialto said. ''We never had a conversation.''

They closed the door on Rialto and went back to the squad room to rest their feet. It was coming up midnight and they'd put in a long day.

''You don't really believe Rialto did that poor sonofabitch?'' Lubbock said.

''I don't think Rialto's got the stones to do a gerbil,'' Jackson said. ''But if he didn't do it that leaves us with nurse Bucket or some person or persons unknown.''

# 19

*Whistler* was ready to wrap it for the night.

The traffic on the freeway was streaming by practically unabated. There'd been a time when you could depend upon some diminishment of noise and congestion after seven or eight o'clock in the evening. Now the river of automobiles and trucks eddied and flowed twenty-four hours a day, with only a thinning of the stream between the hours of three and four in the morning.

He'd gotten used to the roar; he pretended it was the lulling sound of surf like that enjoyed by the wealthy living along the Pacific shore.

Somebody was knocking at his front door. He seldom had visitors, not many came to his house unannounced at any hour let alone at midnight.

"Witches warming up for Halloween," he said to himself as he padded to the door in his stocking feet.

Mary was standing there, looking distraught and apologetic.

"I'm sorry . . . the hour . . . I tried to call—"

"It's all right."

"—but your line was busy," she said. "Probably nothing . . . I had a visit . . . two detectives . . . one named Lubbock . . . had to use my toilet."

"Come on in," Whistler said, taking her by the hand, trying to reduce the flow of words, the explanations tumbling over themselves.

"The other one was Jackson. He talked to me while Lubbock used my bathroom. He was a long time."

"Let me have your coat," Whistler said.

"I don't think he was using the toilet. I think he was nosing around."

"They show you a warrant?"

"All he said was that he'd had his gall bladder removed and when he ate anything greasy he got the shorts."

"You want a cup of coffee? Sit down and I'll make you a cup of coffee."

"No coffee. It'll keep me awake."

"A glass of wine."

"You don't drink wine."

"People bring their own, then leave behind what's left. I can find you a glass of wine, maybe a glass of brandy."

"Should I have asked for a warrant?"

"I don't know why they were at your house."

"I'll have a cup of coffee after all. I don't think I'll be able to sleep tonight."

"So, sit down. It'll only take a minute. Instant, okay?"

"Sure, instant."

While Whistler went out to the kitchen to microwave two cups of water and drop a teaspoon of instant coffee into each one, Mary called out from the living room, "Looks like I won the bet."

"What?"

"This place is a pigsty."

"You take sugar or sweetener?"

"Neither."

"You take milk or whitener?"

"Neither."

He walked back into the living room with the two cups. She was standing by the sliding doors leading to the deck. She raised her arms and stretched them out, indicating the condition of the room, her Halloween pumpkin grin on her face.

The place was a mess, magazines, newspapers, soiled clothes and the remains of a couple of TV dinners scattered everywhere. Louise had disappointed him again. She was supposed to stop by every Wednesday—and today was Wednesday—and give the house a going-over, four hours in the morning, but it was pretty clear that she'd failed to show up.

"We should have put up stakes for the bet," he said, crossing the room and handing her the mug.

Mary turned around and faced the glass doors.

"You've got a view."

"It used to be better than it is now," he said, coming up behind her and putting his hand on her shoulder.

"Hey," she said.

"You want to tell me what brings you here?"

"Two homicide detectives—"

"Yes. Lubbock and Jackson."

"—came to question me."

"Question you about what?"

"Kenny Gotch's death."

"Since when do homicide detectives come around asking questions about patients who die of incurable diseases in hospitals?"

"Kenny Gotch didn't die of Kaposi's sarcoma, he died from having his throat cut."

"Why the hell would anybody cut a dying man's throat?" he said, but that was just an automatic response, like the jerking of a knee. "To keep somebody from confessing to something that'd drop somebody else in the soup," he said, answering his own question. "Gotch ever confess anything to you?"

"Just that he was sorry for the life he lived. Toward the end there he thought AIDS was God's punishment."

"Well, that's the party line, isn't it? All the thin-lipped, tight-assed eunuchs and professional virgins gloating over things that happen to people who don't live their lives the way they think they should be lived? Any way you want to look at it, you've got to pay a price for being human."

"Original sin?"

"Whatever you want to call it. So, Lubbock and Jackson?"

"They came around asking about your friend. They wanted to know what he was doing there. Do you know what he was doing there?"

"Doing a favor for Gotch's relative. Doing a favor for Abe Forstman."

"What kind of favor?"

"Gotch had told Forstman part, but not all, of something that was troubling his soul. Rialto holds a private license, just like I do, and maybe Forstman thought a professional could get it out of Kenny."

"Do you think he did?"

"Rialto says he didn't."

He touched her arm and she started, as though he'd shocked her.

They walked over to the couch and sat down.

"So that's all the homicide cops wanted?" he asked.

"They hinted."

"What do you mean hinted?"

"They talked about caregivers who give people who are suffering under their care a little nudge."

"You?"

"Me or somebody at the hospice. But, yes, me. That's what frightened me. That's why I ran to you. I don't know what you can do."

"Maybe you thought I could give you a little comfort."

"Maybe that's it," she said.

"Is something going on here?" he asked.

"I've read about it, but I always thought it was a fairy tale or at least a commodity too scarce to think about."

"What's that?"

"I'm not going to say love at first sight. Something else. Instant attraction."

"We going to do anything about it?"

"The name of the game's been changed, Whistler. People can't just hit and run. We've all got to grow up."

She leaned over and kissed him on the corner of his mouth, moving in quick, lingering for what seemed a little while, then moving out again before he could turn it into something bigger.

He tried to get rid of the mugs in their hands gracefully. It was awkward but at least it got their hands free.

"I didn't make the bed," he said.

"How do you feel about using a condom?"

In the still that followed a satisfying exploration and culmination, sex as practiced by unboastful lovers, they lay on their backs, listening to their hearts and the undiminished rout of traffic along the freeway.

"Sounds like the surf," she said.

"I think so," he said.

"Was it good for you?" she asked.

"What?"

"I thought I'd beat you to it."

"I never ask was it good," he said.

"How about did the earth move?" she said, giggling softly.

"Only if I think there's been a quake."

Whistler felt so damned comfortable and sated and content he could have cried.

"You remember the man in the lunchroom?" Whistler asked.

He couldn't see but could imagine the little frown of thoughtful effort on her forehead.

"Yes," she said. "Yes. Kenny Gotch's landlady described the man I saw in the restaurant."

"And?"

"And what? Wait. I've got it. When I saw that man with the black hair and red tieback in the restaurant I remembered that I'd seen him before, but I couldn't remember just when or where."

"Do you remember now?"

"In the hospice. I passed him in the corridor early in the morning. I thought he was visiting someone."

"Early in the morning?"

"If someone's about to die and if there's time to call the next of kin or closest friend, we do it and never mind about visiting hours. I saw him in the corridor and then in the restaurant and before I could place him the thought must have come to me that it was perfectly natural for somebody visiting the hospice to stop in for a bite in a restaurant so close by. That's what must have passed through my mind before I dropped it altogether. You don't think he was visiting a patient about to die, do you?"

"I think that's just what he was doing. And I think he came back to get Gotch's things."

"For Gaea's sake, the world's gone mad," she said.

Sometime in the night Whistler dreamt or thought he dreamt that someone, a woman, was chanting softly into his ear.

". . . and wonders of his love,

And wonders of his love,

And wonders and wonders of his love."

The words were sung to the tune of a Christmas carol, but he couldn't remember the name of it.

# 20

*I* never said I had a conversation with Kenny Gotch," Rialto told Isaac Canaan as they sat across from each other at the scarred and abused table in one of the interrogation rooms at Hollywood station.

Canaan had called in a request to Hollywood station that one Mike Rialto be picked up and held without charge until

Canaan had a chance to have a little talk with him, when much to his surprise he was told that Rialto was already enjoying the hospitality of their holding cell.

Rialto had been called out from a fitful sleep on a thin mattress tossed on the floor of an overcrowded holding tank, the smell of vomit seeping into his clothes, at six o'clock in the morning.

"If you didn't have a conversation with this Kenny Gotch, what did you tell Lubbock and Jackson?" Canaan asked.

"I told them that when I walked into the room, Kenny Gotch, this person I didn't even know—who I was stopping by to visit as a favor to a friend—was lying on his side all curled up—"

"In the fetal position?"

"—with his knees . . . that's right, in that position which is, I understand, the position that persons take before they die."

"They don't always die throwing up blood inside the next five minutes. I mean with a knife in their throat," Canaan said.

"I know this. This I know. What I'm saying is, he could have been on his last legs from the blade in the throat. I didn't know he had a blade in his throat. He was facing away from me and it was as gloomy as a cellar in the room."

"You turned him over on his back?"

"I didn't exactly turn him over. I touched him on the shoulder. I nudged him a little to see if he was awake and he made a sound. So I figured he maybe needed a little help rolling over onto his back. So, very gently, I took his shoulder and pulled a little bit and he tipped right over. He turned his head toward me—"

"So, he was still alive."

"Wait a second. See, I don't know that. You understand what I'm saying here? There was a pillow propping up his knees, which could have had him off balance, so all it needed was a touch to roll him over. When he turned his head toward me, I thought he was looking to see who it was. I mean his eyes was half-opened, half-closed. What am I supposed to think about that? I mean I didn't wait for him to blink, anything like that."

He was running off at the mouth and he knew it, but he'd been so goddamn glad to see a friendly face when it turned out to be Canaan sitting there in the visitor's room waiting for him that he'd started talking and now he couldn't stop. Canaan was just sitting there listening, nudging him every now and then with a nod, a grunt or a word just to keep him going, but Rialto didn't need nudging. He couldn't help rattling on. The only thing he hoped was that Canaan wouldn't ask the question Rialto didn't want asked, about the thing Whistler told him to forget about.

"I didn't think about was he alive, wasn't he alive. I just wanted to do what I went there to do—"

"Say hello because your friend asked you to stop by?"

"—and get the hell out of there. That's right."

"See, Mike, that's the part . . . well, all right, go on."

"What?"

"I said go on, so go on."

"He made a noise. I thought he wanted to tell me something."

"Was he breathing?"

"I don't know."

"So, maybe the sound you heard was his lungs filling up with blood."

Rialto winced and wiped his hand across his face.

That's the way Wally Beery used to wipe his hand across his face, Canaan thought, and immediately wondered how many people out on the stroll would remember Wally Beery, would even know who he was.

"You touch him again?" Canaan asked.

"I bent over to put my ear close to his mouth because I thought his voice was weak—"

"Because it could be—"

"—and he threw up all—"

"—you touched him when his lungs had sucked air—"

"—over me, my face and neck."

"—when he turned over and then the blood drained down in there on top of the air and you could've just barely touched him and the air was expelled with the blood in front of it."

"That's what I'm saying. He could've been dead when I walked into that room," Rialto said, beside himself with the joy of seeing a way out.

"It could've happened that way," Canaan said. "The man could've been already dead or just on the edge of dying when you stepped into the room."

"That's what I've been trying to tell Lubbock and Jackson," Rialto exclaimed with this big heaving sigh of relief because the cavalry had finally arrived and he'd be out of there in ten, fifteen minutes.

"Or it could be the nurse bent over him and did the job with you standing there scared to death with Gotch's blood all over you," Canaan said.

"I'd like to grab hold of that, Isaac," Rialto said. "I really would like to agree with you, but I got to be honest here. I got to tell you that I had my eye on her and I can't honestly say she could've done it. Not after I was already in the room, I mean."

"If they decide you ain't the man who done it, they'll be looking at the nurse next anyway."

"If they decide to charge her with anything, I'll tell them I had my eye on her. What more can I say?"

Isaac had been nodding like a wise old rabbi all through Rialto's stammering, stumbling dissertation.

"There's one thing I'm having a little trouble with, Mike," Canaan said.

"What's that?"

"Back there when you said you'd stopped by to visit this friend you didn't even know, never even met, because another friend—"

"An old, old friend from over to the poker games in Gardena."

"—asked you to drop by. That don't strike me as the sort of thing you're known to do. You understand what I'm saying?"

"You think I'm lying."

"I think you're not exactly telling me the truth, which ain't quite the same thing. So, now you tell me what you were talking about with Whistler and Bosco when I walked in and you said you wasn't feeling too good and then took off. Why were you over there trying to talk to this Kenny Gotch?"

"You understand, it wasn't me wanted to keep this from you," Rialto said, suddenly deciding to give it up. "It was Whistler. He said it was better left alone."

"You could say that about practically anything and everything," Canaan said, "and I'm certainly not going to get mad at anybody for trying to keep me from hearing bad news, but I'm going to find out sooner or later, one way or another, and if it's you decides to tell me what I want to know—to do me that favor—then it's you I'm going to owe a favor in return."

"My friend, Abe Forstman—"

"From over in Gardena."

"—who was related to Kenny Gotch by marriage, told me that he was worried and didn't know what he should do because Kenny Gotch told him something one day when Abe—who hardly knew Kenny either—was visiting him because his wife—Abe's wife—told him to."

"What did Kenny Gotch tell Abe Forstman?" Canaan said very softly, very patiently.

"He told him he knew who it was that stole your brother's little girl . . ."

Canaan straightened up in the chair as though setting himself for the blow.

". . . and did things to her before she was killed . . ."

Tears were filling Canaan's eyes. Tears of grief and tears of rage, Rialto thought.

". . . and put her in the cemetery on the tombstone."

Canaan was on his feet, his body propped up on his arms, his hands flat on the table.

"Where can I find this Abe Forstman?"

"He don't know the name of the person Kenny Gotch was talking about. He never told him. That's why I was over there. I wanted to see if there was anything to it—that the poor gazooney wasn't just delirious when he talked to his cousin—before I turned it over to you. But when I didn't get anything, there was nothing to tell you."

"I want Abe Forstman's address and telephone number, if you got them."

"Okay."

"And the same for this Kenny Gotch."

"I ain't got that."

"All right. That's no trouble. I'm willing to bet a dollar to a dime I got him on a card, young Kenny Gotch. Young Harriet LaRue in his purple dress and rhinestone shoes."

He straightened up and settled his hands in his pockets as though they were weapons he meant to conceal. "You got anything else you want to tell me, Mike?"

Rialto reached into his back pocket and took out the card and envelope. There was no reason to hold it back anymore. If anyone was going to do him any good, it was Isaac Canaan, so he might as well buy all the good will he could get. Handing over the card he said, "This was under Kenny Gotch's pillow. I saw it while I was sitting there waiting for him to wake up. I was just curious, you know how it is, so I had a look and the next thing I know he's puking up all over me and I must've shoved it into my back pocket."

Canaan examined the envelope and then opened the card and read the message.

"Thanks," he said. "I owe you."

"How big?"

It was easy for Canaan to read Rialto's mind.

"I don't think Lubbock and Jackson seriously believe you filled a contract. They just want you twisting in the wind for a while."

"I'd just as soon not."

"I'll see what I can do," Canaan said, "but you got to understand, it ain't up to me."

# *21*

*Mary* Bucket was gone when Whistler woke up.

The tune but not the words someone had sung into his sleeping ear, in or out of a dream, lingered like the scent of the soap she used, reminding him she'd been there.

She'd been a quiet, tender lover with something else going on underneath, an urgency she wouldn't express, a fury she wouldn't release.

He rolled out of bed, and when his feet hit the floor he cringed from the chill. If it wasn't that he had to pee so bad, he'd have just as soon got back under the covers and slept another hour, another day, another week.

But that wouldn't take care of a thing.

He showered, shaved and got himself moving by eight o'clock.

Call it triage, call it prioritizing. One thing everybody's got to figure out, if they want to do their job with any reasonable degree of efficiency, is what comes first and what comes next.

But when you've got nothing but a paper bag filled with scraps, all you can do is lay them out and sort them out, matching color to color, shape to shape, hunch to hunch. Like doing a jigsaw puzzle. Waiting for one or two pieces to connect up and make a bigger something that you can build upon.

He thought about calling Abe Forstman and breaking the unhappy news, but he didn't feel himself up to dealing with anyone's grief, no matter how mild and abstract, just that minute and put it on mental hold. He was feeling fragile, as though a bout with the flu were coming on.

He tried the unanswered numbers again, risking the anger of people not yet up for strange callers.

He finally got to talk to Bobby L, who sleepily invited him over to share her bed, and Bobby D, who told him to go fuck himself. What did he think he was doing waking up a working girl so early in the morning?

# 22

*Charlie* Chickering, the attendant at the morgue, was not a friend; he was not even an acquaintance. He was a contact. Whistler sometimes bullied him, sometimes coddled him, according to Charlie's mood, but always ended up slipping him a ten or a twenty, for he'd long since learned that though sugar might keep somebody's temper sweet and vinegar might scare them into cooperation, when all was said and done, only money could guarantee answers that bore any resemblance to the truth.

He carried a paper bag under his arm when he walked into the dank confines of the dead house. It contained a pastrami on rye, two bottles of Dr. Brown's cream soda and a cheese Danish, brought from Cantor's Delicatessen in the Fairfax district of Hollywood. Money aside, Chickering was also vulnerable to delicatessen sandwiches and Dr. Brown's cream soda.

Chickering had his feet up on his desk and was looking at the pictures in a crotch magazine.

"You ever read a book?" Whistler asked.

"I read a book once. It was full of words that made no sense. It went on and on for page after page about how if you worked hard, kept your nose clean, respected the female sex, was good to your old man and old lady and never told a lie, you'd end up being president of some big savings and loan. So I knew that was bullshit right there. The only ones who ever get to be the head of big savings and loans lie, cheat, rat on their fathers, leave their mothers rot in the worst slums and tell women they love them just so they can get a shot at their puppies."

"Their what?"

"Their puppies. I'm sick and tired how everybody says the same old things the same old way. You're all the time hearing about pussies. Well, I say, let's hear it for the puppies."

Whistler put the bag down on the cluttered desktop.

Chickering peered inside the sack from behind a pair of lenses like bottle bottoms and gave a sniff. He grinned, showing the wire braces he'd been wearing on his teeth for as long as Whistler had known him.

"You want something from me?" Chickering said.

"I want to ask about a certain Kenny Gotch who was delivered to your establishment from Angeles Hospice."

"Angeles's got its own morgue."

"I don't think they do posts on patients that were murdered."

"Oh, that one," Chickering said.

Whistler took out his slender roll and peeled off a ten.

"Has he been done yet?"

"Nobody said there was a particular hurry. You see a blade in somebody's throat you got to figure that's what killed him."

"I'd like to have a look."

"What for?"

"How the hell do I know? Just so I know what I'm talking about if anybody asks me what a valvulotome looks like."

"So, you already know about that."

Charlie sat there munching on the sandwich, his feet comfortably placed on his desk, and it looked like he wasn't going to move.

"Didn't you bring something for yourself?" he asked.

"It's too early for me to eat," Whistler replied.

"You see, there's the trouble, Whistler. You ain't sociable. You don't bring a sandwich along for yourself so we can eat lunch together."

"The sun's hardly up," Whistler said, handing over another ten.

"So breakfast, then," Chickering said, putting his feet on the floor. Holding the sandwich in his mouth, he opened a drawer, took out a pass, filled it out and handed it to Whistler.

He took the sandwich out of a mouth smeared with mustard.

"Authorization in case somebody should ask," he said.

Whistler pinned the plastic sleeve with the instant pass in it to his lapel.

Chickering put on a pair of surgical gloves and a paper mask. He handed a pair of gloves and a mask to Whistler, who donned the mask but put the gloves into his pocket.

"I'm not going to touch anything," he said.

They walked down the corridor and went into the keeping room. It was very cold; their breaths puffed out in small streams around the edges of the masks. Chickering grabbed a chart off the wall beside the entrance door and checked the tag numbers, then started walking toward the back. There were draped bodies lying on gurneys along the sides; one hand was dangling out from beneath the sheet. Chickering tucked it back.

"They move sometimes," he said, his eyes crinkling up, grinning behind the mask.

He pushed aside a gurney to get at one of the refrigerated drawers that contained the last remains of Kenny Gotch. It was red tagged TAKE WARNING. The drawer was on a safety lock that moved at the pressure of his thumb; it gave easily at a tug and whispered out on its rails.

Chickering pulled back the concealing sheet. "How much you want to see?"

"Just down past the cut."

Chickering draped the sheet just below the collarbones.

Whistler bent over the pale figure, which looked like a painting of the dead Christ in some ancient altarpiece. The blood had been wiped off, though stains and dried patches had been left behind.

The blade, of course, was gone, taken for evidence and riding around in Lubbock's pocket at the moment.

A knife such as Mary had described could have easily been missed or mistaken for something else.

"How long would it'd've been, this valvulotome?" Whistler asked.

"Just about the length of the first joint of your thumb," a voice said at their backs.

They both jumped away and backed off a step.

A young guy in a white coat, with sandy hair and the expression of an irritated cat on his face, was standing there.

"How the hell do you do that?" Whistler asked.

"Crepe-soled shoes. Who are you and what're you doing here?"

"He had an authorization," Chickering said.

"Oh, yeah?" he said, looking closer. "I can't make out the signature."

"It was signed by Ernest Lubbock," Whistler said.

"Who's Ernest Lubbock?"

"Detective of homicide, Hollywood station," Whistler said.

"I won't bother checking," the white coat said, glancing at Chickering. "It looks like one of Charlie's instant passes available for a fee."

"No, sir," Chickering said, throwing up his hands palms out as though warding off a blow.

"Never mind," the white coat said, facing Whistler as though confronting him. "You still haven't introduced yourself."

Whistler had met the type before. They were usually merely irritating but not altogether harmless. He went into his billfold and scrabbled around looking for one of his cards, figuring it would impress this gazooney more than a verbal introduction would do. He found one, stained and dog-eared from riding around in his pocket too long.

The white coat gave it a look and handed it back.

"You've only got one name?" he asked, as though that were an accusation of some kind.

"One does okay by me."

"What are you, a musician or a model on the side?" he asked, needling Whistler.

"You want to give me *your* name?" Whistler asked. "Just one'll do."

"Patterson. My name's Joel Patterson and I work here."

"Dr. Patterson's an assistant medical examiner," Chickering quickly said.

Patterson tapped the red tag. "This the reason for all the masks and gloves? There's no need, as long as you don't start playing in the man's blood or body fluids."

"Are you the man who's going to have to do that?"

"When the time comes he could be on my rotation, yes. But I can already tell you what happened. Somebody punched a valvulotome into the hollow above the clavicle, twisted the blade around, hooked the carotid and sliced it. Ka-bam!"

"Is there a chance that Mr. Gotch got his hands on the valvulotome"—Patterson's eyebrows shot up—"and did the job on himself?" Whistler asked. "I mean would there have been so much pain that the first stab would've stopped him?"

"Probably less pain than you'd have slitting your wrists," Patterson said. "So, you're thinking suicide?"

"I can understand a man so afraid of pain to come or so disgusted by the physical indignities laid on him by his disease that he'd do such a thing."

"So can I," Patterson said, the testy expression gone from his face like a magic trick.

Whistler found himself liking him a little better.

"There's something else you could help me with," Whistler said.

"I've got a minute."

Whistler looked at Chickering. "Why don't you go finish your snack, Charlie, before the rye bread gets dry around the edges?"

Chickering shrugged and walked away.

Whistler reached into his pocket and took out the folded handkerchief that held the mummified finger. He unwrapped it and held it out on his flattened palm.

Patterson first bent down to peer at it, then picked it up very delicately.

"Where'd you find this?"

"Can you tell me if it's what I think it is?"

"What do you think it is?"

"It looks like a mummified finger."

"That's what it is. A child's finger."

"I was hoping you'd say it was something made out of plastic. You know these joke shops sell things that look so real—"

"Coffee spills and dog turds?"

"—that they'd fool an expert. Yes, things like that," Whistler said, catching up with Patterson's remark.

"Where'd you get this?"

"I found it in the apartment of that man in the drawer."

"Do you have any idea where he got it?"

"No."

"Then you didn't go to this man's apartment specifically in search of this?"

"No. I just happened to find it."

"Were you working on a case involving the dead man?"

"There was no case. It was more like I was doing a small favor for a friend which led to an involvement."

Patterson had that catlike frown back on his kisser and Whistler was liking him less again.

"Curiosity would describe it best," he said.

"I understand. When you got nothing to do you rattle doorknobs and peek in garbage cans. You never know when a scrap of money might show up."

"I'm not a civil service employee," Whistler said. "My work isn't waiting for me on the desk every morning. I've got to do a certain amount of mining, but that wasn't what I had in mind this time. The only one who might've been a client was already dead. Kenny Gotch there could use a detective or at least a friend to find out who done him if he didn't do himself. I was just doing a favor for a friend and went walking down the road, putting one foot after the other, until I landed here with a kid's finger in my pocket."

Patterson reached into the pocket of his smock with his empty hand and drew out a glassine Ziploc bag. "I'd better hold on to this."

Whistler plucked the tiny finger from Patterson's palm,

then snatched the bag from the fingers of the doctor's other hand.

"I don't think so."

"This could be evidence in a homicide."

"It wasn't found at the murder scene."

"Even so it might—it certainly would—have a bearing on the circumstances, it seems to me."

"You could be right, but it's not evidence at the moment."

Whistler dropped the finger into the bag and put it into his pocket.

"I'm going to report this," Patterson said.

"I understand."

"When I said it was evidence in a homicide, I didn't mean the possible murder of Mr. Gotch, I mean the murder of the child from whom this finger was taken."

"I understand that, too. I'm pretty certain I knew the child. I don't want a little piece of her kicking around some property room down at the station or dumped in some drawer here at the morgue. I don't want it to be an item tagged and filed. When I think the time's right, I'll give it to the proper person for burial. You can report it to whoever you want."

They stood there playing the game of stares. Patterson blinked first. He went into his pocket and took out a small pad and a ballpoint pen, and quickly wrote something down.

"All right. I'll leave it up to you. But, if I were you, I'd at least talk to Sergeant Harry Essex. You ever met him?"

"No, but I've heard about him."

"So, you know what he does?"

"I've been told. He's the Satan maven."

Patterson must have heard an edge of disbelief, even of ridicule, in Whistler's voice.

"That's right, they've got a special unit or at least a special cop. There are a lot of people taking this business of satanism very seriously. I'm not talking about congressmen's wives who want to put warning labels on music albums. I'm not talking about professional witnesses. I'm talking about cops who pick up dead teenagers and mutilated babies. I'm talking about priests asked to cleanse houses that are possessed. I'm talking about a cop like Essex, who is the last man in the world you'd expect to believe in ghosts and ghoulies."

He turned away and pushed the drawer holding Kenny Gotch back into safekeeping, then turned back to Whistler, who'd removed his mask and was standing there like a stone.

"Nothing new under the sun, Whistler. We're still painting ourselves blue and hiding in the dark.

"You getting a cold?" Patterson suddenly asked.

"Feels like it. You got any suggestions?"

"Take two aspirin and call me in the morning," Patterson said, finally giving Whistler a grin.

# 23

*It's* easy to get lost on the campus of UCLA. One parking lot looks like another and visitors usually have to park so far away from their destinations that half a dozen can be seen wandering around, asking directions from students as confused as they, practically any hour of the day and evening.

Thirty-six thousand students and faculty; a small city larger than neighboring Beverly Hills.

Whistler parked the Chevy after picking a parking ticket out of the machine. You wanted anything nowadays, you had to pay, one way or another. The world was running on funds provided by parking meters, traffic fines and three-dollar admissions to museums that once invited the people in for free.

It took Whistler three-quarters of an hour to find the right office at the end of the right corridor in the right building in the correct complex. There was a cardboard sign taped to the pebbled glass that gave notice that the office was assigned to James Kilroy, associate professor, department of the humanities. Whistler rapped on the glass and got a "Come in," for his trouble.

It was worse than a rat's nest inside. The window was open, letting in the fine weather, otherwise the room would have been unbearable with the odor of tuna fish, onions, book dust and stale socks.

A frail young man with red hair that looked like a fright wig and granny glasses perched on the end of a snub nose was sitting back in an oak swivel chair. His feet, in size fourteen felony flyers, were up on a square foot of clear space on the desk. He was munching tuna and onions on a kaiser roll and reading some sort of journal.

He glanced up at Whistler and waved the magazine in the air.

"Shroud of Turin," he said. "They're at it again. Is it, ain't it, the shroud in which Jesus Christ was wrapped when they placed him in the tomb? A perennial. It pops up every few years. New scientific studies. New conclusive evidence. You interested in the shroud of Turin?"

"I heard about it but I'm not particularly interested," Whistler said.

"Can I interest you in the Nag Hammadi Library?"

"What?"

"What's your discipline?"

"Keeping my weight under a hundred and eighty pounds," Whistler said.

"That's good. It'll save your heart," Kilroy said. "What do you want to know?"

"Mummified fingers. The finger of a child."

"Ah," Kilroy said, dropping his feet to the floor and straightening his long, skinny body into an upright position.

"I'm also interested in *Magick in Theory and Practice*," Whistler said.

"Spelled *i-c-k*?"

"That's the one."

"Satanism. Very popular subject. What specifically do you want to know?"

"I don't know what I want to know. Except for the finger

and the book, I haven't got any experience with that kind of strange."

"You've probably had more experience than you're aware of. This is the Age of Aquarius."

"I thought that wasn't coming until the year two thousand."

"Give or take," Kilroy said, grinning.

"I also thought the Age of Aquarius was going to be marked by international harmony and service to others."

"You see? You see? I told you that you probably knew more than you thought you knew."

"I've got a friend reads everything in print and then tells me about it," Whistler said. "So what's Aquarius got to do with satanism?"

Kilroy picked up a broad-pointed carpenter's pencil and drew a wide line on a sheet of paper, pressing down hard at first and then letting up the pressure so it ended light. It looked like an artist's value scale.

"You say something's good, somebody else makes it bad. Any human activity you want to examine can be described on a scale of values. Up here it's light, down here it's dark." He touched a place midway with his finger. "If you pick a point along the scale, you have to decide for yourself if it's more light than dark, more dark than light. Some people have nice things to say about the coming Age of Aquarius, some people claim there's going to be an explosion of evil."

Kilroy talked like a man in a hurry. He gave the impression of somebody running like hell dropping pearls of wisdom and information in his wake. Whistler tried to take it all in but it was hard going and it showed on his face.

"The Christians have the cross as their symbol of faith," Kilroy said. "The satanists turn it upside down in the Black Mass and make it a symbol of derision. You following me?"

"Well, I'm limping along," Whistler said.

"If there is no God, there is no Satan, and vice versa. You follow the logic?"

Whistler shrugged.

"What you want is an overview," Kilroy said.

"I'd like to know about the finger."

"Have you heard of the Hand of Glory?" Kilroy asked.

"No."

"How about necromancy?"

"I've heard about that. I used to know a woman who claimed she could speak to the spirits of the dead and cast spells."

"So, you know about communicating with the dead in order to tell the future because the dead are no longer bound by mortal limitations and can foresee events?"

"Well, no, I didn't exactly say I knew anything like that. I just remember her mentioning it once or twice."

"The Hand of Glory is used in necromancy. In the original ancient ritual, the sorcerer obtained the hand of a hanged man, wrapped it in a piece of shroud, pickled it in a jar for two weeks, then dried it out. Since then there have been a lot of variations introduced."

"Every cook likes to change the recipe a little?" Whistler said.

"Was that a joke?" Kilroy asked.

"I don't know what we're talking about here. It's like a crappy movie. I'm sitting here listening to you talking about the pickled hands of hanged men and—"

"Life's a crappy movie—"

"—talking to the dead."

"—didn't you know?"

They both stopped talking and stared at one another, as though amused and stunned by the truth of their remarks. One comment was just as true as the other; they *were* talking like a couple of characters in a B picture and life *was* sometimes as bad or worse than any B picture ever made.

"I mean I don't like the variation you're about to tell me about in detail," Whistler said.

"Using the hands of children?" Kilroy said.

Whistler waited for him to go on.

"There's a special innocence attached to children and therefore they are supposed to have access to greater truths. There's a history of it that goes all the way back to the Salem witch trials in this country. Beyond that to the Old Country and over in Asia, the Middle East, Africa. The same talismans and charms and rituals pop up everywhere. All the way back to the Paleolithic Age," Kilroy said.

"Can we stick to now?" Whistler asked. "I've got a feeling it's about all I can handle."

"You can't separate now from then. It's been going on for a long time. Children found mutilated and murdered in this state and other states are very often found with a hand missing."

"You say the hands are being used for witchcraft?"

"That depends on what you mean by witchcraft. Obeah, originated by the Ashanti and practiced by West Indian slaves, is not the voodoo from Dahomey, which is also practiced in the West Indies. Nor is it Espiritismo, a cult rooted in both, but people mix them up and together all the time.

"In the same way, witches figure in satanism and any number of primitive pagan nature religions but a witch is also said to be a female magician who practices white magic and the healing arts. Not all or even many practicing witches call upon Satan, but a severed hand or a finger could be used in satanic rituals. It's confusing. Like every other human enterprise, matters of religion and antireligion lie on a scale of values."

"For Christ's sake," Whistler said, "isn't witchcraft all just a lot of mumbo-jumbo? Frustrated women and horny men jumping over candle flames and swords, kissing the master's ass, laying virgins out on a slab. Just a lot of kinky fucking. Kids listening to records that are supposed to tell them how to summon the devil, do a Black Mass, if they run the record backward?"

"Why shouldn't they believe in messages revealed when a record's played backward or ritual incantations or symbols carved into their cheeks? We've all had enough training in such things. I give you the Gregorian chants. I give you *shin* and *daleth* and *yod.*"

Whistler made a sound, asking for an explanation.

"Hebrew pictographs drawn on the arms of Jews with the strings of the *t'filin.* Seven wraps of the strings on the arm. I give you Tibetan monks on their knees spinning prayer wheels and old Catholic women on their knees telling the prayer beads." He paused, stuck out his nose and peered at Whistler in a challenging way. "Are you a believer?"

"I haven't made up my mind," Whistler said.

"Most people haven't made up their mind. Jews eat pork and Catholics use contraceptives. Only the fundamentalists, the ones we call fanatics, believe strictly in the rules laid down by the Koran or the Talmud or the Bible. But we say 'for Christ's sake' automatically, a call for protection against the madness of the world. We also knock on wood. Do you know why we knock on wood? It comes from the old Druid faith. When a priest died it was believed that his spirit entered an oak in the sacred grove. When we knock on wood, we're waking him up, so that he'll hear our petitions. Our days are filled with automatic rituals like that. A little wine poured on the ground at wedding feasts. A pinch of salt thrown over the shoulder when it's spilled."

"Harmless."

"Of course harmless. I'm simply saying the line between the really ancient religions; the corn festivals; *la vecchia religione;* the veneration of trees; the live sacrifice of animals; Druids; witches; the adoration of Satan, disappears without trace into the sacrifice of Lot's wife and Aaron's daughter and the crucifixion of Jesus Christ himself."

"The Bible stories are metaphors, moral fables," Whistler said.

Kilroy's eyebrows flicked up in amused disagreement. "Do you know about the receiving of the host in the Catholic mass?"

"I was raised Roman Catholic."

"Did you have your First Communion?"

"I was confirmed, too."

"Do you remember what you were told about the host?"

"That it represented the body and blood of Christ."

"No. You were told that it *was* the body and blood of Christ. By the miracle of transubstantiation the wafer of bread has literally been transformed into the body and blood of Christ. That's one of the reasons why Catholics were persecuted so vigorously. They were said to be flesh eaters. Cannibals. All the devils and demons you'd care to count are out there waiting in the dark in a thousand disguises."

Whistler nodded. Kilroy was right. You saw the everyday horrors and told yourself that was all of it, the worst of it, some poor bastard gone mad. You never wanted to look for deeper reasons. The possibility that evil was as real and well defined as good, and that there were thousands who worshipped Satan in their hearts or in fact.

Kilroy suddenly started scrambling around in the clutter on his desk and came up with a wristwatch.

"Got to deliver a lecture."

"I still don't know—"

"What's your name?" Kilroy asked, interrupting him as he scrambled through the room's mess, picking up a book here and a book there, riffling through them swiftly, marking titles and page numbers down on the top sheet of a legal pad.

"Whistler."

"Just Whistler? That your street name?"

"I never thought about it."

"That's interesting. You thinking of taking classes? I'm going to teach an extension course next term."

"I'll think about it."

"Well, lifelong learning keeps you young, isn't that what they say?" Kilroy said. "I've got to give a lecture in two minutes and then I've got a date. So we'll have to talk again some other time. You take this list and go down to the college bookstore. They'll have them all, they're on my reading list. You've got to have a little background, a smattering of ignorance, at least a small vocabulary. Some definitions. You don't have to read just the pages I've noted or read them in the order that I've marked them down, but if you follow those leads you'll get the information you're looking for in some kind of sequence."

"It's nice of you to take the time," Whistler said.

Kilroy stopped short, as though what Whistler had just said came as a great surprise. "Hey," he said, "I'm a teacher. It's what I do and it's a pleasure to meet somebody with a greater interest in the subject—any subject—than most of my students demonstrate. By the way, what do you do?"

"I'm a private detective."

"You don't say."

"One more thing," Whistler said. "Do you happen to know anybody by the same of Kenny Gotch?"

There was a moment of stillness, a little shift in time, before Kilroy put his fingertips to his forehead, the gesture universally understood to be a stimulation to memory, miming the effort of giving Whistler's question some thought. An actor's gesture.

"I guess you don't know him," Whistler said. "Anybody ever met somebody by the name of Gotch, I'm pretty sure they'd remember."

"Hold it," Kilroy said. "Gotch. Just a kid. This is seven, eight years ago. I remember. Like you say, a name like that's hard to forget. He came into my extension class, attended class once or twice and then dropped out. That happens all the time, they sign up and then they drop out."

"He dropped out altogether. He's dead."

"It happens," Kilroy said.


As he hurried along the corridor toward the lecture hall— where he would no doubt be greeted by half a dozen disinterested students ready to fall asleep and one homely goggle-eyed girl ready to kiss his feet—Kilroy thought about this wild card that had suddenly intruded itself into the game.

Gotch had apparently confessed to more people than just the priest out in the valley. To whom and how many was the question.

He'd brought all this trouble on himself, giving way to a tender feeling, giving the finger of the little girl to Kenny as a love token.

On the other hand the danger out there, evidenced by the appearance of this Whistler, gave him a thrill, a challenge. He was up to it. He could conquer the world given half a chance and any reason at all.

# 24

*Canaan* had been right, he'd had a card on Kenny Gotch also known as Harriet LaRue. He had a picture of him in his mind, tilting along the boulevard in his purple dresses and rhinestone shoes.

Canaan went to Abe Forstman's house, introduced himself and told him to tell his wife that he was a friend from the card parlor over in Gardena who happened to be in the neighborhood and stopped by to see if Abe wanted to join him for a cup of coffee.

In the car on the way over to Gotch's apartment, he told Forstman about the way his nephew had left this life. The shock on the man's face was severe. For a minute Canaan thought he was having a heart attack.

"There should be an easier way to break the news but I been doing this more than thirty years and I never found it. I'm sorry to be the one to bring you heartache."

"It's just a kind of general shock, the way people die. The violence all around. I came out here for the sun. I didn't expect smog and muggings and young boys and girls selling their bodies on the street corners."

"Who could have dreamed?" Canaan murmured.

"Shooting poison in their veins and sniffing it up their noses. Movie stars . . . they ain't even married . . . having babies. Bragging about it like it's a badge of courage. Remarkable. My cousin—my wife's cousin three times removed—was just a child. She tells me he could sing and dance and play the piano. I mean that's entertainment. What was this other with the purple dresses and rhinestone shoes?" He looked around at the passing houses and apartment buildings and asked, "Where are we going for a coffee?"

"You want a coffee somewhere, we can have a coffee," Canaan said, "but I hoped you wouldn't mind if we went over to your cousin's place."

"What for?"

"I'd like to look around, get a feeling."

"If you want." After a few minutes Forstman said, "Well, here we are," as though he'd been brought along to show Canaan the way.

Somebody had been there. There was no television set and no telephone. Gotch's clothes had been piled in a large carton, with Kleenex printed in blue on the side, ready to be carted away by Goodwill or whoever. Books were piled on the floor, some in smaller cartons, but the job had been given up before it was finished.

"I've been going at it a little and a little," Forstman said.

Canaan stood in the middle of the living room and turned slowly in a circle, looking at everything, the books, the ratty couch, the posters on the wall, waiting for something to speak to him before he waded in, hoping for a little magic.

He went into the cubicle of a kitchen. A swarm of flies rose up from the garbage in the sink.

At his shoulder, Frostman said, "Filthy. I should have cleaned that up."

Canaan brushed the flies away, the sudden thought of Beelzebub, literally translated from the Hebrew as the Lord of the Flies, flashing through his mind.

The bedroom smelled of old restless sleepings and awakenings.

"Our friend, Rialto, told me your cousin never gave you a name when he told you he was there when the little girl was killed years ago," Canaan said, inflecting it so it seemed a question or an appeal for honesty.

"He never told me," Forstman said. "That's why I told Mike. I thought he'd know what to do."

"You should have called me. I mean the police."

"I can see that now, but how should I know about such things?"

"The name of whoever it was should be around here some-where," Canaan said, in the voice of a man who hoped that simply saying something would make it happen.

But, except for the grinning demon faces of the rock musi-cians and three books on satanism and magic, there was nothing he could find.

When he left the apartment there was an old woman in a wrapper standing at the bottom of the stairs.

"Is it you, Mr. Forstman?" she said.

"It's me," Forstman said. "I'd introduce you but I forgot your name."

"Mrs. Prager."

"Mrs. Prager, this is Mr. Canaan."

She looked Canaan over as though searching for possi-bilities.

"You helping your friend clean out Kenny's apartment?"

"I'm doing what I can to clear up a few things," Canaan said.

"Well, you can take your time, the rent's paid up till the end of the month."

"All I'll need is another day or two, Mrs. Prager," Forstman said, "and everything that was Kenny's will be gone and the place cleaned up."

# 25

*It's* no trouble finding an address when all you've got is a telephone number if you have access to a reverse directory, which lists the numbers first and the names and addresses after.

Gambler lived in the Silver Lake district, among the His-panics, where cheap rents were to be had.

Whistler called first to see if Gambler was home. He wasn't. But Whistler drove on over to a street called Sunflower anyway, to a decaying apartment building that looked like a moldy wedding cake that was practically underneath the Glendale Freeway. Talking to neighbors can often be more profitable than talking to the subject.

The mailboxes and nameplates had been torn out. At the end of a long hallway that smelled of rat droppings he found the door to the manager's apartment. The bell didn't work but repeated knocking finally roused somebody. Whistler could hear someone shuffling along the hall on the other side of the door and then sensed that an eye had been placed to the peephole.

"Who are you?" a voice asked.

"I'm looking for George Gambler."

"You mean George Gomble?"

"That could be him."

"He likes to be called Gambler. Second floor, apartment eight."

"He's not home."

"You checked?"

"I called before I drove over."

"So how come you drove over if he wasn't home?"

"I took the chance."

"How long it take you to drive over?"

The voice was the querulous voice of an old man or woman who'd just been awakened from a sleep or someone whose voice had grown rusty and thin from disuse.

"Twenty minutes," Whistler said.

"Maybe he's back. Did you go upstairs and knock?"

"No. I didn't know his apartment number."

"So, go up and knock on his door and if he isn't home you better go away and come back another time."

"I'd like to ask you a couple of questions about George."

"You know George?"

"I only spoke to him on the phone once."

"Why should I answer any questions about one of my tenants? What's in it for me, you want me to give away a man's business?"

156

Whistler took his money clip out of his pocket and peeled off a ten-dollar bill. He folded it in half and in half again, bent down and slipped it under the door. It disappeared like it'd been snapped up by a lizard.

"So what do you want to know about George?" the ancient voice asked.

"He work?"

"You mean has he got a job?"

"That's what I mean."

"He shakes his booty on the Hollywood Boulevard stroll."

"He what?"

"He's a twangy boy."

"He's a what?" Whistler said, playing dumb.

"You don't know what is a twangy boy?"

"I've heard the word but I'm not exactly sure about what it means. I mean different words mean different things to different people."

"Are you a philosopher?"

"I'm interested in language."

"A twangy boy's a male who sells his ass for the carnal delectation and entertainment of men of the homosexual persuasion but claims not to be a homosexual himself. You understand what I'm saying here? It's like a hooker going down on another hooker for show. She isn't necessarily bent that way but does it to please the customer and make an extra dollar. A twangy boy's different in so much as he isn't selling his tender ass to persons of the opposite sex but persons of his own gender. There's not much call for male prostitutes among young women—who can get it when and where they please—you understand?"

"Sounds reasonable to me."

"Managers I know who've tried to run male prostitutes say they got a lot of complaints from older women who used the service. The young studs couldn't get it up."

Whistler said, "Men have that problem."

"That's what's known as a social quandary."

"You seem to know a lot about sexual customs and behavior," Whistler said.

"I was in the trade a hundred years ago."

"Would it be possible for you to open the door?"

"What for?"

"Well, we could hear one another better without having to shout."

"I don't mind speaking up. If you mind speaking up, we can end this conversation right now and you can go away."

"I just thought we'd both be more comfortable talking face-to-face."

"I wouldn't be more comfortable and I'm pretty sure you wouldn't be more comfortable. All right, now, do you know enough about George Gomble?"

"Did you ever meet his friend Kenny Gotch?"

"That depends on what you mean by meet, since you're so interested in language and the exact meaning of words. When he came around and George wasn't home, I talked to George's friend, Kenny Gotch, through the door, just like I'm talking to you."

"Did you know that Gotch was dead?"

"Was it in the papers?"

"I doubt it."

"Was it on the television?"

"I don't think anybody much noticed."

"Then I wouldn't know about it."

"I thought maybe George might have mentioned it to you."

"We don't talk a lot, George and me," the voice said, growing a little stronger with use, smoothing out, "but I can tell you that this Gotch hasn't been around for a while. They probably had a quarrel. Twangy boys are like whores. They're always having quarrels."

"Do you know if he ever went to see Kenny in the hospice?"

"I wouldn't know anything like that."

"Well, I guess that's all I can think of for the moment."

"You're not a customer, are you," the voice said. It wasn't a question.

"No. I'm trying to find out some things about this Kenny Gotch and George is one of my only leads."

"You're not a cop, though?"

"I've got a private license."

158

"So, that's okay."

"Thank you," Whistler said.

"Hey," the manager said, turning Whistler back as he started to walk away. There was the whisper of the ten-dollar bill being shoved back under the door.

"You want to go buy a bottle with this tenner, you can come back and we can talk some more. Maybe I can tell you a couple of things you didn't think to ask and had no idea I'd even know."

Whistler bent down and picked up the money.

"What's your pleasure?" he asked.

"What's yours?"

"I gave up my rights to drink a while back."

"Vodka then. It goes good with practically anything."

"Where can I—"

"Just turn right at the entrance, go down to the corner and turn right again. There's a package shop about halfway down the block. When you come back just walk in. I'll leave the door open."

Whistler took the walk, bought the bottle and was back in twenty minutes. The door was open just like the manager said it would be.

It smelled sweet and spicy inside the apartment with just a little fustiness, like a Kitty Litter box, lingering underneath the incense.

He could hear her singing softly in another room. It was the song he'd heard during the night.

"And wonders, and wonders of his love," she sang.

When she heard his footsteps on the hardwood floors of the hallway, she stopped and called out, "In here. To the right."

The short hallway branched out at the end, one door leading to a kitchen and the other to a living room.

There were curtains at the kitchen windows, a quart mayonnaise jar full of daisies on the bare pine table, which had been scrubbed white. A white cat dozed next to the daisies in a pool of sunlight puddled there. It looked at him with a cat's disdain, eyes as green as bottle glass, then blinked twice before it closed its eyes and napped again.

Green shades, like those householders pull down to save the rugs from summer fading back east, concealed the windows in the living room. It was like walking underwater; the air had weight.

Six or seven cats sat or lay on chairs and bookshelves. The one that lounged in the lap of the woman sitting in the chair in the farthest corner of the room was black and stared at Whistler with an unwavering gaze.

The woman looked like a monument, robed as she was in dark green and scarlet brocade. Her hands, catching what light there was in the room, were beautiful and beautifully kept. The robe revealed a good deal of her bosom and the swell of her breasts. Her head and face were covered by a purple scarf that allowed her to look out but didn't allow anyone to see in.

"I put out some Seven-Up, some orange juice and some tonic on that tray over there, in case you change your mind," she said.

"What can I make for you?" he asked.

"Splash it with Seven-Up."

Beside the mixes on the sideboard there was a teak ice bucket filled with ice cubes.

Whistler made her a drink and poured some Seven-Up over ice for himself.

"What's the name of that Christmas carol you were singing?" he asked.

"It was part of the temple rite of the winter solstice long before it was a Christmas Carol," she said.

When he didn't ask for an explanation—because he was wondering where Mary Bucket had come by it if she hadn't just been singing Christmas Carols out of season—she made a sound like a sighing laugh.

He handed her the drink he'd made for her and their fingertips accidentally touched as she took her glass from his hand. He could see down the front of her robe. Her breasts were solid and conical, the breasts of someone young or in very good shape.

"I always had great tits," she said, as though she knew exactly where he was looking.

He moved away and sat down and said, "I can see that."

"Winners. That's what I called them. My breadwinners. Men don't really like huge ones. That's just a lot of propaganda. What they like is flesh that pushes back when they grab hold."

Whistler felt himself blushing. It startled him.

"Am I embarrassing you, or are you just getting all hot and bothered?" she asked. There was amusement in her voice.

He touched his face and laughed. "I didn't expect that. I don't usually do that."

"I caught you by surprise. You come in here expecting to see some old woman—my voice gets to sounding ancient when I don't use it very much—with a big fat body and a head of hair like a worn-out mop"—she reached back behind her head, underneath the scarf, and drew forth a heavy plait of black, black hair and draped it over her shoulder so that it curved around one breast—"and instead you find a woman with a veil over her face and a pair of tits any woman would be proud to own. And who's not a bit shy about talking about them. I believe in being frank. I saw where you were looking and I said so."

"I think you meant for me to look, you don't mind my saying," Whistler said. "As long as we're being frank."

"I guess I did. I haven't had a man look at me for a long time. I don't want to forget altogether what I had once upon a time." She slipped the glass under the veil, hand and glass disappearing like a magic trick, and sipped at her drink.

"You had the power," Whistler said.

"Understand that do you? Understand that it isn't all drug habits and early incest and brutal men that lead some women into prostitution."

"It's the power."

"That's right. The power. Any woman with two tits and a treasure can make practically any man sit up and beg for it like a puppy dog."

"There's the power and there's the danger," Whistler said.

"You got that right, too. Playing with fire. Teasing the beasts. Lying with strangers. All very dangerous."

"You met someone you couldn't control? A pimp punish you?"

"A kinky john pointed a finger at me. I didn't understand."

"Neither do I."

"He had a knife on the end of his finger."

She pulled at the edge of the veil and it slithered off her face like a rush of dark water. The kinky john had done terrible things to her face.

"My name's Ardella," she said.

He looked at her as levelly as he could, hoping that his instinctive feelings of horror, pity and disgust weren't showing on his face. That she couldn't read the thoughts he couldn't help thinking. Here was this monstrously ugly face sitting on top of this incredibly lush body.

"My name's Whistler," he said.

"I'm a witch," Ardella said. "I could make you a spell or mix you a potion for that flu you've got."

It didn't take a witch to figure out he was coming down with something. He sounded like hell and probably looked the same.

"I thought I'd go home and pump up on vitamin C," he said, "but thanks for the offer."

She took a long pull on her vodka and Seven, then replaced the veil.

"We always called my grandmother Teague a witch," Whistler said. "She'd suddenly stop whatever she was doing and say, 'Cousin Charlotte's coming,' and the next thing you know Cousin Charlotte—who hadn't stopped by in six, seven months—would come knocking at the door. Once she said 'Billy's dead.' Billy was her brother and was over in Korea. Two days later she got the visit from the army informing her that Corporal William Teague had died in battle."

"Precognition. Second sight," Ardella said. "It run in the family?"

"Not that I know about."

"You never had a premonition come true?"

"Come to think of it . . ." Whistler paused, the memories flooding back, wondering how come he hadn't thought of the funny things that had happened when he was just a kid, so long ago, for maybe twenty, thirty years.

"You remember something?" she asked.

"I think so."

"Oh?"

"When I was a little boy, maybe five or six, I used to have these horrible dreams before anybody in the family died."

"In what way horrible?"

"Just before my grandfather Teague died I had a dream where I woke up in my room and heard talking. I got out of bed and walked down the hall toward the lighted kitchen, which seemed longer in the dream than it really was. When I reached the doorway I could see my brother sitting on my grandfather's knees. Well, I couldn't really see his knees because the table was in the way. I took a step into the kitchen and turned my head. My mother and father were sitting there drinking coffee like they did at night. They smiled at me and my mother told my brother to get off my grandfather's lap and let me climb up and give my grandfather a hug. My brother got off his lap and when I went over to climb up, I saw that there was no flesh on his legs and knees. They were just bones. Then, in the dream, I remembered that my brother was dead. He'd died when he was only a couple of years old, before I was even born, and this was—in the dream— eight years later, which would've made my brother ten if he hadn't died. A couple of days later my grandfather died of cancer up in a hospital in Connecticut somewhere."

"Did you know he was in the hospital?"

"I don't remember. Probably."

"That's what everyone told you, isn't it? They told you that you knew your grandfather was in hospital and your worry cast up the dream."

"That would be a reasonable assumption."

She leaned forward and touched his hand.

"There you go. But it might have been second sight. A lot of us have it, but usually it gets knocked out of us because people laugh or tell us we're making up stories, so we stop having dreams and premonitions."

"When you tell me you're a witch, I'm assuming—"

"That I'm a good witch?"

"I mean I knew a girl in town once who said she knew spells that'd call up devils."

"Maybe she did, maybe she did," Ardella said, "but, you're right, I'm a good witch. The magic I do is white magic. I'm a priestess of Wicca."

"You were going to tell me a couple of things about George?" Whistler said.

"Kenny Gotch was trying to recruit him."

"Recruit him into what?"

"The service of Satan."

"Like the Church of Satan up in San Francisco?"

Ardella laughed. It was throaty and seductive.

"That's just playacting. The satanists around La-La Land play a different game."

"How different?"

"They mean what they say. They believe what they say. Enough of them. They make blood sacrifices. They murder children."

"How do you know that?"

"I have messengers."

"Were these messengers witnesses to any of it? Did they show you any proof? Photographs? Documents? Anything?"

"If secret societies collected such things they wouldn't be secret very long, would they?" Ardella said. "How did Kenny Gotch die?"

"He had AIDS."

"Did he?" Ardella said, sounding arch, sounding mysterious, hinting at secret knowledge.

Playing the game, Whistler thought, hinting at private power and knowledge, the old palm reader's hustle. Be vague enough and you can't go wrong predicting the end of the world. But she was good. She knew he was after something more than doing a favor for a friend the minute he'd walked into the room.

"Well, he was dying of AIDS," he said, "but somebody cut his throat."

She gasped and the veil wavered like a colored waterfall blown by the wind.

"I'm tired," she said. "Talking so much has worn me out. Would you mind?"

Whistler showed himself out and left her to the rest of the bottle.

It was wrong and cruel, but he couldn't help asking himself that if she were a white witch, why didn't she cast a spell, make some magic and do something about her ruined face.

# 26

*Canaan* had an eye. It was no trick at all to pick out William "Pooch" Mandell behind the desk at the AAA office. The kid had the look, the tenderness around the eyes, the softness of the mouth, the narrow shoulders and vulnerable girlish neck. He would have been hit on by boy lovers all his life; he may have started developing some doubts about himself, had experimented more than a little.

Canaan stepped up to the counter where they handed out the maps and a young, black woman came over and asked him what she could do for him.

"I wonder could I talk to that young fella over there," Canaan said.

"William?"

"That's right, William."

She acted doubtful. Street smart and having sensitive antennae, she knew a cop when she saw one. She walked over and told the youngster he was wanted. Mandell looked at Canaan like a startled fawn and almost stumbled getting out of his chair and around the desk.

"Can I help you?" he asked, already out of breath from anxiety.

"Pooch?" Canaan said, smiling.

"What?"

"They call you Pooch?"

"My name's William. William Mandell."

"Here in the office. I understand that. Don't want people calling you Pooch where you work. It wouldn't be dignified. But they call you Pooch out there, don't they?"

"Who calls me Pooch? Out where?"

"Your friends. Out on the street."

"I don't know what you mean out on the street."

"Your friend, Kenny Gotch, called you Pooch when you got together out on the street. Wherever. You know what I mean. Away from work. Away from home. You ever live with Kenny Gotch?"

Mandell looked swiftly both ways, afraid that someone had overheard Canaan, though he'd kept his voice very low, very confidential.

"I don't know what you're talking about."

Canaan put the greeting card and the envelope on the desk. "You've got your return address on this envelope in which you sent this greeting card to your friend telling him that you loved him but that you were afraid."

"I didn't know I wrote down my return address," Mandell said, mortified that he could have done something so stupid.

"Old habits die hard," Canaan said. "I went over to that address and your landlady told me you worked here."

Tears welled up in Mandell's eyes.

"Hey, I'm not out to hurt your feelings, make it hard on you," Canaan said. "Your friend's dead. You know that?"

Mandell nodded.

"Who told you?"

"Somebody called."

"He give a name?"

Mandell looked scared again, as though he feared he'd done something wrong talking on the phone to a stranger.

"So he didn't give you a name. What did he want?"

"I don't know. After he told me Kenny was dead, I hung up on him. I couldn't listen to any more."

"So you didn't tell him anything about you and Kenny?"

"Just that I hadn't seen Kenny in almost a year."

"Why was that? Because he got AIDS?"

"Oh, no. I mean that was awful but . . ."

"But that's not what you were afraid of like you wrote on the card?"

"I don't know who you are," Mandell said, suddenly wary, even defiant.

"I could show you my badge. You want me to do that in front of everybody?"

"No."

"All I want to do is ask you a couple of questions."

"All right."

"Why did you stop seeing him? Why did you send him a card telling him you were afraid?"

"He was involved with some very strange people."

"Did he get involved during the time you were seeing him?"

"Before that. I think long before that, but I never knew about it until one night when he asked me to go to this place with him."

"What place is that?"

"It's a restaurant, a private club or something, down at the beach above Malibu."

"What's the name of this club?"

"Lucifer's."

"And what was there about this club that frightened you?"

"They were passing around photographs of little kids having sex with adults and other little kids. There were nothing but men in the place. There was a lot of weird conversation."

"About what?"

"About the devil and blood sacrifice and Black Masses. That sort of thing. I thought at first it was just a joke, like an initiation, you know. Testing me. Making up silly things like they do in fraternities, making new members kneel blindfolded and drink chicken blood the way you read about sometimes."

"But they weren't joking?"

"I don't think so."

"They wanted you to join the club?"

"That's the impression I got."

"And Kenny Gotch was the recruiter?"

Mandell hesitated, reluctant to accuse the friend who

might have been a lover of such a betrayal. Finally he said, "That's the way it looked."

"You meet anybody that night or any night thereafter?"

"I never went back again. Kenny and I had an argument about it when we got back to town. I told him I didn't appreciate him putting me in that kind of situation."

"So, on that first and only night, then, were you introduced to anybody?"

"There was a man with slick black hair that he wore in a ponytail who told me to call him Rahab."

"Anybody else?"

"There was some skinny guy with red hair, looked like Howdy-Doody, I didn't get his name. There was a fat man by the name of Lester."

"Just Lester?"

"That's all the name he gave me. Nobody ever gave me their whole name. Just one name. I couldn't tell sometimes if it was the first or last name they were giving me. Except this one very old man. Somebody called him Mr. Cape and he'd already told me his name was Walter."

Canaan straightened up as though some tightness across his chest had to be relieved.

"You all right?" Mandell asked.

"I'm all right, William," Canaan said. "You seem to remember a lot about Lucifer's after only one visit."

"It made an impression," Mandell said, smiling nervously. "Besides, I'm good at remembering names. My father always told me remembering names would be a big help no matter what business or profession you ended up in."

"Your father's right. It's helped me in my business."

They stood there smiling at each other.

"Thanks for telling me what you remembered," Canaan said.

Mandell colored at the praise.

Canaan started to leave, then stepped back to the counter.

"Hey, William, don't be ashamed you told Kenny Gotch you loved him. You understand what I'm saying? There ain't so much love going around we can keep it to ourselves."

# 27

*St.* Jude's in Van Nuys, a smallish stucco church of Spanish Missionary design, stood in the middle of a wasteland on a dusty side road off Roscoe near the Van Nuys Airport.

There was another building, a very large wooden shack, about fifty yards down the road; after that nothing but the scrub around the airport and way beyond that a line of power towers like a bunch of Star Wars tanks with legs—striding off into the distance.

In the other direction, grubby shacks and houses, wrecked cars and old abandoned Dumpsters beyond the empty fields, were nothing but a smudge of ochre smeared between earth and sky.

Whistler pulled up in front of the church, parking on a broiling patch of cracked blacktop that had the dusky look of a white-hot cast-iron frying pan.

The clear, smogless sky, a blessing to the thousands of naked bodies piled up down on the beaches, a wonder to the citizens of most of the L.A. Basin and a pleasant shock to the grifters, drifters and dream dogs sitting and standing along the Hollywood stroll, faces raised to the unfiltered sun for the fourth day in a row, was a curse out here in the San Fernando Valley. If any church in the vast city—which was also a county—needed air-conditioning, it was St. Jude's.

The rectory and church offices were around back. Someone, once upon a time, had tried to make a little enclosed garden with a well and flower beds between the church and the priest's house, but the badly made adobe bricks had fallen down and melted away. Nothing but some cactus and stones grew in the sandy earth. As he passed by, Whistler glanced in and saw the well was dry and, in fact, had never even been a working well but just an artifact meant to bring a comforting feeling, and perhaps a nostalgic tear, to the eyes of the Mexicans, legal and illegal, who packed into this little corner of the great metropolis. He wondered how come, since Mexicans were supposed to work wonders with brick, tile, adobe and stone, they'd done such a lousy job on the garden walls.

While he was standing there thinking about that, the door to the back building opened and a nervous woman in a sheer black dress and white collar and cuffs stood there, squinting against the glare of the sun. She was an Anglo, as pale as a ghost. You could see, even from a distance, how badly she would suffer from exposure to the sun. She looked like a woman from Minnesota or Maine, tall and spare. You had to wonder what she was doing in Southern California.

"Yes? Yes?" she said, a whine in her voice, as though she'd never before seen anyone invade the garden by merely stepping over the broken wall and walking up to the back door.

"My name's Whistler? I had an appointment?" he said, lifting the end of the sentences in that way people of no confidence have, an impersonation meant to make him appear nonthreatening and put her at her ease.

"Oh, yes. Are you early?"

"I could be."

"I think you're early. I'll check Father's book."

"Didn't I make the appointment with you?" Whistler asked.

"I know, but I jotted the information down on a piece of paper and put it on Father's desk. I'm not sure if he put it in his book. I'll check."

"You don't have to bother. I'll wait out here until he can get to me."

"Is it very hot out there?" she asked, squinting out into the white sunlight from the shaded shelter of the doorway.

"I don't mind."

"I'd ask you to come in, except . . ."

She ran down like a top, never finishing the sentence, never telling him what the exception was, just putting out a little fear there, telling him that she didn't like the idea of letting a strange man into the building when Father wasn't there.

"Well, maybe if you could give me an idea of how long Father'll be," Whistler said.

"Ahhh," she said. "Father Mitchum's over at the chicken market."

"The what?"

"Down there," she said, pointing to the shack down the road.

"Is it public?"

"Oh, yes."

"Then, I'll just go on down there and introduce myself. Will he be wearing his collar?"

"Oh, you'll know it's him," she said, and smiled.

Whistler crossed the garden, stepping over a break in the wall, and walked across the stubble field. There were old sedans buffed matte by sun and sand and several pickup trucks sagging on their springs slouching on the clay and gravel around the shed. The closer he got the louder the sounds of chicken cackle and men's voices rose.

He walked around to the front. The door was partially open, stopped by a brick. It was gloomy inside and shadows were dancing around. He stepped over the threshold into a sea of white shirts stained with sweat, straw Stetsons and silver-tipped boots, brown Aztec and Mayan faces, a few Caucasians, the whites of everybody's eyes and teeth almost phosphorescent in the gloom; he stepped into a roar of Spanish; into a choking ammoniac cloud of chicken shit dust, kicked up by the thrashing of hundreds of chickens in cages piled up on three sides of the building ten and twelve cages high.

Whistler had the feeling that if one of them slipped out of place, teetered, tumbled and crashed, all the others would come down as well, and they'd all be slashed to death by the army of suddenly liberated, crazed fowl.

A rough arena had been constructed out of two-by-fours and it was around this space that fifty or sixty men were gathered, those in front kneeling down, their heads resting on their crossed forearms, watching fighting cocks going at it. Rising up in puffs of feathers, iridescent black and brown splashed with scarlet here and there, crimson wattles gorged with enraged blood, vermilion eyes blazing. Going at it while the brown men laid down their paper dollars and silver coins on this goddamn hot, clear afternoon out in San Fernando Valley, just spitting distance from La-La Land.

Whistler stood up in the rear rank, taller than practically every other standing man in the place, and looked all around for Father Mitchum. There was no one wearing a collar but there was an Anglo with white hair and a ruddy face sitting on a folding chair beside the little gate where the contestants were brought in and out. He was watching the fighting birds with a pained, yet resigned, expression on a face stamped with the map of Ireland. A man of sixty-five, maybe seventy, in a pair of jeans and a sweatshirt with the logo of Loyola University on the front.

His eyes flickered up from the violent attack of bird on bird, seeking relief. He saw Whistler and nodded, then held up a finger, knowing at once that Whistler was the man marked down on his daily calendar. He looked into the arena again.

So did Whistler.

A man, apparently the referee, yelled out, and two other men picked up the birds. One took a mouthful of water from a bottle and sprayed it into his rooster's face. The bird closed its eyes like a child taking the cooling spray of an open fire hydrant in the summer. The other stuck his bird's entire head in his mouth, breathing oxygen into the tiring creature. The word was given, the birds dropped into the arena again. The flurry of violence was brief. The spur of the brown bird caught in the throat of the black one and was dragged around by the dying loser until the handlers disengaged them.

The winning handler held his victorious bird over his head. It crowed wildly, thrashing its wings, declaring itself.

The losing handler held the black bird for a moment, looked into its eyes, the light fading out like sparks whirled from a fire into the night air and, holding it with apparent gentleness, wrung its neck. The fighting cock died without a murmur. The man threw the carcass into a basket, half-filled with such carcasses, which lay at Father Mitchum's feet.

It was the last bout of the day, the fights having probably started early in the morning when it was still dark, before the sun heated up the landscape.

Money was changing hands. Now that the fights were over and the need for shouted encouragements past, the white-shirted, straw-hatted sons of conquistadores and Indians spoke in soft voices that seemed almost shy, people who knew how to take small satisfactions from the hard lives they led even here in the land of milk and honey beyond the border of their impoverished country.

One old man went over to the priest and apparently offered to carry the basket filled with the fallen warriors, but Father Mitchum declined. He grabbed the two handles of the basket and stood up, lifting the carcasses of the fighting cocks in one easy movement. The old man glared at the priest's back, as though wishing him dead as Father Mitchum walked toward the exit.

Whistler stepped up and asked Mitchum if he could use a hand.

"I can carry the weight but it makes for an awkward balance," Father Mitchum said, giving up one handle.

They walked with the basket between them along the field back the way Whistler had come.

"That old man who offered to help you carry the basket was looking holes through you," Whistler said.

Father Mitchum grinned. "Old Ortega imagines himself my rival and my enemy. He's the local high priest of Espiritismo."

"Is he trying to put a curse on you?"

"He's trying to convince me that I should give him all the black cocks. He claims they're useful in his ceremonies and very hard to come by. He insists that my refusal to give away any of my chickens is a breech of professional courtesy."

Whistler glanced down into the basket at the feathers glimmering and shining like wet black coal and the hides of roan horses and the heads of green bottle flies, splashed with scarlet and rust.

"They're tough as harness straps," Father Mitchum said, "but, made up into a stew, there are those who can still be coaxed into believing in God's bounty."

"Here in America," Whistler said.

"If we can put a man on the moon and fight foreign wars, why can't we provide for the poor and homeless," Father Mitchum said, an edge of bright ironical humor gleaming around the edges of his words, mocking the equation that do-gooders expressed in their thousands.

Father Mitchum maneuvered them along the field so that they stepped into the garden across the fallen wall as Whistler had done.

"I hope Mrs. Margaret didn't see us. She gets pissed off when I take the shortcuts over the wall," Father Mitchum said. "Why didn't you wait for me in the rectory? It's a little cooler."

"I got the idea that your secretary wouldn't like having a strange man in the house with you not there."

Father Mitchum tossed Whistler a glance, having another look at a man who could have read that about Mrs. Margaret at first glance.

"I've got no secretary, Lord knows. What I've got—and lucky to have her—is Mrs. Margaret. I took her off the streets in downtown L.A. She'd been a patient in a state mental hospital and when the facility was closed she was put out on the street."

"Where local government would care for her," Whistler said with mild bitterness in his voice.

"She made her way downtown around the financial district where she lived in a cardboard box in sight of the branch office of the largest bank in the world."

"Japanese?"

"Of course."

They reached the back door and set the basket of vanquished cocks on a stone slab beneath an outside hose bib. There was a faded blue-painted bench up against the wall. Father Mitchum sat down, dragging a red bandana from the back pocket of his black trousers and mopping his face.

"She's afraid of being molested inside the house," Father

Mitchum said. "She's perfectly unafraid if she meets a stranger—anyone—out of doors, but I think she'd panic if anybody tried to get inside when she was alone. You want something cold?"

"It might help," Whistler said. Then he pointed to the priest's arms with his chin and said, "You've got blood on you, Father."

Mitchum stared at Whistler for a moment, then turned his attention to the spigot, turning it on and washing his hands and forearms under the flow. He looked up and over his shoulder at Whistler. "It make you uncomfortable calling a man Father?"

"I don't know about titles," Whistler said.

Father Mitchum nodded his head vigorously, as though agreeing with that point of view. "Mrs. Margaret," he called. "Mrs. Margaret?"

"What is it?" Mrs. Margaret said from the doorway.

With the priest there to protect her, she presented a different person to the world, self-confident and just a little bit impatient.

"Have we got a couple of Carta Blancas in the fridge?" Father Mitchum asked.

"I don't drink beer," Whistler said.

"Something stronger?"

"I don't drink at all."

Father Mitchum stood up, holding his arms out from the sides, shaking the water from his hands, looking at Whistler with a stare of shrewd appraisal.

"I made some lemonade," Mrs. Margaret said, and left the doorway to fetch the drinks.

"It give you any trouble?" Father Mitchum asked.

"There are moments."

"I know the burning. Not booze, but other appetites. I mean I knew it. When I was a young priest. The young women wondering about you, testing your commitment to your faith. You know what I mean?"

"Some women would think it was a hell of a triumph, seducing a priest."

"And some would think it an even greater one when they

didn't succeed. That's why they try. We don't really trust people. We're always testing them. It's the modern failing. Do you know that?" he asked.

"So the young women would tease the young priest," he went on, "wanting him to fall from grace, not wanting him to fall from grace, never realizing what a torture they were to him." He sat down on the blue bench again. "We might as well sit right here and have our refreshment. It won't really be any cooler inside. I only like to think it is."

Whistler sat down beside him—there was plenty of room for two—and Father Mitchum said, "Mrs. Margaret told me you were asking about spiritual guidance. I don't think that's what you're after."

"I'm after information."

"Oh, that stuff," Father Mitchum said, laughing softly.

"You have a parishioner by the name of Kenny Gotch?"

"The inference being that my congregation being so small I'd remember each and every one of them by name?"

Whistler knew the priest was running around the mulberry bush a little, sorting out some impressions he'd not yet finished sorting out, buying a little time.

"The inference being that a name like Gotch isn't forgotten so easily," Whistler said. "Now that I see the neighborhood I'd say an Anglo named Gotch might even be unforgettable."

"He wasn't a parishioner. He was a . . . petitioner."

"Petitioning for what?"

"A hearing."

"A hearing with who?"

"With anyone who would show him the way."

"Where was he going?"

Father Mitchum studied his hands, hunched over them, his elbows on his knees, fingers splayed out before him. "It's a very funny thing about blood," he said. "No matter how often I wash my hands, there's always a trace of it left imbedded in the cuticle, under the fingernails. Like traces of a faith you were raised in but you thought you'd washed all away." He glanced up at Whistler, looking arch and conspiratorial. "I'm not going to give you any of that chicken shit about the hope of heaven and saving your soul while you've got the chance. There's a tendency among priests to use the untimely death of anyone as a kind of example, a laudatory lesson placed there for their convenience in pursuit of the conversion or recapture of souls. Kenny Gotch was frightened as only a human being staring into the pit can be frightened. He'd done things."

"He told me," Whistler said, stretching the truth more than a little.

"Oh?"

"And I found out a little more."

"And?"

"I didn't find out enough."

"How did you come to me? I don't think Kenny Gotch lived around here."

"He lived over in West Hollywood. After he died, I had a look in his apartment. Your number was programmed into his phone."

A little smile touched Father Mitchum's mouth, as though that news both pleased and saddened him.

"He called a lot at first. Sometimes in the middle of the night. Drunk sometimes. High on drugs. Full of remorse. Then the calls dwindled away to practically nothing."

"How long had he been calling?"

"More than two years. I save my old telephone and appointment books. It'll be recorded there, the first time he called, if that'll be of any use to you."

Whistler shrugged, seeing no relevance in it.

"That may have been when he first tested HIV positive," he said.

"Perhaps. It's the sort of scare that sends lost sheep running back to the fold."

"Is that what Kenny Gotch was, a lost sheep?" Whistler asked, making it sound as though the priest had a little box of handy homilies and labels that he pasted on the world and the people in it as they passed by, some stopping and bowing their heads for his blessing. Making the priest and his way of looking at things trivial and shallow.

"It's just a way of speaking," Father Mitchum said. "I'll bet you've got a phrase or two in your profession that falls trippingly from the tongue. What brought Kenny back to the church was a lot uglier than the image of woolly sheep coming home across a green meadow."

Mrs. Margaret appeared with a tray on which sat a frosted glass of lemonade with a red plastic straw in it and another empty frosted glass with a bottle of Carta Blanca beer uncapped beside it. She'd put on a small white apron to protect her black dress from any drips or to make a little ceremony out of serving the guest. She even smiled at him when Whistler took the glass and thanked her, watching him with careful eyes until he'd taken a sip from the straw and declared it good with a nod and a smile.

"Maybe I should have made it hot," she said. "It might have done your cold some good."

"Thank you anyway," Whistler said, "but this'll go down a lot better."

"When you go to bed tonight you might make yourself a hot lemonade with some honey in it," she said.

"I'll do that."

She went back inside.

"Well, it looks like you have a way with the ladies yourself," Father Mitchum said.

"How's that?"

"Mrs. Margaret put on her best apron. Little things like that say much about the way some people give their trust."

"How did Kenny Gotch do that?"

"He finally came to see me and asked me to tell him what I knew about salvation. I explained the value of confession and sincere repentance."

Whistler waited but the priest didn't add anything. Whistler had to ask.

"Did you hear his confession?"

"Not then. That first meeting, and those that came after, was just the overture. I think he wanted to test my sincerity. He wanted to see if I'd jump on his back, knock him to the ground and wrestle Satan for his soul."

"Did he believe in Satan?"

The flash of shrewdness lit up the priest's eyes again. "You mean literally?"

"We could fool around. Play word games. Do *you* believe in Satan? Literally?"

"Would I were a Jesuit," Father Mitchum said, smiling a quirky smile. "Those boys know how to play word games. Do you remember that motion picture? *The Exorcist?*"

"It's a film everybody's seen or at least heard about."

"You remember that when the mother appealed to the church, they referred her first to a Jesuit who made the case that the child was in need of psychiatric care and consultation? They don't go throwing myth made corporeal around the way some priests and ministers do. Couldn't help her, that Jesuit. They finally had to drag that old priest all the way back from Egypt, where he was digging up old bones, to do the job. To wrestle with the devil in her."

"Possession. That's another thing. You can make a case from the evidence either way," Whistler said. "Either it's literal or it's a metaphor."

"That's the whole argument in a nutshell. On most matters of belief you can make a case from the facts either way. That's the wellspring of religion. What comes after. What it comes down to when you run out of arguments one way and the other. Faith. Blind faith. I haven't got blind faith."

Father Mitchum seemed amused at the startled expression he saw on Whistler's face.

"You're surprised," he said. "Here I am a priest, if not a Jesuit, instructed in the faith more than any layman, admitting to one of those layman that I'm not strong in faith. Well, that's not exactly what I said. I said I didn't have the gift of blind faith, just like I never had the gift of willing celibacy. But that's not to say that I haven't been able to act appropriately and wisely. I haven't known a woman. In the biblical sense," he added with another little smile. "And I haven't discounted or discarded the actuality of Satan with all the confusion and contradiction surrounding that eminence."

"You're sounding like a Jesuit," Whistler said.

"I'm simply saying that I don't have to necessarily believe in the miracle of the loaves and fishes by which Christ fed the multitude as long as I can feed some of my poor with fighting chickens slain in battle. I don't have to have blind faith in all the ceremony, ritual and complicated theology that's formed, over the centuries, like incrustations of sea creatures on a ship's bottom, around a seed of revelation. All I have to believe in are simple acts of goodness and mercy. To be trustworthy in all confidences. Which does, I think, bring us to your question."

"Did you?"

"Did I hear Kenny Gotch's confession? You already have your answer."

"You mean that you did but that you won't break the vow of confidentiality."

"You understand me exactly."

"Even if I told you that his confession might have clues that could lead to the arrest of a child molester and murderer?"

"If I heard his confession, I think I'd know that," Father Mitchum said. "How would that change the contract between Kenny and myself?"

"We owe more to the living than the dead."

"In my faith there is no death. Neither Kenny Gotch nor the child are dead. I pray for them equally."

"There's the child's family still suffering."

"Thirsting and hungering for vengeance?" Father Mitchum asked.

"We make up our own minds about what we want, a God of mercy or a God of vengeance."

"That's the subject of another Jesuitical debate. This much I think I can safely tell you without breaking the implied contract I had with Kenny Gotch. In the last communication we had, Kenny asked me about the progression of events that preceded an exorcism."

"He thought he was possessed?"

"He never said that in so many words but if I were a man who read between the lines, I'd say that was the fact of the matter. One way or the other he was having intercourse or thought he was having intercourse with demons." He stood up and, ignoring the glass, drank the last of the beer from the bottle.

"Then, according to your own tenets, Kenny Gotch might

have been possessed, under the orders of something evil. Reason enough to fight against what it brought to pass, to steal its victory over Kenny. Reason enough to break the vow of the confessional."

"Balancing out the betrayals?"

"I'd say so."

Mitchum looked thoughtful, suddenly doubtful about the simple rules laid upon him by his faith and the demands of his office, which any priest knew were not so simple.

"I'll pray on it. I'll ask for guidance." He smiled. "Would you like to stay for dinner?" he asked.

"I have to be getting back to Hollywood," Whistler said.

"Too bad. You could've helped me pluck some chickens."

"I'd like to come back after you've prayed on it."

"Yes, whenever you like. Give me tonight."

# 28

*The* sky was so clear Whistler was tempted to drive out north of Malibu where he knew about a deserted curl of beach a short walk down the coast from the wreck of a mansion once owned and operated by some child guru and a private restaurant said to be the haunt of pederasts, pedophiles and other assorted ginks, hoping that the salt air might break up the congestion in his nose that was moving down into his chest.

Instead he drove back into town, heading for Gentry's, going home. For if home was where comfort and sympathetic friends were to be found, the coffee shop was all the home he really had.

He wasn't quite certain why Kilroy had loaded him with book titles or why he'd even want to buy them as he'd done, but he'd asked questions as though the answers were simple ones and he understood that at least a minor education was required before he could understand the significance of the severed finger and the mutilation done to little Sarah by those who'd taken her innocence and her life.

Bosco, reading his own book, *The Masks of God: Primitive Mythology* by Joseph Campbell, noted the armload of books Whistler carried in and piled on the table in his favorite booth but made no comment, simply bringing a cup of coffee and nodding approvingly at Whistler's studious concentration, as though he were the parent and Whistler a favorite child finally discovering the joys of reading.

"You got the flu coming on," he said. "Too bad I can't give you a shot of brandy in your coffee."

"I know the cure. I used it many a time," Whistler said, not even lifting his eye from the page.

He was wearing a pair of reading glasses, just lately acquired and required. It felt strange to be seeking information through the agency of books rather than the give-and-take of interrogation. Not that he was altogether ignorant of books, but he was simply more comfortable being a hunter than a gleaner. Bosco was the boy for shaping a world and a philosophy from the subtle comparisons and opinions available in books; Whistler's way was rougher and readier.

He coughed discreetly into his hand, trying to be quiet about it, because if Bosco kicked into his motherly mode, he'd be sent home to bed with a container of chicken soup and orders to stay in bed.

Jeanne Millholme thought about the erotic hour with Rahab, the conflict of emotions.

Stripped naked—because that was the only way she knew to get him to strip naked as well—she was nearly overwhelmed by a tide of lust coupled with the most profound desire to surrender. Whether to the sudden demands of her flesh and his flesh or to the overpowering desire of her soul to turn over her fate to someone or something else, she couldn't say.

Desperate for repose, she was all too ready, here at the end of her long search to give it up, and deny the evidence of her eyes as she approached the buttocks he presented to her, the ass with the burgundy stain like a crouching spider emerging from his anus.

But, if love had prompted her unrelenting hunt, a rushing flood of rage reinspired her appetite for revenge.

She remembered the capture of the child stealer. His name had been Harry Atlanta. When the Indians had dragged him back into the village with a thong of leather around his neck, he was already running red with blood. The chief had questioned him and threatened him and when all the answers he could or would give had been extracted, they'd hacked at him with their machetes until there was nothing but dog meat left of him.

She'd watched it all and exulted in it.

Despair came after when something that might have been her son's body was found.

Between the two, she thought, staring at her paintings of rampant men and threatened women, gibbering beasts and lost children, she wondered if all of that and all that came after had driven her mad.

"After the blood of a sacrificial child has been mixed with the contents of the chalice, these words are used to accompany the offerings made to Satan: Astaroth, Asmodeus, I beg you to accept the sacrifice of this child which we now offer to you, so that we may receive the thanks we ask," Whistler read in *The Dictionary of Satanism.*

He'd been reading such stuff for two hours, extracts from *The Book of Mormon, The Book of the Apocalypse,* the *Kabala* and half a dozen more dealing with the fallen angel who was Lucifer or Satan or the devil and the thousand names of his servants, until the words had started to become gibberish.

He pushed the glasses to the top of his head and grasped the bridge of his nose with his thumb and forefinger, trying to press away the weariness that fogged his brain. His chest was filled with cotton and he was breathing through his mouth.

Bosco slipped into the booth across the table from Whistler. He adjusted Whistler's book so he could read the title on the spine. He quickly checked the other titles as well.

"I didn't know you had an interest," Bosco said.

"I found something that gave me an interest," Whistler replied, reaching over to tap the cover of Bosco's book. "I notice you've been reading in the subject yourself."

"I'm doing a comparison of religions."

"By way of choosing a church to join?"

"I'm not a joiner. I ain't a believer neither. What I am is a secular humanist with a wide open mind. Truth and wisdom is where you find it."

"So what's this, you reading about religions and me reading about religions?"

"Synchronicity."

"What?"

"Synchronicity. The workings of chance. What you would call coincidence. Random happenings coming together at the intersection of a point in time."

"Should we be impressed?"

"No. It happens all the time. It's like you suddenly get thinking about hippopotamuses because you just bought a stuffed toy hippopotamus for your favorite niece or whoever. I mean, you don't give a lot of thought to hippopotamuses, right? Then all of a sudden you notice there's a hippopotamus on the cover of *People* and there's a PBS special on hippopotamuses and you go to a restaurant and they got hippopotamus on the menu."

"Hey."

"I exaggerate. But you get my meaning? You ain't had a thought about hippopotamuses in years and you figure that nobody else is paying much attention to hippopotamuses either, and then you buy a stuffed toy and all of a sudden, everywhere you look, hippopotamuses."

"Synchronicity."

"You got it. So my interest in religions old and new comes out of my reading and thinking, where most of my interests come from. Where did your interest come from?"

"I found a mummified finger—like a doll's finger—in

Kenny Gotch's apartment. If he really had a connection with whoever it was killed Sarah Canaan, the finger could be . . ."

He left it there. Not finishing the thought because just identifying it as hers gave him a lot of pain.

Bosco waved at the books. "So, this?"

"I went asking questions of a professor and this is what I got. You ever hear of the Hand of Glory?"

"Necromancy."

"Well, this Professor Kilroy says the finger could be a version of that."

Bosco nodded.

"None of this seems to surprise you."

"What do you want me to be surprised about? That the world's filled with lunatics? I always knew that. I always knew that there were more crazies outside than inside. I always knew that people were desperate to find something to hold on to, belong to, and if they couldn't believe in something saintly, they'd believe in something evil. You should talk to Sergeant Harry Essex, the Satan maven."

"He's been recommended."

"He works out of the Plaza. Give him a call. Mention my name."

Bitchie Boo, one of the Heavy Metal Fates, leather skirt just barely covering her glorious ass, came in then, loudly calling, "Innkeeper, innkeeper, I need something tall and cool."

She spotted Bosco sitting with Whistler and toddled over on her spiked heels.

"You make me a diet cola, Bosco. You make me a glass of ice tea."

"Make up your mind, darling," Bosco said, "or do you want a glass of each?"

"That's good. Put them in containers to go."

She smiled at Whistler as though waiting for an invitation as Bosco slid out and went to get her refreshment.

Whistler nodded and Bitchie Boo sat down, her eyes flickering over the pages of the open books.

"You shouldn't read that stuff," she said.

"You read upside down?" Whistler said, feigning great admiration.

"You doubt I could read at all," she said. "I can read upside down, sideways and standing on my head. I'm telling you, watch that witchcraft and don't mess with Satan. There's girls and boys on the street mess with Satan and it don't do them no good."

"Like who, Bitchie Boo?"

"You even say the names you can get the blame, bring down a curse on you. Oh, no, no, oh, hon, no," she said, waving a hand tipped with blood red fingernails in the air.

Bosco came back with the two tall plastic cups with straws poking up out of the lids. She sipped one and then the other. "That's cola and that's tea. That's good, that's good."

She stood up and settled her short skirt over the curve of her rump, patting herself there in appreciation of what it earned for her.

"You going to see Rialto down at Hollywood station?" she asked.

"What's Rialto doing down at Hollywood station?"

"They say he cut a man's throat. You go down and see him, you say hello for me. But, if I was you, I'd go home, get into bed and take care of that cold."

She picked up the two cups and walked on out, her hips shattering the air all the way down the aisle to the door.

# 29

So, now it's all over the street that I'm an assassin," Rialto said, wiping his face with his hands as though trying to work some life into his flesh. "It's going to have a serious impact on my business."

"Nobody's going to believe you cut anybody's throat," Whistler said.

"Gossip stains a man, proved or otherwise," Rialto insisted. "Everybody'll think, 'where there's smoke there's fire.' "

"So maybe it'll do you some good. They think, 'where there's smoke there's fire,' it'll maybe give you a reputation among the hookers."

"It could do that," Rialto agreed after a little pause, seeming to be momentarily uplifted by the thought that something good might come out of all this after all. "But if I don't get out of here, how am I going to capitalize on my notoriety? You think I should call a lawyer?"

"They keep you more than seventy-two, they have to book you," Whistler said. "I'd wait and see. So, what did you tell Canaan?"

"I told him what I had to tell him. There's no keeping anything from Isaac when he wants to know."

"So, exactly what did you tell him?"

"I told him that Kenny Gotch told Abe Forstman who told me that he knew who abducted, tortured and killed a little girl, then threw her body in Hollywood Cemetery ten years ago."

"What else?"

"I told him that Kenny Gotch rolled over and threw up on me."

"What else?" Whistler asked again, staring into Rialto's eyes, not giving him space to figure out should he shouldn't he tell Whistler everything without asking a price.

"I gave him a greeting card I found under Gotch's pillow and stuffed into my pocket."

"What greeting card?"

"One of them greeting cards with a sweet poem on it."

"Was it signed?"

"It said something about this person who sent the card sending their love but being afraid to come visit. Something like that."

"Was it signed?"

Rialto, being a man who never gave away something for nothing, decided Whistler had all he was going to get. He thought a minute and then shook his head.

Whistler read his eyes and knew he was holding back, but there wasn't much he could do; you couldn't choke something out of somebody in a police station.

He got ready to go.

"I don't have to tell you, do I?"

"Tell me what?"

"Canaan's out there looking for the person who sent that card to Kenny Gotch. He's out there trying to find the end of the string, just like I'm trying to do. If he finds—when he finds—whoever's on the other end of it I don't know what he's going to do. What do you think he's going to do?"

"Waste the sonofabitch who murdered Sarah."

"That's what I think he's going to do. And that'll be the end of Isaac. A cop that takes trial and punishment into his own hands that way is giving up everything in which he ever believed."

"Pooch. The name on the card was Pooch," Rialto said.

"Ah, Jesus H. Christ," Whistler said, remembering his conversation on the telephone with William Mandell, "why am I so bad at picking the right door?"

"You got a bad cold there," Rialto said. "I hope you didn't give it to me."

\*    \*    \*

Whistler got William "Pooch" Mandell's address out of the reverse directory. He went to Mandell's house and found out from his landlady that he'd come home from work at midafternoon, packed a bag, tossed it in the back of his Ford and took off on what he told her was an unexpected summons home.

The landlady read his voice, his eyes and his running nose, and kept her distance. All she knew was that home for Mandell was somewhere back in the Midwest, Ohio, maybe, or Illinois. Too far for Whistler to go chasing after.

Canaan had gotten to something through Rialto that Whistler had missed because he'd never been told. Who would've thought of asking Rialto if he'd picked up a letter in the dead man's room?

Whistler went over to Hollywood station, approached Captain Hensler in the squad room and found out that Canaan had walked in and told the captain that he was taking a week, maybe two weeks, of accumulated sick leave.

"Didn't you think that pretty funny?"

"He said he felt a cold coming on. You give him your cold?"

"I didn't have my cold or flu or whatever when I saw him last," Whistler said. "But sick or not, I don't think Isaac's taken a day's sick leave or even a day's personal time in ten years. I've seen him walking around with a temperature of a hundred and two."

"That's the trouble. A man gives you something extra every day for ten years, you expect him to go on doing it forever. Maybe he did feel a cold coming on. Maybe he wanted to eat up some of his sick time because if he don't there's a good chance he'll never get paid for it when he retires. Maybe he wanted to shack up for a week, a couple weeks, get his carburetor adjusted. Let the man have some free time. Unless there's something you know, I don't know."

Whistler put up his hands, denying that he had any special knowledge or special concern.

"You sure you're not worried about him?" Hensler asked.

"Why would I be worried about him?"

"Because Isaac's not getting any younger. Because ever since his niece got murdered he's getting older ten to one. Because he could maybe drop dead of a heart attack any minute."

"Jesus Christ, don't say that. Has anybody been over to check his apartment?"

Hensler shook his head. "Have you?"

"I didn't want to butt in until I found out if Isaac was on special assignment, maybe gone undercover, something like that."

"The man's gone less than a day and you're ready to send out an APB. What's going on here, Whistler?"

"If I had anything to tell you, I'd tell you," Whistler said.

Whistler felt very strange going into Canaan's apartment uninvited. In all the years they'd known one another Canaan had never asked him over, though Whistler had asked the old detective over to his house many times.

They'd sat around drinking coffee together, listening to the traffic on the freeway, pretending it was surf, and although Canaan had never stayed long he'd acted as though he'd been grateful for the company.

Whistler luded the Yale with a credit card, amazed that a cop wouldn't have better security. Then he saw there was nothing for a self-respecting thief—not even a drug addict looking for the price of a fix or a bindle of blow—to turn into cash. The black-and-white television set was so old you'd have to pay somebody to take it off your hands and junk it. Maybe the only things worth a gonnif's glance were the framed inscriptions on the walls, beautifully executed in illuminated calligraphy, but then again very few addicts appreciated ancient quotations.

"All my life I grew up among the sages and have found nothing better for anybody than silence," said one.

"Keep far away from an evil neighbor, do not associate with the wicked, and do not shrug off all thought of calamity," said another.

Whistler understood the irony of that, the kiddie vice cop, who had to confront the worst depravities of a sick society every day of his life, admonishing himself to have nothing to do with the villains he dealt with. The last few words were the snapper though, turning the warning around, saying that there was really no place to hide and you'd better be ready for that too. Calamity. Plenty of that to go around.

He went into the kitchen and started opening drawers and cabinets, having no idea what he was looking for, but hoping he'd recognize something significant when he saw it.

There were a few pots and pans, just enough to warm up a can of stew or fry an egg. A half-pint microwave probably used for nothing more than TV dinners and heating water for tea and coffee sat on the counter along with a toaster.

There was the usual collection of utensils and stainless steel flatware purchased from a five and dime.

Nothing in the refrigerator, not even a tray of ice cubes. Whistler ran himself a glass of water from the tap. It smelled and tasted of unknown bugs and gases overlaid with chemicals. The pleasures of modern life, even a glass of water blasted by the crush of too much demand.

He examined his anxiety. Canaan had been gone, at most, the few hours since he'd questioned Rialto and learned the truth about what they'd tried to keep from him.

As he got ready to leave he noticed the parchment and the pens and ink on the table. Canaan had been at work on another of his quotations; had sketched this one in pencil. It was only half completed if Whistler remembered the much-repeated Old Testament quote correctly.

"Vengeance is mine . . ."

". . . sayeth the Lord," Whistler murmured.

# 30

*Diana* was twenty-five and had been in La-La Land two
years, during which time she'd made half a dozen friends,
three hundred acquaintances and had endured and profited
by twelve hundred passing collisions with hungry, horny,
lonely men.

The Bobbys, Darnel and Lamay, were two of her friends.
Kenny Gotch and Joe, the day man at the bar at the Luau,
were two others. The head nurse at the Angeles, Mary
Bucket, was another, and a photographer by the name of Raymond Raditski, who called himself Rahab on his business
cards, monogrammed shirts and the gold lettering on the
window of his storefront studio in West Hollywood, was
something else again; a relationship she'd yet to describe or
qualify. Sometimes he gave her the giggles and sometimes
the chills.

He was sitting on the daybed playing with his camera, the
open case beside him, taking pictures of her standing in front
of the glass sliding doors of her apartment on Sweetzer overlooking the city. It was a nice apartment with a balcony. On
a clear day like today you could see the tower of the city
hall in Beverly Hills.

There were framed prints of flowers in the living room,
puppy dogs and kittens in the kitchen, the famous picture of
the suffering Jesus, with blood dripping into his eyes, mouth
agape in pain and near-death ecstasy, and another of a bleed-
ing heart, wrapped in thorns and surmounted by a crown,
on the wall above her bed. She rarely conducted business
at home.

"The life's gone out of the city," she said.

"How's that?" Rahab asked.

"It's got no flavor. It's like a piece of chewing gum what's lost all its peppermint and sugar."

"You thinking of taking a trip?"

"Why not. My inventory travels with me."

"You got a place in mind?"

"I was thinking American Samoa."

"What the hell ever put that notion into your head?"

"I noticed it when I was making out my income tax return."

"Let me understand this? You make out an income tax return?"

"Certainly, I do. I pay into Social Security."

"What do you put down under occupation?"

"Therapist."

He laughed and she stared at him, not being one who saw the humor in irony.

Since Schedule C for self-employed persons asks for a business code in the upper right-hand corner, she'd looked up the categories and decided that what she did properly came under the heading of therapy and that was that.

"So, what do you think?" she asked.

"About you being a therapist?"

"About going to American Samoa. I met some guys from there. They was as big as barns."

"That what turns you on, Dee? Guys as big as barns?"

"Turns me on?" The idea of getting turned on didn't have much meaning to her anymore.

"I mean it don't necessarily follow that a man as big as a barn has a cock as big as a horse," he went on.

"I wish you'd watch your mouth," she said. "I ain't looking for men with big things. All I'm looking for is a place where I can lay down on the sand and go to sleep."

The phone rang. She let the message click in but picked up before her voice had finished the news that Diana Corday was not at home at the moment.

"I'm here, I'm here," she said with a little lift to her voice, a little invitation, eager anticipation, which didn't quite conceal her boredom with it all. "Who's this?"

She and the caller waited until her message stopped.

"I got to get that fixed," she said, sitting down on the day-bed next to Rahab. "It's not supposed to do that. It's supposed to stop on the dot when I pick up. So, I'm sorry. Who's this?"

Rahab was inspecting his fingernails, beautifully mani-cured into points like those guitarists flashed on their strum-ming hand, pleased because everything about him was neat and trim.

"Whistler? That your first name, your last name, or do they call you that because of what you do when a pretty woman passes by?" Diana asked.

Rahab looked at her with more than a little interest. He'd had a call on his mobile phone. Whistler's name had been mentioned as someone to be watched.

"Somebody refer you to me?" she went on.

Her face moved, a little tick of pain or anguish.

"Who? Kenny Gotch? Kenny Gotch's dead," she said. She placed her palm on the mouthpiece and turned her head to Rahab. "Is it on the street that Kenny Gotch is dead?"

Rahab nodded and moved over, putting his ear close to the earpiece so he could hear the other end of the conversation.

"I was a friend of Kenny's," Whistler's voice said. "I'd like to talk to you about him, if that's all right."

"What do you want to talk about?" Diana said, removing her hand from the mouthpiece.

"Well, you were a friend of Kenny's and I was a friend of Kenny's, so I just thought . . ."

"You mean you want to talk about Kenny just like that? You didn't call because Kenny referred you to me for any services?"

"Services? No. What services?"

"Never mind," she said. "I'm just wondering how come if you were a friend of Kenny's I never heard about you. I mean if he told you about me, how come he didn't tell me about you? Especially with a name like Whistler and all. I mean that's something one friend would mention to another friend, like it was a curiosity. You know what I mean?"

Whistler laughed. "Well, maybe it was one of those cases

where Kenny didn't want one of his friends meeting another one of his friends for reasons we'll never know."

"I don't see how we got anything to talk—"

Rahab had her by the wrist, putting his other hand over the mouthpiece, nodding his head vigorously, telling her to say yes to a meeting. He let her go and leaned back on his elbows, watching her.

"Okay," she said, frowning a little, not wanting to be told what to do. "What's today? Wednesday, right? Okay. How about six o'clock tonight? What? You'll buy me dinner? Well, you want to buy me something, you can buy me breakfast. Because I work nights and that's when I have my breakfast. So, where? Gentry's Coffee Shop? Yeah, I know the joint. I'm glad to see you're a big spender." She hung up and got off the bed. "Fuck him. He wants to talk about Kenny Gotch and I don't want to talk about Kenny Gotch. I was there when Kenny Gotch died. He was all over blood."

Rahab got up off the bed, launching himself neatly to his feet like a tumbler doing a flip.

Diana turned to the window again and stared off across the city.

"You meet with this guy tonight," Rahab said. "I'd like to have a look at him."

"What for?"

He shrugged. "You never know. You go meet this Whistler tonight. I'd like to have a look. What're you doing Halloween?"

"I don't know. Working the hotel bars. Wimps wearing masks get very brave and do what they wouldn't have the balls to do in their bare faces. Why?"

"I got a little job for you, if you want it. Private show."

"What kind of show?"

"Initiation into the Church of Satan."

"This going to be one of them up the walls, on the ceiling, twenty pairs of hands groping and twenty assholes popping?" she asked.

"No, this is going to be a big production. Private club. It'll be like an acting job, you know what I mean?"

"Would I be the star?" she asked, looking at him slant-eyed.

"Well, maybe not *the* star but at least a costar."

"Who else'll be in the cast?"

"Maybe the dwarf. Maybe the giantess. I could use your friends, the two Bobbys. In fact, you don't want the gig," he said, making it sound as though it was a nightclub booking he was offering here, "I could offer your part to one of them."

"One of them wouldn't remember all the mumbo-jumbo necessary for a Black Mass," she said.

"You think you still remember the routine?"

"I don't need any rehearsals, for Christ's sake."

"For Lucifer's sake. You've got to watch your habits. You don't want to fuck things up with a slip of the tongue."

"Just tell me when and where."

"Be ready Halloween night around six o'clock and I'll pick you up. If I can't make it, somebody else'll drive you down there."

"Where?"

"Lucifer's."

"That kink club down on the beach above Malibu?"

He smiled.

"You know some very funny people, Ray."

"This isn't vaudeville," he said, warning her that she should take things a little more seriously.

"Don't tell me you're starting to believe this crap," she said, striking a pose, her head tilted to one side.

"Are you telling me none of this attracts you?"

"Attract? What attract? You think I get off lying naked on a marble slab—getting a goddamn chill—and having some woman kiss my twat?"

He threw back his head and laughed. She started laughing, too, but wasn't sure what they were laughing at.

# 31

*There* were rumors out on the stroll that old-line whores and newly turned out hookers were giving it away in a rush of good feeling, the clean air having washed their souls and restored their innocence if not their maidenheads.

Whistler could give himself every reason for leaving the city behind and going down to the beach and joining the armies of city refugees down at the seaside, covering every inch of sand with their bodies, ready to rise up in one great celebration before marching into the sea and swimming toward the rising moon until the millennium arrived, or he could go home and crawl into bed the way everybody was telling him to do. But he had the bone in his teeth and couldn't let go. He took a hit of the twelve-hour decongestant inhalator—his third in five hours—and felt his sinuses open up so he could stop breathing through his mouth like a beached fish. He popped an oral anesthetic lozenge to soothe the sore throat that was working its way toward his ears.

"Feelin' good," he murmured, trying to psych himself, but what with his clogged sinuses he didn't sound very convincing.

A woman with a twenty-year-old body, a thirty-year-old face and hundred-year-old eyes walked through the open door and stopped three strides inside the coffee shop, feet planted, quietly turning her head one way and the other, scanning the place in search of someone.

Whistler recognized her as one of those rare professional women who'd literally seen it all, back rooms and bawdy houses, on call and convention cruising, sodomy, lesbian acts, triples, acrobatics and maybe even a little bestiality thrown in during extra hard times, and yet had somehow come through it all untouched at the center of her, changing her skin each night and morning, creating anew a kind of cynical, skeptical honesty with which to face the world.

Bosco had glanced up from his book and was looking at her with a look that was interested, wary, admiring and lecherous all at the same time.

He glanced at Whistler, who was on his feet waiting for her approach, and saw that she'd made an impression on Whistler as well.

Diana put out her hand, not like some suburban housewife meeting a strange man for lunch but like an equal ready to sit down and cut some kind of deal.

"You want a menu?" Whistler asked.

"Tea. I'd like some herb tea, if they got it," Diana said.

Bosco was right there at her shoulder. "Mint? Chamomile? Orange Spice? My own?" he offered.

She looked at him, her eyes flickering to his empty sleeve. "What's 'My Own'?"

"I mix it myself. A little valerian to soothe the nerves, a sprinkle of peppermint for zest, thirty Colombian dark-roasted coffee beans for balance—"

"You know coffee's an herb?" she said, widening her eyes and smiling.

"I made a study."

"So, that's what I'll have."

She turned away and sat down, waiting for Whistler to sit down opposite.

"You wanted to talk about Kenny?" she said.

"Were you good friends?"

She shrugged her shoulders.

"I figured you must've been a good friend."

"How'd you figure that?"

"Kenny had ten personal numbers programmed into his telephone speed dialer. One of them was a relative and another was probably his drug connection. Two were—"

She put up her hand and waved it from side to side, making a face of minor annoyance.

"I don't want to hear—"

"—ex-boyfriends and—"

"—about who he had in his telephone directory."

"—I haven't been able to make contact with two more. Why not? Why don't you want to hear about the people Kenny knew?"

"Because you start asking me questions about people Kenny knew, I won't tell you anything. I'll tell you anything I know about Kenny and me but I won't go pointing any fingers."

"I understand. That's good. I was just trying to explain how come I figured you must've been a good friend."

"I was a friend for the wee smalls."

"Do you mind explaining that?"

"He wasn't a best friend. You'll drop what you're doing and run to a best friend when they're in trouble. He wasn't even a good friend. You'll send a good friend a check when they're needy. He wasn't a new acquaintance, more like an old one. You've got some hope for better and more with a new acquaintance."

"So what was he, this old acquaintance?"

She smiled and her face lost ten years, maybe a little more. Especially around the mouth. She was a child having fun, teasing a grown-up. "An old acquaintance with a bullet."

"Meaning he was on his way to becoming a friend?"

"We talked a lot in the mornings sometimes, just before we went to bed to get some sleep. It ain't natural being a night worker. Cops on graveyard and last out, clerks in all-night drugstores and coffee shops, emergency workers and hookers know how hard it is to get your nerves sorted out at the end of a long night. You know?"

Whistler nodded. "What did you talk about in the wee smalls?"

"Going home. Walking through the door on your mother's birthday or when your sister's getting married or on Christmas day and having everybody hug you and kiss you and say how much they've missed you."

"So?"

"So, what?"

"Why don't you do it? Why didn't Kenny do it?"

"Grow up. What I just talked about are pictures torn out of a magazine. There was nothing like that waiting for Kenny or me. It was just what we talked about in the wee smalls. You asked what we talked about and I just told you what we talked about."

Her face had grown solemn and hard, all the impish pleasure she'd revealed for a few moments all tucked away again.

"Did you ever talk about anything else?"

"Sure, we talked about how freaky some of the trade was getting to be out there. It's these terrible movies and awful books excite the crazies out there. Somebody ought to do something about it."

"You ever talk about religion?"

"What?" The word went up like a shield.

"You ever talk about God?"

"That's very private. I don't talk about my religion and I don't talk about my private life to strangers."

"That's too bad, because that's what I've really got to know about if I'm going to find out who cut Kenny's throat."

The color faded—"What're you talking about? Kenny had AIDS"—and returned to her face like a tide. She was a quick recovery, Whistler thought.

"You're sure of that?" he asked.

"I volunteer my time over there at Angeles. I was there the morning they found him dead. I walked in on him to say good morning a minute after he died in his own blood. It was AIDS."

"He was going to die of AIDS," he agreed. "He was maybe a couple of days away from dying of AIDS, but he died of a little blade in the throat."

She was looking down at the table between her clasped hands. "Oh, my God," she murmured.

"What?" Whistler asked, leaning forward. "What did you say?"

When she looked up, her eyes seemed stunned. "Nobody said anything about Kenny being knifed to death."

"It wasn't a knife exactly. It was a surgeon's blade they don't even use anymore. It's a blade with a little cage on the back of it which slips on the surgeon's finger."

Bosco was back with the tea and coffee. Diana stuck her nose into the mug, inhaling the soothing vapors.

Bosco looked at Whistler and Whistler gave him the nod to sit down. Bosco slipped into the booth next to Whistler as Diana took a long sip of the tea.

"Very good. Very good," she said.

"I didn't ask, I just put in some honey."

"What kind of honey?"

"Sage."

"Yeah, that's good, that's good," she said.

Whistler took his three-by-five cards, secured by a rubber band, out of his pocket. "Can I read off a few names and you tell me if Kenny ever talked to you about any of these people?"

She nodded.

"George Gomble."

"Sure. Kenny lived with him for a while and then they had a lover's quarrel."

"Jane."

"That's all? Just Jane? I must know a hundred Janes. I don't remember Kenny ever told me anything or talked about any special Jane."

"We'll get back to it," Whistler said. "Kilroy."

She shook her head.

"Bobby L and Bobby D."

"They work the streets, a couple of young hookers. Bobby Lamay arrived maybe a year ago. The other one, Bobby Darnel, a little after. Kenny used to hang around with them when he was all dressed up in girl clothes. They passed johns off to one another. You know? Kenny would maybe get some interest, but when he said he was in costume—he was very honest that way—and the customer said he wasn't into boys, Kenny'd hand him off to one of the Bobbys. And vise versa. No sense letting one get away because you ain't got the proper merchandise."

"You ever trade any action with any of them?"

"I don't work the streets anymore. My business is practically all referrals nowadays. I don't even hang out in lounges or bars very much except for recreation."

"Okay. Next one is somebody by the name of Mike."

Again she shook her head. "Same thing like with Jane. How many Mikes you think I know? Fifty if I bothered to count?"

"Pooch."

"He's some kid don't know is he isn't he."

"Is he isn't he what?"

"A homosexual, a bisexual, a straight or what. He's fooling around, trying to make up his mind. He was fooling around with Kenny's affections and it bothered Kenny. He didn't want to seduce anybody, you understand what I mean, just because the person was lonely or something. It bothered Kenny a lot. This was before he got sick. After that, I don't know how he handled the relationship."

"Jet."

She gave Whistler a knowing look. "That's your drug connection?"

"I figure."

"Well, you figure right. He was Kenny's man, one of your minority entrepreneurs."

"You know where I can find him?" Whistler asked.

"Put out the word you're looking for a buy and Jet'll find you."

"You deal with him?"

"Only sometimes. When I got the blues. Life ain't all peaches and cream. You know?"

Whistler nodded and went back to his cards.

"You have any idea why Kenny would have a photography studio on his speed dial?"

"A photography studio?" she echoed.

"Someplace by the name of Rahab's?"

"Haven't got a clue." She looked at her watch. "I've got a date."

"We haven't had a chance to talk," Whistler said.

"Sure we have. Thanks for the tea."

She was out of the booth and out the door before Whistler could move to stop her.

"I feel lousy," Whistler said. "I'm going home. Anybody asks you don't know that."

# 32

**Some** research psychologists maintain that the sense of déjà vu, that odd wrinkle in time by which something seen for apparently the first time seems so familiar that a person believes it must have been visited before, is really a product of the way the brain processes information. Every once in a great while information is recorded and immediately forgotten—we're talking nanoseconds here—and instantly recorded again, compared against data already in the memory bank but not consciously known to be there, and then thrown into the front of the brain as a memory of something experienced at another time and place in another life.

Making the turn onto the long winding road that led to the top of the Hollywood hill where Walter Cape's mansion perched like the monster's castle in a Disney movie gave Canaan just such a feeling of a past life revisited without at first glance having a truly vivid memory of having been there before. He had to struggle to bring back recall, but it came.

Had it been only ten years before—shortly after the discovery of his niece's broken little body—that he and Bellerose, a fat cop in a white suit from New Orleans, and Whistler, holding an aluminum case in which a woman's head rested in dry ice, had driven up this road on the way to punish a monster by the name of Walter Cape with an act of horror because they could not otherwise bring him to justice?

There was a realtor's sign on a stake hammered into the ground. It was weathered, as though it had been standing there unmoved a long time.

He drove on, pulling up before the massive wrought-iron gates set in the stone columns of the wall that kept out the world. They were closed and padlocked, but there was no-body in the squat gatehouse; no guard toting a shotgun in the crook of his arm coming out to challenge him as there had been before.

He got out of his car and tested the chain and lock. The shank hadn't been driven home; the lock was merely hooked between the links of chain, making it easy for anyone going in or out to merely unloose the barrier without bothering with a key.

Going up the shorter circular drive to the front door, there was evidence of neglect everywhere, plants rotting in their beds, trees stunned with disease, showing half-faces of bare decay and half-faces of lushly struggling life on the side clos-est to the sun. Someone had left a wheeled garbage bin on the side of the wide apron where a dozen cars could be parked side by side.

There was a light on in a room on the top floor, another in a room beyond a small walled garden; he could just see the top of the French doors.

He went up to the door and pushed the bell button. He heard nothing from inside. He put his ear to the door and pressed the button again. It might not be working or it might be sounding in some servant's post deep in the house. He waited two minutes, and then he used the knocker shaped in the form of several small boys engaged in sexual play. He felt saddened by the foolishness of such coy advertisement. Cape would have called it a conversation piece, he knew. Party guests would comment about it and think it amusing.

He knocked once every minute and waited in between. Five minutes passed.

He walked around to the side of the house and found a way into the small private garden, walked up to the French doors and looked into the room. An old man was sitting before a fire, staring at his lap.

He realized that it was Walter Cape, a man once vigorous and powerful, now grown old, fallen into decay.

Canaan rattled on the pane with his fingernails. Cape whirled around and stared, throwing up his hands, his eyes wide and terrified. He was holding a little notebook in his one hand. It fluttered like a flag in his distress.

Canaan quickly removed his badge holder, flipped it opened and held the shield to the windowpane, mouthing, "Police. Police."

Cape fumbled for the telephone beside his chair, the notebook falling unnoticed to the carpet, and pressed a button. They stared at each other while they waited. After a while a big man wearing a black vest, his sleeves rolled up, came into the room, saw Canaan in the garden, frowned, nodded at something Cape said to him and came to open the French door.

"Police," Canaan said.

"Nobody called for the police," the servant said.

"He never hears anybody at the door," Cape complained, as though Canaan were an ally. "Malcolm never hears anything. Somebody could come in and murder me and Malcolm wouldn't hear."

"I came to ask Mr. Cape a few questions," Canaan said.

"About what?" Malcolm asked.

"About something that's none of your business," Canaan said.

"You're in my house. Whatever you have to ask can be asked in front of Malcolm," Cape said.

"I've come about a child who was mutilated and murdered," Canaan said, sitting down in the other chair by the fire without being invited.

"I don't know anything about a child," Cape said, his voice rising, growing irritated now that his initial terror was subsiding and his protector was in the room.

"It happened a long time ago."

"How long ago?"

"A year or so before I came to visit you with some friends of mine. You were having a dinner party. My friend rolled a memento mori across the linen and into your lap."

The fear flooded back into Cape's face again.

"I wanted to remind you of that, but it's not why I'm here," Canaan said.

"I remember you now," Cape said. "You haven't changed much."

He waited, cocking his head archly. Canaan understood that the old man wanted to be told that neither had he changed. Was it necessary to his survival that Cape believe he was successfully fending off time? If he were told the truth would he crumble into dust? Canaan said nothing.

"You're the cop who found his niece mutilated and murdered. I looked you up, you and that one, Whistler, and the other one from the south."

"Bellerose."

"Yes, him. I looked you up and found out all about you."

"We already knew all about you."

"For all the good it did you."

"It was enough to take the starch out of you. I can see that things haven't been the same."

"You didn't ruin me, if that's what you think."

"We weren't trying to ruin you, if you mean take your money. It looks like we did what we wanted to do. We made you afraid."

Cape's face screwed up like a fist; like the face of an enraged baby. He raved on incoherently, spittle gathering at the corners of his mouth, for a full minute or more. Malcolm went to bring him a glass of brandy and made him take a sip. Cape's eyes were mad.

He looked up at his servant with a child's expression.

"I have to take a pee," he whined. "I have to take a pee right now or I'll do it in my pants."

Malcolm hesitated, glancing at Canaan.

"Don't look at him," Cape said, suddenly enraged, "look at me. I said I have to go to the bathroom right this minute."

Malcolm helped the old man out of the chair. Cape jittered and skittered as they made their way across the room. They went out into the marble-floored entry and disappeared behind the door jamb.

Canaan leaned forward, reached down and picked up the notebook. It was wire spiral-bound. He flipped over the pages.

Out in the entry Malcolm said, "Not here."

"Well, I couldn't hold it, goddammit. You weren't fast enough when I told you I had to go."

The pages were filled with poems. Canaan read one. It was very sentimental, full of self-pity. Very badly done.

"Why won't you wear your diaper?" Malcolm said, as though not expecting an answer.

Canaan flipped to the front page.

"Watch yourself. You think I'm senile and crazy, but don't depend upon it," Cape said in a voice grown amazingly and instantly powerful.

There was an inscription on the first page saying that the notebook belonged to Harriet LaRue and Kenneth Gotch.

"Let's get back inside before that sonofabitch steals the silver," Cape said.

Canaan put the notebook into his pocket.

They came back into the room. There was a dark stain in front of Cape's trousers.

"Get me that dressing gown," Cape said.

Malcolm took a red and gold brocaded robe from a hat tree and helped Cape get into it. He sat down in his chair again, arranging the skirts of the robe over his lap to conceal his accident.

"So, you're still obsessed with the murder of your niece?"

"She never leaves my thoughts."

"Well, what makes you think I'd know anything about it? I'm sure you looked me up and know that I don't like little girls."

"Oh, I know what you like," Canaan said. "But I know you know the men who like little girls. You know all the strange ones. All the sick ones."

"Aren't we all?" Cape said. "Sick and strange, one way or another."

"You knew a young man by the name of Kenny Gotch. He called himself Harriet LaRue sometime."

"I met him once or twice. He was a little old for me."

"But somebody to trade with a friend."

"Oh, yes. He had his value."

"Who valued him?"

Cape smiled.

"You walk in here with nothing but your hate and hope,

expecting me to give up the name of someone I know who might—I say might—have had something to do with the death of your niece—what?—nine or ten years ago?"

"That's what I expect," Canaan said.

"What can you pay me for the information?"

Canaan reached into his pocket and took out a small pistol.

"You should have left the room when I asked you to, Malcolm. Now, after I've killed this old man, I'll have to kill you. If you'd left the room we could have agreed that he'd committed suicide with this unregistered gun because of something I revealed to him."

"I could leave the room right now," Malcolm said, surprisingly calm in the face of what was going down.

"Jesus Christ, Jesus Christ, would you do that?" Cape asked, his voice growing thin and frayed.

Malcolm made a sound like a cough or a laugh.

"Who'd believe I'd take my own life because of something you said?" Cape screamed at Canaan.

Canaan took out the notebook and threw it into Cape's lap.

"You had Kenny Gotch, a dying man, killed—his throat cut—because he meant to betray you before he died. He wanted to save his immortal soul from hell."

"Not I. I had nothing to do with it."

"I found you out and confronted you with it. You begged to be allowed to take your own life, an old man like you about to die. I decided to save the city the cost of a trial. Now I'll have to kill your man and you myself and make up another story. The authorities'll believe anything I tell them."

"I'll give you the name of the killer. That's really who you want."

Canaan waited. It wasn't necessary for him to agree to the deal, Cape had nowhere else to go.

"A man by the name of Raymond Raditski who calls himself Rahab cut Gotch's throat."

"Why?"

"Because Gotch knew the name of the man who killed your niece. He knew he was dying and was desperate to confess his sins."

"That's the name I want," Canaan said.

Cape hesitated. His mouth trembled and then grew firm. He'd made up his mind how much he'd give and no more, not through any loyalty to Sarah Canaan's killer but because it was his nature to give away as little as possible in every transaction, even to a man who'd clearly kill him if he chose to.

"You can get it from Rahab."

Canaan understood. He could threaten Cape with death but the man had come to the sticking point, the exercise of pride more important even than his life.

"Where is this Raymond Raditski?"

"He's a photographer. Do you know Lucifer's, the private restaurant above Malibu?"

"Yes, I know it."

"He'll be there tonight, taking pictures."

Canaan stood up.

"So we're quits," Cape said, making it a statement.

"We'll see."

"You're looking for vengeance not justice. Besides, I'm an old man about to die."

Canaan stared at Cape with infinite loathing and compassion.

"You really should wear your diapers," he said.

# 33

*Feeling* bad finally became more than he could handle, so Whistler made his way home, set out the cough syrup, the aspirin, the vitamin C and the nasal decongestant spray. He made himself a hot lemonade and put some honey in it, regretting the alcoholism that prevented his using the cold cure he'd once sworn by, a pint of rock and rye in just such a hot toddy as he now drank down like medicine, after drawing the drapes against the light; after undressing; before taking a hit of the nasal spray and crawling, naked, into his unmade bed.

He suffered bad dreams, not really sleeping, but drifting around in a sea of discomfort until he became aware that there were footsteps stealthily crossing the living room. His ears sent signals to his brain and his brain determined there was danger and sent signals to his motor centers, but then something went awry and he lay there paralyzed, unable to move a finger.

Bosco had once told him about theories concerning the phenomenon, that in the ancient beginnings of humankind when the tribe all slept together in a huddle like a pack of wolves there may have been occasions when a male, awakened from a deep sleep under the perceived threat of attack, lashed out and killed a female or a child or a weaker male before the enemy, or lack of one, had been identified. So nature had provided this trigger delay, a split second that seemed like minutes, which gave a little time, at least, for evaluation.

But lying there thinking about another one of Bosco's arcane bits of information scarcely eased the painful beat of his heart and the surge of adrenaline that pulsed against his eyelids and numbed his lips.

When at last the blockage broke apart and he was able to open his eyes and see the figure hovering over him, one hand reaching out toward his face, he struck with his own hand, grasping the invader's wrist and drawing a cry from the shadows.

"Hold it," Mary Bucket cried, "I'm not attacking."

"Who? Who?"

"Mary. It's only Mary."

"Light," he said, letting go of her and fumbling for the switch on the bedside lamp.

She was already over to the windows, drawing the drapes aside, opening the window.

"Fresh air. You've got to get some fresh air in here," she said.

After examining the bottles and containers, making a commentary face at each one of them, she disposed of all of them in the wastebasket by the door.

"Hey," Whistler exclaimed, peering out from the cocoon of sweaty, tangled sheets.

"Get out of that bed," she said. "How can you expect to get any rest in a tangle like that? Sheets?"

"Bottom drawer," he said, crawling out of bed and dragging the top blanket with him for the sake of modesty.

She stripped the bed and remade it with the clean sheets, folding the hospital corners with the quick, neat movements of someone who knew exactly what they were doing.

"Stay there," she ordered and disappeared into the bathroom.

Whistler heard the water running and she was back in a minute with two washcloths and a hand towel.

Kneeling beside him, she pulled the blanket away.

"Hey," he said, feeling foolish and managed.

"Get real," she said. "I've seen you bare-assed."

"But then you were bare-assed, too."

"Well, you'll just have to wait on that. I don't think you're up to any action."

She washed him down with the washcloths.

"I suppose you don't own any pajamas," she said.

"Second drawer from the bottom."

She went to get them, bending over from the waist.

Looking at the curve of her rump, Whistler felt a stirring and smiled, reckoning he was already feeling better.

The action didn't go unnoticed. She grinned and said, "Maybe I'm wrong about the action, but we'll have to wait on it anyway." She tossed the pajamas at him. "Put these on and get into bed. I'll be right back."

"How'd you get in?" he called after her, standing up and getting into the pajamas as he'd been told.

"Door was off the latch."

"Jesus Christ."

"What's that?" she called, from the bathroom.

"It's a hell of a thing for a detective to do, leaving his house unlocked."

"It's a hell of a thing for anyone to do," she replied.

There were sounds of running water and rattling pans. She appeared in the doorway right after he slipped between the sheets, closing his eyes in pleasure. The sheets and pillowcases were cool and smooth. He closed his eyes and remembered how it felt to be nursed by his mother when he'd been a child.

There'd been a summer when he'd gone to visit his uncle, aunt and cousins on their farm. The very first day he'd gone out running through the fields and along the river with his cousins and the family dog, shirtless as they had been, and had come back with a case of sun poisoning and the worst dose of poison oak they'd ever seen.

His aunt could have nursed him right there but it was clear that he wanted to go home, so they sent him back on the train. He remembered arriving in the city with a rash that had spread all over his sunburned body, his legs swollen from the effects of the sun.

His mother had bathed him in cool water with boric acid salts in it and blotted the pustules that plagued him with calamine lotion that dried and caked on him from the radiant heat of the burn. Every half hour she cooled him with the lotion, all through the day and evening, until he fell asleep feeling safe and comforted.

"Feeling better?" Mary asked.

He knew he was grinning.

"How'd you know I was home?" he asked.

"I stopped in at Gentry's. Bosco figured you'd get here sooner or later. Here, drink this."

He opened his eyes to see her sitting in the chair, which she'd drawn up beside the bed. She had a steaming cup in her hands and held it out to him.

"What is it?" he asked, the way patients have asked since the beginning of time.

"Hyssop, valerian, sage, rose hips—"

"Eye of newt?"

"—rosemary and violets. What makes you say that?"

"Say what?"

"Eye of newt."

"I was making a joke. You know, like you're offering me a witch's brew."

"How did you know I was a witch?"

"I didn't. I was just trying to be mildly funny. Are you telling me that you are a witch?"

"Yes, I am. Does that seem odd?"

"The only thing that seems odd is that you're the second witch that declared herself to me today."

"Oh?"

"I was looking for a kid that knew Kenny Gotch, might even have been an ex-lover, and the manager of the apartment house where this kid, George Gomble, lives told me she was a witch. Her name's Ardella and she said her face had been ruined by a customer who used a blade on her."

"I know Ardella," Mary said.

"How's that?"

"We've studied together and, before her face was ruined, we sometimes met at conventions."

"You're serious about this being a witch?"

"You belong to Alcoholics Anonymous, don't you?" she said.

"More or less. I don't go to meetings much anymore but I went plenty in my time."

"Are you serious about it?"

"Of course I am."

"Then why do you think it so strange that I should believe in the power and benevolence of a world created by a higher power as I understand it?"

She was using the statement from the AA big book, the bible of the organization, the belief in a higher power as each individual understands whatever that is to be.

"I wasn't making fun of what you believe," he said.

"I know you weren't. Drink this, now. It will make you sleep."

There was the smell of flowers and grass and the taste of spring water laced with oranges and cherries as he drank.

She drew the drapes together, cutting out some of the light but not all of the fresh air. The thrum of the traffic along the freeway did, indeed, sound like distant surf.

Just before he slept, he heard Mary humming the old melody.

"And wonders, and wonders of his love."

## 34

*Mary* Bucket knocked on Ardella's door.

Ardella's rusty, seldom-used voice asked, "Who's there?"

"Mary Bucket," Mary said.

"A minute," Ardella said.

Mary knew she was getting a scarf to drape over her face, old memories of past beauty dying last of all.

It was dark inside the apartment, the fusty smell of cats clinging to the drapes closed against the last light of evening.

They embraced, cheek touching cheek through the veil that draped Ardella's ruined face.

"I'll make some tea," Ardella said. "Will you wait for me in the parlor?"

"I'll sit with you in the kitchen," Mary said.

"Do you want me to help you cast a spell?"

"What kind of spell did you have in mind?"

"How about the one that binds a lover to you?"

"Does it show?"

Mary knew that Ardella was smiling her wise, all-knowing smile behind her veil. It was part of the game Ardella played, that wise, all-knowing smile.

Ardella put the kettle on as Mary brushed a cat off one of the kitchen chairs and sat down.

"How are you keeping?" Mary asked.

"Not too well. I am visited by incubi. They tempt me into intercourse."

"Do you refuse them?"

"They're very sly. They don't come right out and demand it, you know."

"What form do they take?"

"One came to me just today, calling himself Whistler. That's a demonic name I've not heard before." She placed herbs and tea leaves in a brown earthenware pot.

"What did you talk about, this Whistler and you?" Mary asked.

"He wanted to know about a friend of a friend. Do you remember Kenny Gotch?"

"He died in the hospice. I was the one who found him dead."

"Oh, yes," Ardella said. "The demon told me. The poor child died of AIDS, he said."

"He was dying of AIDS but someone cut his throat."

Ardella snatched the veil from her face as though it was suddenly smothering her and half-turned her face away.

"I could feel the evil when he told me about Kenny Gotch's death," Ardella said.

"Evil coming from Whistler?"

"Not coming from him. Surrounding him. Waiting for him."

"What did you tell him about Kenny?"

"That he was doing the devil's work."

"My God, he was nothing but a lost child," Mary said.

"Lost children are easily corrupted," Ardella said.

"Do you really think this Whistler is an incubus?"

Ardella smiled. It twisted the side of her face grotesquely and she jerked her head aside again, trying to conceal it. All the same, the smile was somehow impish.

"Maybe not an evil spirit sent to have intercourse with sleeping women, but a very tempting man. Wouldn't you say?"

Mary put a hand to her cheek, as though testing the temperature of her skin, afraid it had given her away.

"Some time ago, you described the man who cut you," Mary suddenly said, as though changing the subject with the first thing that came to mind.

Ardella poured boiling water from the kettle into the pot and sat down to wait for it to steep. "Yes?" she said.

"A dark man with black hair—"

"Who dressed in black—"

"—that he wore in a short pigtail—"

"—and wore dark glasses—"

"—tied back with a colored cord."

"—and took pictures," Ardella finished, the fear sparkling in her voice. "Have you seen him?"

"I think so. I think I've seen him twice. Once—so briefly I thought I'd only imagined it or had mistaken someone else for him—turning a corner in the hospice early in the morning and once in a restaurant near the hospice."

"What was the knife that he cut you with like?" Mary asked.

"It was a curved blade attached to a little clamp or cage that fit on the tip of his finger," Ardella said. "Stay away from that one. He calls himself Bennu Rahab now. His name was Raditski when he bought an hour of my time and then went crazy and cut my face when I asked for my money. Stay away from him. If he ever comes near you, run away. He's worse than the incubi."

"Do you want me to stay and help you cast a spell against the incubi?" Mary asked.

"You don't believe in any of it, the magic and the spells."

"I believe there's something in prayer of any kind."

"They all come together in the end," Ardella said, "the sciences and the religions. It's all a matter of blind faith in the end."

"I'll stay if you want me to."

"To keep away the incubi?" Ardella laughed. "You know the only way to defend against the incubi is to have a satisfying sex life." She touched her face. "Better the incubi than nothing. Let's do a periwinkle spell," she said, "in hopes that we may find suitable lovers." She poured the tea into porcelain cups without handles and sprinkled dried leaves taken from a jar of iridescent glass into them.

"A loving lad, a loving lass/Periwinkle brings love to pass," she crooned.

They sipped the tea.

"You don't happen to have any Valium or Halcion with you, do you?" Ardella asked offhandedly. "I have trouble sleeping."

"Valerian leaves steeped in wine with this periwinkle would do you better," Mary said.

# 35

*When* Whistler awoke, it was dark outside. The headlights of the traffic along the freeway cast moving patterns on the ceiling and the shape sitting in the chair.

"Have you been sitting there all this time, Mary?" he asked.

"There's no Mary here," a rough, husky voice replied.

Whistler reached toward the night table.

"You don't keep a gun there, fella. The only gun I found was the one you stash in the planter by the door."

Now that he was focused, and even in the gloom, Whistler could see the intruder's eyes, the kind of water-colored eyes that gathered every stray speck of light from the surroundings and magnified it by a factor of two. They shone out of a face that was like one of Georgia O'Keeffe's animal skulls, every bony plane as sharp as the chisel in a sculptor's hand could make it.

"That's a dumb place to stash a gun," the man went on. "It's the first place a fool would hide one and the first place another fool would look. So, I guess we're just a couple of fools."

"Do me a favor?"

"Name it?"

"I'd like to know what you're doing here."

"That's interesting."

"What's interesting?"

"You don't ask me who I am. The first thing you ask is what I'm doing here. So, what I'm doing here is I've been recommended to you by a couple of people. My name's Essex. Sergeant Harry Essex. I know who you are."

"Was there anybody else here when you came?"

"This Mary? No, there was nobody else here."

"Was the door off the latch?"

"No, she locked it behind her when she left. I just used a little savvy."

"You mind if I get up and get dressed?"

"I'm not threatening you or anything. Do what you want."

"You want anything? Coffee? Tea?" Whistler asked, throwing the covers aside and putting his feet on the floor. There was no sign of dizziness or weakness. "I don't keep any booze around the house," he added.

"You a friend of Bill Wilson's?" Essex asked.

"I never knew the man but I'm a friend," Whistler said, giving a correct response to the AA question.

"Me too. Fifteen years."

"Eleven. Twelve. I don't count."

"I can't help it. I always keep count of everything. It's like a disease. I'll go make myself a cup of coffee, you don't mind. Can I make one for you?"

"Sure. Make mine black."

"Me, too," Essex said and left the bedroom.

By the time Whistler was dressed and out in the living room, Essex was sitting in the best easy chair with a cup of coffee in front of him on the coffee table. There was another one waiting for Whistler.

"So sit down and tell me what I can do for you," Essex said.

"You're the Satan maven for the LAPD, is that right?"

"The Satan maven. That's Yiddish for expert, right? You mind if I use that?"

Whistler made a gesture of permission, a shrug of the shoulders, a wave of the hand, responding to sarcasm with a little of his own. He sat down, as though he were a guest in his own house. He didn't turn on any lights; the low-wattage lamp beside the window, which was always kept burning, was enough.

"You probably wouldn't remember a little kid—"

"By the name of Sarah Canaan? I remember. Why wouldn't I remember?"

"One kid out of how many every year?" Whistler asked.

"It's not as bad as the media makes out. They're into this way of doing business: the disease of the week, the crime of the week, the social injustice of the week, the outrage of the week. A couple of years back they reported five million children lost and missing in the United States every year. Made it sound like they were all kidnapped, probably murdered. Most of the kids were in their early teens. Runaways. A lot of the kids were picked up by a mother or father who lost custody after a divorce. And so on and so forth. The public likes big numbers. They like drama."

He took a long swallow of the hot coffee.

"Besides, how could I forget what happened to a cop's baby? A cop's brother's baby?" he added.

"But you weren't on the case?" Whistler said.

"No, I was working Lofts and Warehouses at the time."

"When did you take up witch hunting?"

"About the same time you did."

"What do you mean?"

"When you got started on that case involving the Vietnamese whore without a head. It took you down to New Orleans. I know you saw a little juju, a little gris-gris, down there. Voodoo magic."

"How did you find out about that?" Whistler asked.

"I'd just been told to set up the special unit. I had some men to fill it out back then. It's just me now. I'm not a budget item. I took out everything that had anything to do with the cults. There was a file on that girl without a head and mention that a private license by the name of Whistler had an interest. You went down to Rampart and talked to Carl Corvallis, the leader of that satanic group who were prosecuted for a series of mutilation killings, right?"

"Isaac Canaan got me in."

"He told me."

"He tell you about New Orleans?"

"No, Lieutenant Bellerose told me. I was networking. A lot of that devil shit down there. Also that talk show host?"

"Twelvetrees?"

"Yeah, that one. There were rumors. He was into beating

up on whores but there were whispers that he was into worse."

"I didn't know that," Whistler said.

"I didn't say you did. I'm just saying everybody's brushing shoulders with it every day and they don't even know it. You knew about that crazy bitch, Eve Choyren, who was involved with Paul Hobby? You remember an immigrant by the name of Bolivia hung around with those two?"

"Yes."

"He was a *hungan*."

"A what?"

"A voodoo priest. And that other one, the goat sticker from Appalachia . . ."

Whistler moved back a little into the shadows, as though trying to hide from the past at the mention of the man who had once stolen away the heart of Whistler's own true love.

". . . that Younger? I never could make up my mind if he was a son of Satan or just a sonofabitch playing the game."

"There a lot of these devil worshipers around?"

"More than you might expect. Why shouldn't there be? The devil's been around a long time. The old religions even longer. There's been plenty of times when Christians, particularly Catholics, were considered nothing but members of evil cults. I'm not talking ancient history here. I'm not talking about the Dark Ages. I'm talking about right here in the good old U. S. of A. Back in the eighteen thirties, eighteen forties."

"A hundred and fifty years ago?"

"Sure, a hundred and fifty years ago. Why not a hundred and fifty years ago? You think things have changed all that much? There was a wave of anti-Catholic hysteria going on back then. There were a lot of books written by women claiming to have escaped from forced confinement in convents, where they'd been forced to witness and join in on sexual orgies and torture sessions. Where they were forced to watch the slaughter of newborn infants," Essex said.

"The Jews have also been accused of eating children. It's still not hard to find thousands of people ready to believe both stories on practically no evidence except maybe that a priest or two, a psychiatrist or two, have passed on a load of bullshit they went and bought," he went on.

Whistler nodded his head.

"You're agreeing?" Essex said.

"I'm remembering after Blatty's picture, *The Exorcist,* came out. I'll bet I met a hundred people after that who swore they knew the real family back in Brooklyn. It got funny thinking about all of them living next door to this girl and her mother."

"People believe what they want to believe," Essex said. "Sometimes all they want is everybody's attention while they're telling how they were involved—no matter how slightly—in some extraordinary event. For a minute there they feel like somebody with everybody going 'ooo' and 'ah' or even going 'bullshit.'

"Sometimes people believe or say they believe because they can make a buck out of it," Essex said. "Say you got a situation where you're a psychiatrist and you got a patient comes to you with multiple personality disorder," he went on, warming to his own explanation, getting into it.

You didn't have to be smart to understand that Essex's job was his hobby and his passion.

"So you're a psychiatrist or a therapist who's having trouble with your wife, who's sick and tired of you explaining why you can't get it up or why you lust after little girls or why you don't put your dirty socks in the hamper or whatever domestic hang-up you've got going there that's just the excuse for the fact that you don't love each other anymore, and you're both looking for a way out. So this patient who walks around being three, four, twelve people? This is an exciting woman and also a woman who thinks you are the cat's meow. Also maybe she's got a nice pair of tits and a pretty face."

"So, one day she lays a story on you, the big breakthrough memory that she's been blocking all these years," Essex said.

"Which made her go all to pieces," Whistler said.

"I like that. That's funny. Can I use that?"

Whistler nodded.

"She tells you how she was sexually abused and tortured

as a child by a secret group of satanists to which her parents belonged," Essex went on, as though he'd not really been interrupted. "She claims she saw people ritually murdered. Babies and adults, too. She says she was once fed ashes from the burned remains of a victim and another time was smeared with the blood and guts of a fetus that had been sliced in half right in front of her very eyes. You get the picture?"

Whistler nodded.

"The big moment comes when Satan himself arrives to personally torture her," Essex said, "but Jesus and the Virgin Mary intercede on her behalf and save her at the eleventh hour."

"Is this a hypothetical?" Whistler asked again, putting it another way.

"This is an alleged true life story published maybe ten years ago by a couple of big New York publishers who would, we know, publish the rape and murder of their own mothers if they could make a dollar. The psychiatrist in the case divorced his wife and married his patient," Essex said.

"Make up any variation thereof. But that's not the point I'm getting to. The point I'm getting to is that all of a sudden we got multiple personality disorder spreading like a common cold in a grammar school. The funny thing is how many of these MPDs—you see it's getting so common you got to have initials for it—tell tales of abuse by satanic cults. The next thing you know, you got an organization by the name of the International Society for the Study of Multiple Personality and Dissociation sponsoring conferences and workshops on satanic cult abuse at three hundred fifty dollars for a fun weekend. You got important psychiatrists and psychologists sitting there pursing their lips, knitting their brows and nodding their heads like a bunch of yo-yos."

Essex leaned back.

"Usually sensible people say there's got to be something to it. Otherwise why would these intelligent people go along with such a load of horse puckie? I tell them because they don't want to be left out. I tell them because they get caught up in group-think just like everybody else. I know cops in other cities believe they got Satan in the slam. I tell them because there's a lot of money to be made out of people's fear and longing. You understand what I'm saying here? It's like people say to me how come somebody like Shirley Maclaine opens herself up to ridicule and criticism talking about this channeling, this out-of-body experience, this previous-life caper, when she's a movie star, makes all this money, got a house down in Malibu and so forth, if it wasn't the truth? I tell them because she's got people who set up these weekend seminars for five hundred bucks a pop. They talk about this and they talk about that. At the end of the last day all these people are in the auditorium, wherever, looking at an empty white wingback chair on the stage or platform and out comes Shirley in a white pants outfit and tells them all this stuff they want to hear. How she took a trip out of her body. How she met a channeler—they used to call them mediums—who gave her the word that she was Cleopatra in another life or that her daughter was her mother in another life. It gets complicated but anything goes when you're making it up. A million dollars a season for sitting in a white wingbacked chair telling people fairy tales. Why not?"

"She was great in *The Apartment* with Jack Lemmon."

"Yeah, I think she's really cute," Essex said.

"So the way you're talking," Whistler said, "whether you believe in it or not—these satanic cult outfits are all over the place."

"Sure they are. So what? It doesn't mean a hellofalot. Don't misunderstand me. I take them seriously. I'm just saying that there might be killers who are worshipers of Satan but it doesn't necessarily follow that all satanists are killers. The ones who want to kill use the faith as an excuse."

"You telling me that believing that dreck doesn't encourage murder?"

"I'm telling you that anybody wants to do something, they'll find a reason and a faith that lets them do it," Essex said. "When these serial killers and mass murderers confess, most of them say that God told them to do it. A lot more believe they are actually Jesus Christ back for the Second Coming." He stood up. "Was I any help? Not much, right?"

Whistler reached into his pocket and took out the tiny finger in the plastic Baggie. Essex turned on the floor lamp and leaned over to have a closer look.

"You want me to take custody of that? I'll treat it with respect."

"Can you prove if . . ."

Whistler didn't complete the sentence, asking if they could identify the finger as Sarah's.

"Who knows?" Essex said. "They can do amazing things nowadays."

Whistler handed the relic over.

Essex stood up, ready to leave. Whistler walked with him to the door. Essex stopped and looked Whistler over, as if he were making up his mind.

"I tell you what," he said. "Halloween's the night these suckers like to howl. I'm checking out a place with a reputation. Lucifer's. You know Lucifer's?"

"I've heard."

"So I'm going down there to have a look. Me and a couple of friends."

"Curiosity seekers?"

"Vice cops who like to check the scorecard. You can't tell the players without a scorecard. You want to come along, come along."

Whistler hesitated. He was looking for Canaan. He should be looking twenty-four hours a day for as long as it took.

"You think about it, you give me a call," Essex said, handing Whistler his card. "Now, if I was you, I'd go back to sleep. You don't look too swift. I'll find my way out."

# 36

*Canaan* almost missed the sign on the Pacific Coast Highway that marked the turning to Lucifer's. He passed it by a hundred yards and then had to back up, not caring that there might be a car coming over the crest behind him, his belly light with good feelings, reprisal, retribution, revenge, maybe even justice after so many years of worship to the Hebrew God who promised an eye for an eye, his heart pumping with an excitement he hadn't felt in years.

Halfway down the dirt road, with the ruined mansion of the one-time child guru looming above him on the top of the bluff, he stood on the brakes. Otherwise he would have crashed into a tree that had fallen across the road.

It wasn't all that big a tree, though it might have done considerable damage to his car had he run into it, small enough for him to manhandle off to the side.

He got out of the car. A wind coming off the sea with sudden violence rocked him on his feet. He looked up at the mansion at the end of the long drive beyond the twisted, battered gate. There were lights shining from windows on the top floor. A haunted house. Something out of a nightmare.

The wind gusted again. Clouds scudded across the face of the moon and from high above a scream came down the hill, driven by the wind.

It came again. Not the cry of a seabird but the heart-wrenching scream of a woman in great pain and terror.

Canaan went through the gate and ran up the drive. He felt scarcely winded when he reached the courtyard. He was a giant. A hero. Indestructible. A verse from Genesis flashed in his mind.

"Blessed be the most high God, which Hath delivered thine enemies into thy hand."

The front door gave heavily to the pressure of his shoulder. His gun was in his hand. The dark was as black as black velvet.

Lights blazed. Screams assailed his ears. Trumpets blared and cymbals crashed deafeningly. A scene out of Dante's *Inferno,* the worst imaginings of some insane producer of horror films, writhing bodies, tumbling infant corpses, the dismembered, beheaded and disemboweled, rushing toward him from every corner of the vast room.

He reached out a hand as though he meant to grasp reality. He heard a laugh like breaking glass behind him. Something crashed into the back of his head as he turned.

He fell into a pit of black ash.

# 37

*Whistler* had slept like the dead the second time around, lying on his belly, unmoving, the crumpled sheets marking him with a topographical map of the bed's geography when he awakened.

Sometime, while he'd been in the valley of unconsciousness, the phone had rung and his answering machine had picked up. Maybe more than once.

Lying there on his back he examined the pattern of sunlight spilling through the curtains and illuminating the opposite wall. It looked like a cross. With a little imagination you could see a figure hanging on the cross.

If he put out the word he might get two inches in the newspaper, fifteen seconds on the TV news. "Vision appears on wall of house above Cahuenga Boulevard." He could sell tickets at the door. A buck for a peek at the miracle on the wall of his bedroom. Two bucks if you wanted to hang around and pray.

Sometime during the night he'd taken off the pajama top. He looked down and fingered his naked chest and belly, cut into patterns by the folds of the sheets, and saw demons and goblins and flying witches cut into his skin. Visions everywhere.

The first caller during the night had left no message.

The second, in the morning, was Mary Bucket, hoping that her potion had done him good. Something else was in her voice, a certain subtle possessiveness. No suggestion that she was needy for him, no suggestion that one night of sex and another of nursing gave her any hold on him, but, somehow, her hope that it was not going to be just another one-night stand was in it.

He couldn't recognize the gulping, gasping voice of the third caller. Then he managed to piece together the syllables and made out that it was Mrs. Margaret, Father Mitchum's housekeeper and ward. Nearly out of control, whispering her message against a babble of voices, the only thing he could be sure of that she was asking for his help.

If Father Mitchum was in trouble or danger why would Mrs. Margaret appeal first to a stranger?

The sheriff's cars were lined up like stock cars at a rally, enough of them to put together a couple of racks for a couple of races.

In the garden and beyond the crumpling walls, Mitchum's Mexican parishioners, the old women, heads covered with black shawls, old men in cotton trousers and worn leather sandals, little kids, silenced by the silence of their elders, teenaged gang-bangers wearing their colors—leather jackets rich with decoration—even in the heat, young women softly crying, the cock fighters, straw sombreros in their hands, stood, scarcely moving a muscle, mourning.

Even the face of the old high priest of Espiritismo was fixed in lines of grief.

A uniform stopped Whistler at the door.

Whistler showed his license and said he was a friend.

"No friends allowed just yet," the cop said.

"How bad is it?"

"As bad as it can get."

"There was a message on my machine. Mrs. Margaret was asking for me to come."

"I'll tell her you came."

"Can I at least have a couple of words with her, see she's all right?"

"No, you can't do that."

Whistler peered over the young cop's shoulder, looking down the corridor toward the doorway to what he supposed was the priest's sitting room or library. It was jammed with men and women in uniform and other official attendants on the dead.

A big man broke out of the pack, turning his head to look Whistler's way. It was a face Whistler knew.

Lubbock took a step toward him down the corridor.

"What are you doing here, Whistler?" he asked in a voice pitched just loud enough to reach Whistler's ears.

"I could ask you the same thing. Isn't the valley way outside your jurisdiction?"

"Circumstances," Lubbock said, still walking slowly down the corridor, soft-pedaling his voice so it always remained just conversational. "You think you're the only one checked out the numbers on Kenny Gotch's phone?"

"Then you're making the same connections I've been making?"

"Well, I don't know about that," Lubbock said, grinning like a shark. "You want to match peckers?"

"I'd like to speak with Mrs. Margaret before we sit down to swap information."

"Let the man in, officer," Lubbock said. "My responsibility."

Lubbock waved Whistler on ahead of him down the hallway. At the end Whistler could see that he'd guessed right, the room directly off the end of the corridor was a sitting room and study, its walls lined with books, framing a small fireplace and a desk in an alcove. There was a lot of activity around the floor in front of the desk.

When someone got up from his knees, after accomplishing some chore, Whistler could see Mitchum's white hair and the shocking red of blood on the carpet square and tiles, which were the duller red of fired clay.

Lubbock tapped him on the elbow.

"This way," he said.

Whistler turned to his left and went through an arched doorway into a short cross corridor. Another left turn through another doorway took them into a bedroom furnished with nothing but a low wooden trundle bed, a night table, a chest of drawers—the top scattered with brushes and combs and the paraphernalia of a woman's toilet—a tall four-legged stool and another short one, and what looked like a comforter rack, which was being used as a drying rack for light clothing and underwear.

There was also a broken-down wingback easy chair, looking oversize and out of place in the Spartan room, in which Mrs. Margaret sat. She was dressed in the black dress with the white collar and cuffs and was wearing the little white apron she'd worn when she'd served them their refreshments the day before. She lifted her eyes as she covered her mouth and nose with a crumpled handkerchief.

"Do you need a doctor, Mrs. Margaret?" Whistler asked.

"I'm all right."

"Why would she need a doctor, Whistler?" Jackson asked. Lubbock's partner was sitting down on a short-legged stool, looking up into Mrs. Margaret's face. He'd no doubt been questioning her before Whistler and Lubbock entered the room.

"She might be able to use a sedative, something to help her sleep when nighttime comes," Whistler said.

"We'll see about that, if you want it?" Lubbock said.

Mrs. Margaret shook her head no. "I'll be all right."

"You're not staying here alone?" Whistler asked.

"Mrs. Espinoza offered me a bed for as long as I need it." She began to cry. It made her angry to cry because she hadn't cried at all while she'd been out there in the dangerous streets and now she was crying because the comfort and safety she'd found with Father Mitchum had made her soft and more afraid than she'd ever been.

Jackson stood up, as though her weeping embarrassed and distressed him, and moved away to engage Lubbock in murmured conversation in the doorway as though that was the next thing he'd intended to do anyway.

That left room for Whistler to take the stool and reach out for Mrs. Margaret's hand, to take the folded square of paper she'd let him see for a flash when the city cops had been looking elsewhere for a moment.

Lubbock and Jackson asked him to step outside for a minute and Whistler went along, slipping the note into his pocket as he went.


"A twangy boy, about to die of AIDS, takes a funny knife in the throat. A priest what's on his speed dial gets his throat cut a couple of days later. It's a connection, but what it means, your guess is as good as mine," Jackson said.

They were standing outside in the hot sun, Jackson, Lubbock and Whistler.

"What did you ask the priest?" Jackson said.

"I asked him if Kenny Gotch had come to him for counseling. I asked him if he made a confession."

"And?"

"Father Mitchum wouldn't say. Sanctity of the confessional."

"Lawyer-doctor-psychiatrist-client privilege," Jackson said, frustrated by rules that wouldn't let him get through to the facts.

"The church started the idea, I guess," Whistler said.

"Still and all what do you know that maybe we don't know?" Lubbock asked.

"I don't know what you don't know," Whistler said.

"So tell us everything you know—"

"And then you'll tell me everything you know?"

"—and then we'll tell you what we think is good for you to know," Jackson said.

"Tit for tat," Lubbock grinned.

"Cop's tit for tat means you get all the best of it."

Lubbock put away his teasing grin of good fellowship. "You watch it or your tit's going to be in the wringer. Tell us a story, goddammit. Start from the beginning."

Whistler could see no harm. There wasn't a thing in the world he had to hide, no one to protect. For a second there he examined the marvel of cooperating with the police in common cause, seeking a common end.

Whistler told the detectives how Mike Rialto had come busting into Gentry's one morning just two days—could it only be two days?—ago all shook up and babbling on about how this buster dying of AIDS had sprayed him with vomited blood. The dying man, one Kenny Gotch aka Harriet LaRue, a twangy boy who'd often worked the stroll just outside Gentry's door, had told a relative that he had knowledge of a certain murder of a certain child, whose little body had been found mutilated and broken-backed draped over a tombstone in Hollywood Cemetery some ten years before.

"Isaac Canaan's niece," Jackson said, making it a definite comment, not a question.

"That's right, Sarah Canaan, the baby who haunts my friend's dreams and keeps him from sleep."

Lubbock waved a hand as though telling Whistler to hurry on, they knew the circumstances and sympathized but they'd learned, as cops are supposed to learn, not to dwell on things they could do little or nothing about except to exact society's pound of flesh, to wreak vengeance. In the case of a man like Canaan, to do God's work or at least give him a hand.

There'd been so little to go on, Whistler continued, just the vague confession of a frightened kid. Not even that. Just the hint that Gotch knew more than a completely innocent person should have known about a murder. There was hardly the end of a piece of thread to pick up and start winding around your finger, hoping that you could drag a ten-ton solution to an old crime out of the muck.

"But you went to Angeles Hospice to nose around all the same," Lubbock said, as though he were making an accusation.

"Oh, fachrissake, Ernie, let the man tell his story," Jackson said, mildly scolding his partner.

"I figured I owed the effort to Isaac," Whistler said.

"But you didn't tell him what Rialto told you? About what this Kenny Gotch hinted at?" Jackson asked.

"No, but you know Canaan. That man can read things just looking into your eyes. So, I think he knew there was something we weren't telling him that morning."

"I'd say so," Lubbock agreed. "He was on Rialto like a dog on a bone when we jailed him overnight."

"So, keep going," Jackson said.

Whistler told them about taking the supervising nurse, Mary Bucket, to the restaurant and how when they got back to the hospice, with Kenny Gotch's relative Abe Forstman, waiting there to pick up his nephew's, by marriage three times removed, belongings, they found they'd been misplaced or stolen.

While he was telling them about that, Whistler was flashing back on the restaurant and the character dressed in black, hair tied back with a red cord, who'd come into the restaurant and gone right out again, the character Mary had seen creeping around the hospice corridors early in the morning.

He stood there wondering if he should tell Lubbock and Jackson about that or if he'd be opening up a new line of questioning with which the detectives could harass and frighten Mary Bucket.

"You fogging out on us, Whistler?" he heard one of the detectives say.

"Huh?"

"Something come to you all of a sudden you think you should tell us about?" Jackson asked.

In that split second Whistler decided to keep the black-haired man dressed in black to himself. They were already putting the eye on Mary. It wouldn't take much to start them thinking about tying her into a conspiracy to do murder.

"This heat's boiling my brains," Whistler said.

"He's right, Marty," Lubbock said. "Let's move it over into the shade."

"If we can find any," Jackson said.

They walked around looking for a patch out of the sun, under some kind of shelter, big enough to accommodate the three of them.

The note Mrs. Margaret had slipped to him was burning a hole in his pocket, Whistler wanted to read it so bad.

The best they could find was the shadow cast by an old abandoned outhouse. Lubbock opened the rickety door and stuck his nose inside, the automatic response of a cop to closed places, then closed it and put his back against the shady side wall.

"Watch it, that don't fall down on you and drop you down the hole," Jackson said. Then he turned to Whistler and said, "Where were we?"

"Gotch's belongings were missing."

"They still haven't found them," Jackson said. "They had an inventory?"

"Yes," Whistler said.

"You read it?"

"Nothing interesting there except an address book and a twenty-five-cent notebook," Whistler said. "Might have been something useful in there."

"Well, we'll probably never know," Lubbock said. "Then what did you do?"

Whistler hesitated half a beat. He knew what they were doing. They were listening to see if he'd leave out things they already knew he knew or things he'd done or places he'd been. Since he didn't know who they'd questioned and what had been told to them, the truth was better than a lie by omission, even if it looked like he'd stepped over the line a little bit.

"I went over to Kenny Gotch's apartment over the garage with Abe Forstman."

"Without first calling the police?" Lubbock asked quickly, as though he were trying to rattle Whistler.

"Call them about what, some junk and a few bucks belonging to a dead patient, which had probably been tossed down the garbage chute by mistake? Nobody knew that Gotch hadn't died of AIDS at the time."

"So, okay," Lubbock said, glancing at Jackson. Whistler

could read the look. They'd failed to check the hospice garbage. That was something they were going to have to go back and do now that he'd put the thought in their heads. He grinned inside about it until he realized that it was something he, himself, should've thought of two days ago.

"What'd you find over to this Gotch's crash?" Jackson asked.

"A bunch of his things scattered all over the place—"

"It'd been tossed?"

"—and some books on satanism," Whistler finished and then said, "Yes, it'd been tossed."

"When we looked it over somebody'd straightened it up nice and neat," Lubbock said.

"That was me cleaning up behind me as I went," Whistler said. "You saw the posters on the wall?"

"You saying that Gotch was part of some satanic cult that sacrificed him?" Jackson asked.

"No, I'm not saying that."

"What are you saying? You believe in that Satan shit?"

"What I'm saying is 'Chicken or the egg,'" Whistler said. "I don't know if a bunch of control freaks, behind drugs and kinky sex, get people to go for satanic ritual as a kind of faith or if they believe in Satan first and what comes after comes after."

"What are we having here, a religious discussion?" Lubbock asked. "Keep it coming, Whistler. We ain't got all day, fachrissake."

"I took down the list of numbers off the speed dial on his phone," Whistler said.

"What'd it get you?"

Whistler ran the list for them, checking on his three-by-fives so they'd know he was giving them everything. No reason not to give them everything because he figured they had what he had, so if he left anything out they'd know it and wonder why.

"You make contact with any of those numbers?" Lubbock asked.

"I got answers from everybody except somebody by the name of Mike and another one by the name of Jane."

Jackson nodded. Whistler didn't know if that meant they'd made contact with those two people or if they'd tried and failed just the way he had.

"You think you learned anything with these calls you made?" Lubbock asked.

"Well, I learned the kid, this Kenny Gotch, was into sex, drugs and probably satanism."

"You mean the posters and the books in his room? Kids are curious about that," Jackson said. "You ask any library, they'll tell you that they can't keep books on witchcraft and satanism on the shelves. They get stolen. It's kids stealing them."

"He also had a standing order in for some pretty rare and expensive books on the subject down at the bookstore on Hollywood Boulevard. You know the one? The big one—"

"We know the one," Lubbock said. "So he's got an interest."

"These are very expensive books. I think he was putting the order in for someone else. A lot of these people got a thing about keeping secrets."

"We didn't get around to that yet," Jackson said. "Maybe you just gave us an angle."

"I think his drug connection was a dealer calling himself Jet on the streets."

"We already know this gazooney," Jackson said.

"So that was over the phone you talked with this Jet?" Lubbock asked. "How about did you make any contacts face-to-face?"

"So far I talked to Gotch's relative, Abe Forstman."

"Okay," Jackson said.

"And I talked to a professor at UCLA. Kilroy. Teaches comparative religion. Kenny took a couple of classes."

"He had an interest."

"But he didn't go to classes very long," Whistler added.

"Okay," Jackson said again.

"How about the nurse?" Lubbock asked.

"What about her?"

"You got any ideas about her?"

"What kind of ideas?"

"I don't know what kind of ideas. You know she's into witchcraft?"

"What?"

"Oh, yes, she's got all this witchy junk in her apartment."

"Witches aren't satanists," Whistler said.

"You know that, do you?"

"Well, I've been reading up on it."

"Anybody else? You have a face-to-face with anybody else?" Lubbock asked.

Whistler hesitated, making out like he was thinking very hard, wanting to be the soul of cooperation, wondering if there was any reason to mention Ardella or the meeting he'd had with Diana.

"You're fogging out on us again?" Lubbock said.

Jackson pulled a notebook from his pocket, ran his eye down the page, then up again.

"How about this Bobby L or Bobby D?" he asked.

"I only got their answering machines. They're hookers on call," Whistler said.

"How about this Pooch?"

"Also only on the phone. His name's William Mandell. I think he and Kenny Gotch may have been emotionally involved."

"The way you put that, I can see you got a sensitive nature," Lubbock said, sarcastic again, not able to control it.

"How about Diana?" Jackson asked, ignoring his partner.

"Answering machine," Whistler said, having made up his mind not to bring her into it after Lubbock's wisecrack, feeling a lot less cooperative.

"Hey," Jackson said softly, catching the edge of hostility. "Let's keep up the good work, will we? George Gomble?"

"They call him Georgie-Porgie or Gambler on the street," Whistler said, relaxing back into it. "I'm still looking for him."

"Any reason to make somebody special out of him?"

"I just got the idea that he had the strongest connection with Gotch but—"

"What give you that idea?" Lubbock said.

"—don't ask me why. Except when I talked to him on the

phone it sounded like they were best friends or lovers gone sour on one another. At least George was sour on Kenny. Just a vague notion, you know what I mean?"

"I know what you mean," Jackson said, talking about cop instinct, giving Whistler credit for having some of the gift. "We'll keep a special eye out for Georgie-Porgie."

"He likes to be called Gambler better."

"Whatever."

"So who does that leave, outside of the commercial establishments? That leaves Rahab, runs a photo studio."

Whistler saw that Jackson was looking at him without looking at him, watching for a reaction.

"I never made contact with Rahab. Never even tried. Is there something there I should know about?"

Another glance passed between Jackson and Lubbock, talking to each other without having to even open their mouths.

"He's got a sheet on him, this Rahab, this Raymond Raditski, you could put through the wash twenty times and it still wouldn't come out clean," Jackson said.

"So that's that?" Lubbock said.

"Anything you want to share with me?" Whistler asked.

"We just shared. The only thing we got you ain't got is this Raditski and Mary Bucket's religious persuasion," Lubbock said.

"Also you could have some news about Isaac Canaan?" Whistler said.

Jackson and Lubbock shook their heads. They had mournful tight expressions on their faces giving Whistler the idea that they, too, had cause to be concerned.

Sitting in his car in which the heat had built up as the sun rose higher in the sky, Whistler took the crumpled note from his pocket and read what was written there.

We all must struggle to understand what is right. Ancient rules, contracts and covenants often fail us. I've struggled long and hard with the demands of celibacy. A man called Whistler has given me reason to struggle with the principle of the sanctity of the confessional because, as he said, there are other souls in torment to be considered in the matter of Kenny Gotch.

Kenny Gotch came to me for counsel, forgiveness and comfort. I gave him the second, as it is in my power to give it after hearing his confession and offered him counsel, advising him to tell what he knew of the murder of the child to the police. I doubt if I could give him any comfort.

Kenny Gotch also came to me to perform an exorcism. I have no experience in such matters and asked him to come again after I'd sought my own counsel. He never returned.

The note had not been addressed to him. Mrs. Margaret, in her simplicity, had seen Whistler's name on the piece of paper and passed it on to him, believing it would have been Father Mitchum's wish.

The priest had been about to break the sanctity of the confessional and somebody, anticipating that he might do so, had acted to prevent it.

How many other people connected to Kenny Gotch were in danger of being silenced?

# 38

*The* average man goes missing one day and what's to worry? He took a day off and went to a motel to look at some X-rated movies. He went to a ball game, got drunk on beer with some buddies and went home with one of them to sleep it off. He's shacked up with a woman not his wife or girlfriend. He'll come home. Time to worry after seventy-two hours. That's how long Missing Persons asks you to wait before filing a report.

But when somebody's a feature in the landscape, a regular, a tree, a rock, a telephone pole, the kind of person by which the sun and moon tells time, then you got to start worrying after twelve or twenty-four. Thirty-six already smells like a major disruption to the world's smooth operation.

Isaac Canaan's brother and his wife lived in the Los Feliz district of Los Angeles, an old section of the city that had been up and down a dozen times in its lifetime and was now enjoying the fruits of a decorators' boom that had started back in the early eighties. Grand old mansions, used as boardinghouses or broken up into apartments, had been restored to their original grandeur. Along with the newly rich, there were a good many who'd bought into the neighborhood when prices were low, improved their properties with a lot of sweat equity and now lived in houses worth a million and a half, two million dollars, on incomes considerably less than would now be required if they were just buying in. Max and Ruth were a couple who'd done just that, cleverly and energetically building for the future.

Max Canaan's house had a triple garage, a long sweeping flight of steps leading to the front door and a tower. It was painted a cool gray with smart black trim and had a midnight blue door with a lion's head door knocker of bronze—not brass—in the center panel.

Whistler parked on the street instead of driving up to the terrace alongside the garage. He wasn't sure Isaac's sister-in-law would remember him and might be afraid if she saw someone in a car parking outside the house instead of on the street. People were less fearful of someone arriving on foot.

He picked up the ring in the lion's mouth and dropped it twice. Then he waited. He figured the walk from the back of the house to the front would take a minute, but it took a good deal longer than that.

He was about to knock again, when the door to the caged judas hole opened above the lion's head. He could make out a pale face and a dark eye.

"Who are you?" a woman's voice asked.

"Is Mr. or Mrs. Canaan at home?"

"I'm Mrs. Canaan." Her voice had the quality of someone just awakened.

"I'm not sure if you'll remember me," Whistler said.

"Well, tell me your name," she said, impatiently.

"Whistler. I'm a friend of your brother-in-law's."

"Who?"

"Isaac. Isaac Canaan."

She made a sound. She may have been clearing her throat but it sounded like a sob.

The judas hole was shut and the front door opened.

Ruth Canaan stood aside as Whistler stepped across the threshold into a good-size entry that had a door on either side, a staircase winding to the upper floors left center and a corridor leading to another doorway and the back of the house beside it. She was wearing a housecoat. Her hair had been neatly done and the color of her skin was good, yet there was an air about her of an invalid unsound in mind and body.

A man in shirtsleeves, back-lit by the blaze of light in the room beyond, came hurrying down the hallway. Whistler couldn't make out his face, but he assumed it was Isaac's brother, Max.

"What are you doing there, Ruth?" Max said.

"It's me, Max. Isaac's friend, Whistler."

But Max was paying no attention to Whistler. He was reaching out to his wife with one hand, holding a sheaf of papers in the other. "Ruth, what have I told you about opening the door to strangers?"

"I'm Isaac's friend," Whistler said again. "It's been some time but—"

"I know you. I recognize you," Max said, "but that doesn't change the situation."

He had his hand on his wife's shoulder. She sighed and shrugged, as though his warnings had no meaning, were silly precautions. She slipped out from under his hand and went to the door on the left, which Whistler assumed was the door to the living room. She hesitated there, with her hand on the handle, then changed her mind and went over to the stairs instead. She turned around for just a moment before going up. Even from the distance Whistler could see unshed tears glistening in her eyes.

Max watched her mount the flight of stairs until she disappeared off the landing.

"She doesn't care," Max said. "It's almost like she wishes some stranger she lets into the house would kill her. You want to come out back?"

Whistler followed Max through the corridor beside the stairs into the light of a sunporch or garden room, glass all around, that looked out on a garden planted out in raised beds with stone walls around them and paths of decomposed granite in between. There was a wrought-iron bench against the wall that separated their property from the next house farther up the hill. It was all very neat and tidy, very sterile.

"I'm usually not home in the afternoon," Max said, waving Whistler to one of the chairs around a breakfast table. "We have a housekeeper. She had to go to the doctor's today. It was the only appointment she could get, so I came home from the office . . ."

He wound down like a tin toy and looked at Whistler as though he'd already forgotten what it was he'd wanted to say. "It's been a very long time," he said.

"Ten years."

"She would have been almost ready for her Bat Mitzvah. Did I thank you for what you tried to do . . . what you did?"

"I wanted to help. Isaac's a good man and I wanted to help."

"How help?"

"I thought if we could find out who . . ."

Max was shaking his head back and forth like a metronome, slowly, with enough energy to make the bones of his neck snap, his mouth like a wire, his eyes angry, as though Whistler had somehow offended him.

"What good would it have done?" he said. "What good would it do?"

"Sometimes revenge helps to grow scar tissue over the wound," Whistler said.

"Everybody's got a theory," Max said. "You want some coffee?"

Whistler held up his hand, refusing it.

"So, why have you come to the house today?" Max asked, gesturing with the sheaf of papers he still held in his hand, as though telling Whistler that he had work to do and Whistler was wasting his time.

"Isaac told me the other day that he was going off on a little vacation but he forgot to tell me where he'd be in case I wanted to get in touch with him," Whistler lied.

"Why would you want to get in touch with him?"

"Well, you know, this and that. I thought—"

"Hey, don't talk to me—"

"—you might know where—"

"—like I'm some kid."

"—he went."

"What would a private cop have to do with a vice sergeant—I don't care you're friends and maybe even go fishing together, which Isaac doesn't do—except it's got to do with crime?"

"I need his help on something," Whistler said, taking up the idea and fashioning his story around it.

"Tell me the truth," Max said. "Isaac don't take vacations."

"When was the last time you saw your brother?"

"A year, maybe a year and a half. I went down to see him at the station."

"Why?"

"I wanted to see if anything had turned up."

"Even if it wouldn't do any good?"

"So, revenge isn't such a silly thought, after all," Max said. "What I said about revenge not doing any good. I was talking about my wife. Her life's over and getting the one who killed our little Sarah"—he stopped and turned his head away in the same determined way he'd shaken his head—"won't bring either of them back. But revenge will be sweet in my own mouth. It would be a feast that could last me all my life."

"So, the only time you see your brother in a year, a year and a half is to ask him is he still on the job?"

"Isaac's always been welcome in this house. He stays away for his own reasons."

"He feels as though he's to blame. Even though he was a

cop—a protector—he couldn't stop what happened. He couldn't protect his own."

Max put down the sheaf of papers and picked up his coffee cup.

"When was the last time you spoke to Isaac on the phone?" Whistler asked.

"What's the trouble? Has something happened to Isaac?"

"He's gone missing. He told his captain he was coming down with a cold and was taking some sick time and nobody's seen him since."

"What is it you're afraid of? Do you think he's dead?"

"I think he's out there looking to make somebody else dead."

"Do you think he's found out who . . ."

The words wouldn't come. Max was unable to speak again.

"I got hold of the end of a thread that could lead to whoever murdered your daughter," Whistler said. "While I was waiting to find out more, I think Isaac got hold of the same thread. He's got more contacts than me. He's got more experience than me. He's got more smarts than me. He could get where he's going before I get there and I don't know what might happen then. I didn't come to worry you, I came hoping that Isaac might have contacted you and told you there was hope of vengeance."

# 39

*When* a person dies before his time you can usually trace the cause back to some stupidity. With the heat in his blood rushing him along the trail that might lead to the killers of his beloved niece, Canaan had forgotten everything twenty years of being a cop had taught him. Now he was trussed up like a chicken and chained to a wall, bare-assed and shivering, his bladder full and screaming for relief the minute he'd come swimming out of the pit of darkness, head throbbing like a huge heart, eyes filmed over. He suffered a great thirst, his tongue glued to the roof of his mouth with his own thickened spit, which tasted like library paste.

He blinked a dozen times and managed to sweep the veils of mucus aside.

He was in a basement. The smell of dry rot, niter and rat droppings told him that. He could hear the surf booming faintly out there beyond the thick masonry walls, so they hadn't transported him. He was imprisoned where he'd been felled.

The blackness became grayer as his eyes got used to the dark. Little curtains of light crept around the edges of the boards nailed over the basement windows. It was day and he began to see more.

The room was used for storage. There were crates of wine, one or two with their tops knocked loose, straw spilling out, piled against the wall. Some gardening tools, old rusted picks and rakes with broken handles. A few cages for the transport of dogs or cats. Some devices, a chair, a cage, the bulky figure of a woman—the iron maiden, torture machines that looked as flimsy and artificial as stage props.

His thirst was overwhelming him.

He tried to stand up but he was chained so low to the floor that he could only crouch. He couldn't hold his water any-more and let go, splashing his feet, creating a small stream that ran along the cracks in the floor.

With great effort he managed to hook a toe over the edge of a crate and, praying that it was not full of bottles, managed to drag it close enough to touch with his hand.

He removed the straw, putting aside two bottles of wine lying in the bottom of the crate. He mopped up his own urine with straw, then spread what was left to make a nest for his feet. The crate became his stool.

He carefully broke the neck from a bottle. The wine was a red wine. It spilled over his chest the color of blood in the gloom. It didn't slake his thirst but it cleared the gum from his mouth and throat.

He sat there in his nakedness, feeling the cold. He wondered if he should yell out and let his captors know that he was conscious, then decided against it. He wanted to think awhile. Maybe, having been dumb, he could now be smart.

Suddenly he thought of a cartoon he'd seen in a magazine years before. Two prisoners were dangling on the wall in chains, their feet not even touching the floor of the cell. No windows. No furniture. Nothing. One prisoner looks at the other and says, "Now, here's my plan." Canaan started to laugh. He let it go on but kept a close watch on the borders of hysteria.

# 40

*If* you live in a small town five, six years, you know half the people in town and at least have a nodding acquaintance with the other half. You live in a city neighborhood—some of them—in Chicago, New York, Detroit, even L.A., you know maybe ten percent, nod to another ten and watch the other eighty percent out of the corner of your eye.

You live on a street like Hollywood Boulevard—the same number of people as in the small town and city neighborhood, give or take—and you spend sixteen, eighteen hours looking at the faces, you'd think you'd know everybody, at least on sight. But Hollywood Boulevard and the hookers' stroll is an animal that changes color, gender, nationality and composition a hundred times a year, one day to the next, one hour to the next.

Canaan knew practically every one of the baby whores and twangy boys peddling their wares; knew ever gonnif, shark, hustler, bone breaker and ball buster. He was a walking data base.

Whistler knew a great many, but compared to Canaan he knew less than a few; he knew almost nobody.

When he finally caught up with George Gomble—called Georgie-Porgie or Gambler on the street—he wouldn't have bet a quarter that he'd ever seen the kid before. Maybe that was because there were so many pimply faced eighteen-, nineteen-year-old kids, with dirty blond hair and curly lips coming and going on the stroll, one of the hundred Ellis Islands in the cities through which the native immigrants of America circulated; living in closets, sharing cardboard boxes with the mad, the lost and the homeless; available to criminals and thrill killers, corn holers and baby fuckers.

"Gambler?" Whistler said, approaching the kid sideways, cutting him out from his neighbors and fellow ass merchants scouting the flow of traffic on this most perfect of all La-La Land nights.

Gambler gave a little toss to his head, throwing back the fall of hair that obscured one eye, looking, Whistler thought, like that old-time movie star, the one who ended up a saleswoman in a five-and-dime back east somewhere before she died, hair always cutting off half her vision, pouty mouth shaping words like a baby shapes spit bubbles. What was her name? Veronica Lake.

Before George Gomble's time. Before his own time, for that matter, Whistler thought.

Within five seconds the fall of hair slipped down again as Gambler smiled a tentative smile, hoping for a customer but smelling something else about Whistler. Smelling cop.

"Georgie-Porgie?" Whistler asked, reconfirming the identification.

Gambler frowned. "I like to be called Gambler better."

"Sure, whatever you want."

"It ain't what I want," Gambler said, testing the water, allowing himself to simper just a tad. "It's what you want."

"I want you to tell me why you admitted knowing Kenny Gotch but claimed not to know Harriet LaRue when they were one and the same person."

Gambler swung his head and set his weight back on his left foot, ready to run.

Whistler stepped on that foot, not hard but hard enough to keep Gambler from taking the first step. "Hey, don't," he said. "You run and I'll wonder why. I'll get all the news on you. I just want to know a few things. I'm not out to get you."

"Take your foot off my foot," Gambler said.

"You're not going to turn into a greyhound?"

Gambler shook his head, the hair flopping all around like the thrashing of a bird's wing.

Whistler removed his foot and Gambler started to take off, but in the instant when he'd taken the pressure away, Whistler had thrown himself at an angle and stopped Gambler in his tracks.

"For Christ's sake, now I'll never trust you again," Whistler said, taking hold of Gambler's wrist and crushing the nerves into the bones hard enough to make Gambler willing to do what he was told.

"You come with me," Whistler said. "I want to buy you a cup of coffee." He walked him across the boulevard and through the open door into Gentry's, where Bosco sat reading *The Forbidden Gospel.* His favorite booth was taken but he found an empty at the back. He bumped Gambler with his hip and turned him with his wrist, forcing the kid to sit down in the booth. Whistler let go and crowded in.

"Who the fuck you think you are?" Gambler said. "I start yelling bloody murder, I start yelling a fucking faggot rapist is trying to pull my joint under the fucking table, your ass's going to be grass."

"Goddamn, you have a colorful way of talking," Whistler said. "You hear about Benny Rucker?"

"Who?"

"Benny Rucker? Used to cruise the boulevard in his convertible about two, three years ago?"

"I don't know any Benny Rucker. I wasn't around two years ago."

"That's okay. It's the circumstances of his death that's of interest. You want to know how he died?"

"How'd he die?" Gambler asked reluctantly, but still curious enough to ask.

"Killed himself with his pinkie finger."

"What?"

"Hard to believe, isn't it? He was cruising the boulevard, picking his nose with his little finger, when a big Mercedes comes piling out of a side street and crashes into Benny Rucker so fucking hard it drives Benny's pinkie up his nose and into his brain. Killed him on the spot."

"What the hell you talking about?" Gambler said, giving a nervous little half laugh, his cockiness trickling away, leaving nothing but fear behind.

"I'm just pointing out to you how something as small as a pinkie finger can kill a man."

Gambler was the color of old Christmas snow. "I got to take a pee," Gambler said.

"Pee in your sock," Whistler said. "I'm not going to play that game with you, escorting you back and forth, here and there, until you spot a chance to run again. You can't run away from me, Georgie-Porgie, any more than you can run away from your old friends Kenny Gotch and Harriet LaRue."

Gambler made a sound that was like a moan.

"Why did you say you didn't want anything to do with Kenny Gotch? Because he contracted AIDS?"

Gambler kept his head down, the wing of hair falling down straight, staring at his hands with the nails bitten down to the quick. He shook his head and the hair swayed back and forth.

"Come on, kid," Whistler said, "look at me."

Gambler raised his head. His eyes glanced off Whistler's face like a stone skipping on water.

"We broke up before he got sick," he said.

"Broke up? Are you telling me you were a couple?"

"We lived together for a while there."

"You lived with him or he lived with you?"

"I lived with him."

"Were you just friends, or friends and lovers?" Whistler asked very gently.

Tears rose up in Gambler's eyes.

"I loved Harriet LaRue."

"He played that part for you when you were home alone together?"

"Not all the time. I mean he wasn't really a girl, after all."

"But he liked men?"

Gambler shrugged. "He was like me."

"Worked both sides of the street?" Whistler said.

Gambler made an expression of annoyance. "If you want to put it that way."

"I'm not trying to hurt your feelings here," Whistler said, "I'm just trying to get an understanding of the arrangement."

"Black or white, male or female, faggot or straight," Gambler said, with weary contempt. "It ain't that simple."

"I understand that," Whistler said. "So Kenny played the loving wife?"

"We were a couple. Just because he wore dresses and high heels didn't make me the dominator."

Whistler smiled. "Now that I understand," Whistler said, meaning to draw Gambler into the camaraderie of a man's world. "Straight or gay, it's usually the femme who plays the tune and the men who dance to it. So, what did he do to break you up? He cheat on you?"

Gambler looked down at his hands again and shook his head. The wing of hair moved as though trying to take flight.

"Not exactly," Gambler murmured.

"What do you mean by that?"

"He got taken up by this crazy crowd he'd broken with once before. I got him to split with them once but they came back again."

"How much time before he fell in with them the second time?"

"A few years."

"Persistent, weren't they? Didn't want to lose him?"

"They were into things and Kenny was useful, I guess." Gambler got a stubborn look on his face. "Why should I be telling you all this? Why should I be telling you anything?"

"Because you loved Kenny Gotch once upon a time and you want to help me find out who did it to him."

"Gave him AIDS?"

"Put a blade in him."

"What?" The kid's eyes went wide and his face tightened up like a fist. Tears rushed into his eyes and danced there on the lower lids a second before spilling over.

"Somebody stabbed him to death, in the throat," Whistler said.

"What for? What for? He was dying."

"Whoever did it was in a hurry."

"Hurry about what?"

"To shut your friend up. This crowd he left you for. Maybe they were afraid he'd talk about them before he died."

"You mean like to the cops? Kenny wouldn't do that."

"So, all right, somebody else. Like confess it to a priest, for instance, or talk about it to a friend."

Gambler was quiet. The tears no longer flowed but his nose was running. Whistler reached out and took a napkin from the dispenser and handed it to Gambler. Gambler said thanks and blew his nose.

"You still got to go take a pee?"

Gambler nodded and Whistler slid out of the booth and stood up. "There's a door in the back, you know that?" he said.

"Yeah, I know that," Gambler said, getting out from behind the table.

"I'll be waiting for you here. You want a piece of apple pie to go with your coffee?"

"They got anything else?"

"Sometimes they got lemon meringue."

"I'll have a piece of that if they got it."

Whistler signaled Shirley Hightower over and ordered the lemon meringue, a piece of apple for himself and two cups of coffee.

"You seen Isaac around today, Shirley?" Whistler asked.

A little M appeared between her placid eyes. "Not today. Not for a couple of days."

He could see how worried she was. He also knew that Shirley was not the kind who burdened other people with her worries. She was like Canaan that way, keeping practically everything to herself.

"Nothing unusual about that," Whistler said quickly.

"No, nothing unusual," she said. "He don't like me to do it, but I think I'll give him a call at the station anyway."

"I don't see how that could do any harm," he said.

She gave him a grateful smile. "Tell me if you bump into him or hear anything, will you?" Shirley said.

She went away, then came back with the pie and coffee before Gambler returned. When he did he sat down opposite Whistler.

"Kenny ask you to move out, Gambler?" Whistler asked, showing his respect by using the preferred nickname.

"No, it was my decision."

"What made you decide?"

"This crowd . . . they were romancing Kenny? They were into little children."

For Christ's sake, Whistler thought, here's this teenager, a kid himself, drawing the line. It was all right for him to start selling his ass when he was thirteen, fourteen, a couple of years ago, but anybody going after kids eight or nine were really villains to him. Everybody makes a mark along a scale of values from one to a million and where you put your foot is the principle on which you stand. An inch one way is good, an inch the other is bad. So Gambler didn't think much of chicken hawks.

"So, what was Kenny, a recruiter?"

"He might've done some of that, but mostly he was a bird dog."

"That's all?"

"They were into worse."

"How much worse?"

"Satanism. Like that."

"You believe in that stuff, Gambler?"

"I don't think it matters whether you believe it or don't believe it. I think the thing that matters is if the people what fuck around with it believe it."

"That's a pretty sharp observation, Gambler."

"I ain't dumb."

"So, that's what Kenny started bringing home?"

"A lot of that crap, yes. I told him it was bullshit, like playing Wizards and Castles. I tried to laugh him out of it."

"No luck?"

"He wanted to believe it. Maybe he even did. How can you tell what's real and what's a put-on? You know what

I'm saying? Just because somebody goes to church don't mean they actually believe that Jesus Christ woke up and rose from the dead, and just because somebody goes around burning black candles and killing black chickens don't mean they really believe in the devil. The thing is, Kenny was sucked into it. Maybe he didn't want to get out, maybe he didn't know how to get out."

"What was the straw decided you to move out?"

"Kenny showed me a finger. He said it was a real finger. You can buy these fake fingers in the joke shops that look almost like the real thing. Only those fingers are regular size."

"And this finger?"

"Was a little kid's finger."

"He tell you where it came from?"

Gambler shook his head again, so that his hair swept right and left like a tree's crown swayed by the wind.

"I want to tell you something, George," Whistler said, using his real name, psychologically taking them both off the streets into what some would call the real world. "Somebody cut Kenny's throat and somebody thought they had reason to cut the throat of a priest Kenny was talking with out in the Valley. It was like I said, Kenny was talking in the confessional. He talked to you, George."

"But he didn't tell me nothing. He never named any names," Gambler said, as though making a case with Whistler would keep him safe if killers were out there stalking people.

"Sooner or later whoever did Kenny and the priest are going to find out about you, come looking for you. Leave town right now."

"I ain't got the means."

Whistler went into his pocket and gave Gambler what he had, less than fifty dollars.

"This'll get you on a bus to somewhere."

"I ain't going home," Gambler said, as though suddenly believing that Whistler was a social worker tricking him into going home.

"Go where you want. Go to Sacramento and become a politician, but get the hell out of town."

# 41

*Canaan* watched the hours pass, a thin line of light poking through the boarded window marking time as the sun wheeled across the sky.

For hours in the morning after he'd awakened groggy and thirsty but full of the resolve to free himself he imagined how he would talk his way out when they came to feed him, but no one ever came.

Then he thought about tricking his way out by some device like asking for a pack of playing cards with which to while away the hours, peeling the cellulose from the faces, packing it into a hole drilled with broken glass alongside the staple that held the chain into the wall, blowing out his fetters in the best tradition of Houdini or that character on TV who escaped from all kinds of cages, pits and prison cells using nothing but household products readily at hand or bits of string unraveled from his socks. But he was naked and there were no household products except wine and straw close at hand.

He dreamed himself out of there, pretending to be waking from a nightmare, but he was already wide awake and cold and hungry.

He'd scraped away at the adobe brick that secured the staple that held the chain that kept him crouching there, the crate rough on his naked buttocks, but hours of gouging had made scarcely any impression on the old wall.

"Here's my plan," he muttered, beginning, a little, to be afraid as darkness fell outside his prison.

There was the rattle of a key in the lock and the short, rattling run of a chain. The door opened and a figure came in dressed in a scarlet satin cloak with a hood and full face mask, the top half molded, the bottom half a loose curtain.

Canaan leaned back against the wall.

"You'd better have it in mind to kill me because when I get out of here I won't rest—"

"You're threatening me? You won't rest? You won't rest? If you'd let it rest you wouldn't be in the fix you're in right now."

"You're the one killed my niece?"

"What are you talking about? Killing?"

"You said if I'd let it rest. The only thing that keeps me from sleep is the memory of Sarah lying on the slab down at the morgue, that little girl cold and dead."

The masked figure laughed and the short curtain of satin concealing his mouth puffed out.

"I'm cold," Canaan said. "Can you give me my clothes? Can you give me a blanket? I'm thirsty. I want some water."

"Jesus turned water into wine. The least you can do is turn this wine into water," the masquerader joked. Then he suddenly thrust his face, neck and chest close to Canaan's face and screamed, "Tell me, you old sonofabitch. What makes you think I had anything to do with Sarah?"

Canaan threw his legs up and clasped them around the man, crushing him, drawing him closer to his hands, which were limited in reach by the length of the chains. He had a long shard of broken wine bottle in his right hand. He clawed at the cloak and mask, trying to expose the man's neck as the mummer struggled to get free.

The hood and mask were torn away as Kilroy, in a frenzy of terror, finally managed to break away and stood there revealed.

"I've seen your face. I know you now," Canaan said.

"For all the good it'll do you," Kilroy said. He left the room, leaving Canaan in the cold and dark.

# 42

*In* the light of day the hookers' stroll along Hollywood Boulevard looks tired, pale and tattered, as commonplace as a city dump. Ordinary people, with things to buy and business to transact, hurry along, popping into this building or that to get their teeth cleaned, a will drawn up, a tax form checked.

Sight-seers, in pairs and groups like gaggles of geese, make their way through the grifters, bone breakers, pimps, ambitious hookers, lost children, missionaries in their Day-Glo tracksuits and the homeless in their motley, all actors on the stage that they claim as their own when nightfall approaches.

Then the magic happens. The lights come on, making showcases of plenty out of windows filled with merchandise both cheap and dear. The traffic lights dance red, yellow and green along the boulevard. The cars stream by. The tips of cigarettes glow, little beacons of invitation, from alleys and doorways.

And the actors preen and strut and make displays of themselves. There a child in a blond Dynel wig like a cage of electric wire, vest of gold lamé just long enough to cover the bottom of her breasts, held by a single snap, which can be parted if a customer asks to see the fruit, skirt up around the bottom line of her ass cheeks, one leg cocked, as though carrying a grenade between her legs, ready to blow a man's balls off if he's got the guts to pull the pin. Over there a snotty-nosed urchin no more than ten, jingling a pocketful of quarters to spend in the electronic machine arcade, shooting down enemy planes, destroying enemy tanks, chopping up enemy soldiers on the buzzing, blinking screens before going out to sell his sweet patootie to passing chicken hawks.

On Halloween you can't tell the players from the spectators even with a scorecard.

Beverly Hills matrons strut their stuff along the boulevard on the way to somewhere, their tits pushed up and out like the chests of pouter pigeons in dresses of satin and brocade, pretending to be Marie Antoinette, escorted by Louis the whatever, bored husbands going along for the ride.

Ravishing starlets you've seen stripped to the buff and dry fucking in effigy up there on the forty-foot screen go skipping by, Cleopatras with pubic hair shaved away so they might wear their G-strings narrow and low, native girls in nothing but two leaves of palm and a cellophane vest, on the street shaking their booty in the flesh.

Cowboys in chaps with their cocks holstered in glove leather, animals of a dozen sorts pretending, waltzing on the street corners.

Rahab cruised the merchandise. It had been easy to find George Gomble, all he'd had to do was pick up Whistler's trail and follow him to his prey.

Georgie-Porgie, the Gambler, stood with one foot in the gutter and one on the curb, as though hoping that his feet would decide which way to go, across the street and on a bus heading home or up and down the stroll trolling for customers. How far would a forty-seven-dollar handout take him after he'd bought a twenty-dollar rock to clear his head of fear? Maybe Pasadena? Maybe Thousand Oaks? He needed a bigger score if he was to travel any distance at all.

"Are you otherwise engaged?" Rahab asked Gambler in a voice as soft and dark as purple velvet.

It caught Gambler's ear like a song remembered. Had it remembered well enough, he might have walked away. He'd heard the voice in the background, when Kenny Gotch had called or he'd called Kenny, more than once, more than twice, but from one second to the next he remembered and then forgot. He put the foot that was in the gutter up on the curb and was open for business.

"I ain't engaged and I ain't married," Gambler said, lisping a little, playing the whore.

"Can I afford you?" Rahab asked, smiling the serpent's smile.

"Depends on who does what to who."

"Oh, you don't have to do anything. I'll do the doing."

"I don't take the bone up the ass."

"I'm not anal. I'm oral."

This was going to be one of the easy ones, Gambler thought. They'd go back to the customer's car or walk half-way down some dark alley. He'd drop his pants and stand there while the gazooney went down on his knees and copped his joint.

"Fifty bucks," Gambler said.

"Get serious. I'll be doing all the work—"

"—and you'll be having all the fun."

"—and it looks to me like twenty should be plenty."

Gambler turned away, playing hard to get. He hated the bargaining part of it almost more than the doing. Rahab slipped a hand around Gambler's chest and tucked two bills, a twenty and a five, into the pocket of his denim work shirt.

"We'll split the difference," Rahab said.

"What do you mean split the difference?" Gambler said, looking at the bills with a flick of the finger. "I say fifty, you say twenty, and you hand me twenty-five? Split the difference'd be thirty-five."

"I'm splitting the difference between fifty and zero. Nada. Zilch. Take it or leave it."

It was six o'clock in the evening and twenty-five bucks wasn't a bad start on earning his ticket for far away. The quicker the scores, the quicker away from danger. Twenty-five bucks for standing in an alley letting the breeze cool his ass wasn't the worst thing that could happen, Gambler thought.

Rahab reached around again, about to pluck the bills out of Gambler's pocket. Gambler slapped his hand over his chest. "You got it," he said.

They walked down the boulevard together like a couple of strangers. At the corner, they turned north to an alley behind the Capitol Tower, where music was made. Rahab waved Gambler into the alley before him. Gambler unbuckled his belt, opened his fly and dropped his jeans. When he turned he scarcely saw the gleam of the little curved blade before it took his life.

Rahab kneeled down and tore open Gambler's shirt. He took another, longer blade, and opened Gambler's chest as neatly as a surgeon might have done, reached in and cut out the heart and put it in a plastic Baggie.

# 43

*There's* the old saying, What you don't know won't hurt you.

Diana didn't know if that was necessarily true, at least not in every situation, but it was pretty clear that in the present circumstance, this business of Kenny Gotch dying not of the ravages of AIDS—which was bad enough—but by a queer knife in the throat, she wished to high heaven that that Whistler had never told her.

Because now she knew that Kenny Gotch had been murdered with a valvuletome and the only one she ever knew who carried one of those oddities around was Rahab, aka Raditski. She'd asked about the little cage of steel with the blade at the end one night out of nothing but idle curiosity and he'd told her, with an odd kind of relish, as though he wanted to see if it would frighten her, that it was a surgeon's knife which he used as a tool for repairing his cameras. He had a handful of them he'd bought from a surplus medical supply house, he'd said.

She never asked but had more than a vague idea that Rahab had done a lot of bad things, up to and no doubt including murder, so how could she close her eyes to the fact that she probably knew who Kenny's killer was?

Sometimes it was very difficult keeping ideals and necessity separate. Not separating a belief in Jesus Christ and a belief in the older faith of witchcraft; after all, one seemed to follow the other naturally, neither one an offense or a prohibition to the other if you looked at it the right way.

Diana figured Catholics went to fortune-tellers to get their palms read but that didn't mean they took it seriously. Maybe *they* even believed some of it, the lifelines, lovelines in their palms, the fate described in the Tarot and destiny spelled out in the star patterns of astrology, but it wasn't as though *she* planned her life around any of it. Not as much as the old president and his wife had done, for instance. Maybe she tried to make her luck a little better with a spell like the one taught her by that New Orleans hooker, but she didn't actually believe it or depend on any of it; she depended on herself and common sense like she'd always done.

There was one edge, one meeting of borders, that bothered her a little. It was being a practicing Catholic and a make-believe worshiper of Satan at the same time that was causing her some moral confusion.

"I mean it's no more to me, being a naked altar and kissing Rahab's ass, than it would me eating another hooker for a lesbian display," she'd once told Kenny Gotch, her wee small hours of the morning confidant. "It's just doing a job of acting. You don't have to believe it."

"But maybe if you say the words and do the ritual, you're putting your soul in danger, believe it or not," Gotch'd said. "I read once that if you act crazy long enough you'll tip your brain and really go crazy."

"Well, I heard that, too, but I don't believe it, because if I believed it how come I ain't hungry for fucking twenty-four hours a day? It's what I do all the time, acting like I'm wild for it, so how come I ain't wild for it?"

She knew he'd been playing around with that dark shit for real and it worried her; asking his opinion from her point of view was a way of making him think about what he could be getting into without actually coming out and telling him to quit.

Maybe he'd been trying to tell her something else, too,

maybe asking her how to get out from under all that crap, but she hadn't listened close enough. Even if she had, there wasn't a piece of advice—except running forever—that he wouldn't have already thought of.

But something—someone—Rahab!—had killed him and that's what she had to deal with.

It was written in the Old Testament in Numbers, "Whoso killeth any person, the murderer shall be put to death by the mouth of witnesses." She remembered that very well because she'd read through the Bible, looking for mitigation or forgiveness for the life she'd taken back there in New Jersey.

She went to the Bible again to see what else it had to say and was much confused to find that the last part of that line read, "but one witness shall not testify against any person *to cause him* to die."

A lot of preachers and those reborn in Christ said there was no contradiction in the Bible and there it was, in black and white, *in one sentence,* telling you to give up the sucker if you know somebody's a murderer and then telling you not to if it would cause him to die.

Turning to the sisterhood of witches, thinking about becoming a follower of Wicca in an attempt to find some center in her heart, reading all the literature Mary Bucket gave her, didn't give her much guidance.

In the end you had to do what your conscience told you to do, even though the consequences of what you had to do scared you half to death and broke every commandment you'd ever laid on yourself to mind your own business.

So she'd finally picked up the phone and called that joker, Whistler, but only got his machine. She could have taken that as a sign that she'd reached out and been refused. Instead she'd disguised her voice and left a message telling him that if anybody wanted to check out the death of Kenny Gotch they might take a look at a character by the name of Bennu Rahab, aka Raymond Raditski.

Then she had to think about what she should do next, go to this goddamn orgy or don't go.

But even that decision looked like it wasn't really up to her, because if she was a no-show and somebody went after

Rahab, he could very easily put two and two together and come up with Diana Corday as the person who'd finked on him. Then he'd be out there looking for her with that fucking knife on the tip of his finger.

She went looking for the robe she'd put on at the beginning of the Black Mass. At least she didn't have to go worrying about a Halloween costume to wear; she'd be bare-assed most of the time.

The fold of metallic cloth, hanging down like a breech cloth, was so narrow it barely covered Jeanne Millholme's crotch. There was a little vest of the same material that went with it.

Rahab had told her that he was according her a special honor bringing her into the Church of Satan on All Hallows' Eve, a very, very special night in their calendar of ceremony and celebration. She was being doubly honored because the induction was being held in a setting beside the sea that was the most unholy of all the unholy places along the coast, a participant in a larger celebration dedicated to the special holiday.

Which was all very well and good, except the brief costume left no place for concealment. She shuddered at the thought of being out there all but naked in front of so many strange eyes.

She found a black velvet hooded cape lined with wine-colored satin. It had an inner pocket meant for an evening purse. It would do.

She sat down to wait for Rahab to come take her to the midnight meeting of the profane.

# 44

*Tiki* torches lighted the way along the narrow road that wound along the cliff to the beach, past the mansion masquerading as a medieval ruin in Disney-like decay, where bunches of torches were massed on either side of the gateway. Guards in black hooded cloaks and masks, chests crisscrossed with chains and leather, checked the crotch between the thumb and forefinger of the left hand of every guest as they arrived. Upon that web of skin, the lucky guests had transferred the decals that would give them entrance according to the application instructions that had arrived with their invitations.

Nearly invisible in ordinary light, they glowed when a black light was shone upon them so that the guests walked about apparently unmarked but bearing this secret sign that they were of a very special band of brothers and sisters.

The road down to Lucifer's and the footpath beside it were lined with luminaria sporting cutouts of jack-o'-lanterns, black cats with arched backs and witches astride broomsticks.

The restaurant had been cleared of all the usual tables and many of the chairs. Plywood sheets on trestles, draped with orange cloths, were loaded with food and drink of every sort.

It had all the lavish innocence of a Beverly Hills children's party.

Streams of costumed celebrants, men and women, straight and gay, old and young, were in constant motion from one place to another, going to Lucifer's to partake of the elegant refreshments offered there and returning to the mansion as quickly as they could for fear they might miss something notable.

The tableaus and mechanical displays were hidden behind scarlet drapes, and the only adventure to be had in the mansion's musty rooms and corridors at the moment was the scary experience of walking through a maze of swaying, billowing curtains.

They would all be in the mansion, none in Lucifer's, when twelve o'clock came, for that was the announced time of a most unusual entertainment.

Whistler, in jeans and checkered shirt, a bandana around his neck and a Stetson on his head, booted and masked, walked beside Essex, who'd refused to put on any costume at all and had arrived at Whistler's house in a pair of slacks, open-necked shirt, sleeveless sweater and a sport jacket any racetrack tout would have proudly worn.

As they'd driven off in Essex's beat-up city-issue basic black two-door sedan, Whistler asked him who he was supposed to be.

Essex handed over a little square of blank waxy paper, flipped his badge holder out of the handkerchief pocket so it hung out for everyone to see and said, "I'm supposed to be a cop. They'll think it's a joke, just wait and see."

"Are you kidding me?"

"Hell, no. They're in their own crazy world, these people. They'll fly up to the ceiling if someone misses a page in whatever latest ritual somebody's dreamed up like what color hot hankie in which back pocket means what. You know what I mean? What special sex act you looking for, are you giving or taking?

"Other times they'll pop amyl nitrate to relax their sphincters for a little fist fucking with some uniform standing right there at the bar. Nothing happens the same way twice. Anything can start a riot. These people are not in complete control of themselves, you got to understand."

"What's this for?" Whistler asked, holding up the square of paper.

"Black-light sensitive decal. Transfer it onto your hand in the crotch between your thumb and first finger. These assholes'll pay more attention to that than to our faces or this badge dangling out of my pocket. They got great faith in their security methods. They don't know all it takes is one fink to tell the cops everything they got to know. The police artist made these up for me."

"What's it take to transfer the decal?" Whistler asked.

"Anything liquid."

"I don't think I've got enough spit to do the job."

"I could tell you to piss on your hand but I won't," Essex said, grinning. "There's a pint of vodka in the glove compartment."

"Won't the alcohol dissolve it?"

"There's no booze in it, just water. It's my beard when I'm pretending to be on the sauce and don't know what I'm doing in this place or that. Little tricks."

Whistler went into the glove compartment, took out the bottle, uncapped it and smelled it. It was water. He transferred the decal while Essex went back to what he'd been saying before Whistler asked about the transfer.

"I was in this one leather bar one time. I'm wearing vinyl. Who can afford leather? But that's all right. I'm a new face. They're looking me over. But what's making me nervous is nobody's talking. They're just walking around, milling around, without making a peep. Walking around like a bunch of animals on the prowl. I don't know what's going on. There's one buck—a big sonofabitch—slamming his fist into the palm of his hand. Not saying anything, just walking around punching himself in the hand. Very disconcerting. There is absolutely no action, none of the down and dirty. I'm wondering what the hell is going on and then it dawns on me. I'm the new face and they're all waiting for the big guy pounding his fist to initiate me."

"What?" Whistler said.

"He was getting ready to fist fuck me and he was telling me to get ready," Essex said.

"What did you do?"

"Well," Essex said, laughing as though the patrons of that leather bar had only meant to welcome him with a little

innocent fun, "I got the hell out of there. What was I supposed to do, bust him or bend over?"

The rest of the drive down had been easy, two friends
swapping war stories, two street soldiers on a mission.

Now they were walking down the path, both masked, Essex
tapping his badge and getting a laugh from this one and that
one as they passed costumed figures along the way, Whistler
feeling electrified, as though he was coming close to some
hidden source of power or—if he were precognitive as Ardella had hinted he might have been as a child—as though
he was coming close to the friend he sought.

They made their way through the crush around the refreshment table, spearing a shrimp here and a roll of beef around
a cube of cheese there, napkin in one hand and a plastic
flute of domestic champagne in the other. Rubbing asses with
ladies—or whatever—wearing bits of string and patches that
exposed a hell of a lot more skin than they concealed, getting
their own asses rubbed and peckers nudged by disembodied
hands, not knowing from the masked faces and grinning
mouths which of the milling crowd were copping feels.

"Let's break the hell out of this," Essex said. "I'm about
to get smothered by all this tit and belly buttons."

They shouldered their way out.

"Are we looking for something?" Whistler asked when
they'd found a patch of clear air in a corner of the room
where a potted fern stood on a pedestal, a rock in the river of
cowboys, Indians, houris, demons, angels, circus performers,
naked and near-naked bodies swirling through the restaurant,
flowing around the pedestal like water composed of sequins,
feathers, lamé and leather.

"Just showing you a good time," Essex said, "but in case
anything goes down—"

"What's going down?"

"—you take care of yourself, understand? Stay out of the
way."

"What's going down?" Whistler asked again, a little
sharper this time.

"Maybe nothing. We get rumors. We get informants.
There's going to be a show. Like the FBI working up files on

protestors, we like to know who's who; who's onstage, who're the ringmasters. We like to mark our scorecards."

"How many cops have you got undercover here?"

"I ain't got an army, I can tell you that. We're spread very thin on Halloween. We won't do anything foolish, you can bet on that. We just like to know if there're any new players in the Satan game."

Whistler could hardly believe they were talking about things like they were talking about, taking it seriously—well, half-seriously—in this day and age.

"Don't wander off. We get separated in the crowd, check back here eleven forty-five," Essex said.

"I'm a big boy now," Whistler said.

"I know, but I got the transportation," Essex said as he stepped into the flow of bodies again. He turned and said, "Midnight's showtime, the witching hour. Don't want to be late."

Essex and Whistler walked up the path from Lucifer's, having met in the crush around the potted palm, the spot apparently designated by dozens of other trysters as the place of rendezvous. Having arrived first, Whistler had been silently propositioned by half a dozen men and women or whatever before Essex moved up at his shoulder looking troubled.

"The Halloween crazies have started," he said.

"What's that?"

"Six dead so far tonight. A whore was found on a roof hanging by her feet from a stone gargoyle with her guts spilling out of her belly, a baby was found dead in a garbage can with a nail through its eye, and a twangy boy had his heart cut out."

A shudder went up Whistler's spine. He was having strong premonitions of tragedy striking close to home.

"What twangy boy?" he asked as the two of them shuffled along with the crowd, a long worm of flesh covered in scales and rags of many colors, making its way from restaurant to mansion. "You got a name on him?"

"Street name was Georgie-Porgie. You know him?"

"I know him. I was talking to him just a few hours ago."

"Oh? They found him in an alley shoved in between a Dumpster and a wall," Essex said, giving Whistler a look that said that there were no coincidences in the world. Every event fits into every other event somehow in a great web of cause and effect. All you've got to do is listen for the clicks. "The screwballs are just warming up. Six's not so bad so far. It'll get worse when the vampires, ghouls and werewolves really get going after midnight."

They passed through the gates of the mansion and walked up the long drive, the moving mass of people spreading out, seeking momentary relief from the insistent touch of others, then coming together again, funneling through the guarded door, holding out their pale hands, purple spiders shining in the folds of thumb and first finger.

The scarlet curtains had been drawn back to reveal the Satanic tableaus: the wheel of tortured children, the crucified men and women, the fornication among humans and beasts. It was Madame Tussaud's carried to the ultimate degree. As they moved along like cattle, eyes glowing, faces and breasts moist with their own sweat, moving toward some place of ceremony or even death, the guests were assaulted with sounds and smells and images. They were frantically occupied trying to sort out the real from the false. When a figure moved they screamed at one another, asking if it was a human being that leered and beckoned or some clever automaton, a supreme flowering of the special-effect man's art.

Whistler felt a tightness across his chest and suffered a shortness of breath. He was afraid to close his eyes because he might see visions so terrible that he might never erase them from his memory. He listened to the shuffling of the many feet. He felt the flesh of others all around him.

They spilled out into a huge central room like the great room of some ancient castle or the nave of a Greek Orthodox cathedral where the congregation stood at their prayers and fell silent. A rush of cool air surrounded them for a moment. They looked around at scenes of horror and violence projected on the walls.

"For Christ's sake, this cost a bundle," Essex said. "It's as good as fucking Disneyland."

It was as though he had to define the experience they were undergoing as unreal, surreal, manufactured, for fear that it might not be a stage effect after all. As though they may, indeed, have been led into the anteroom of hell.

Jeanne Millholme was waiting in the wings of the small stage, surrounded and concealed by black curtains that thrust out into the huge room, which was quickly filling up with stunned and delighted revelers. The performing stud was there chatting her up, looking over her goodies in a smarmy way, understanding that he'd maybe have a shot at her before the night was over, along with the obligatory poke at one of the Bobbys or Diana herself, according to who played what part. The fact that Diana was going to start the ritual mass meant that she'd probably be able to avoid getting fucked tonight. Hookers were very big on avoiding wear and tear.

Diana started giving orders, sending the dwarf, Billy Bottle, scurrying and the giantess, whose name was Maude Jinks, lumbering here and there setting up a faux marble altar on some boxes draped with a scarlet cloth, arranging and lighting the black candles.

She raised up the black plywood upside-down cross herself. Placed the knife, a papier-mâché goat's head, a chalice with a lump of chicken fat (substituting for human fat), and an artificial blood-red rose on the faux marble.

She asked the two Bobbys which one of them was going to be the naked altar.

"I can't do it," Bobby L said. "I got a cold coming on. All I need is lying there through the whole damn thing without a stitch on."

"Well, you got to run around naked anyway, so what's the difference?" Bobby D argued. "One way or the other you're going to get a chill and you know how ticklish I am when people start screwing around putting things on my belly."

"So how come this fucking place ain't heated?" Bobby L asked.

"Well, it's as big as a barn," Diana said. "You could pump five hundred bucks worth of hot air into here and it still wouldn't get warm. So make up your minds. Remember the one who ain't the altar has to do the bit with the chalice."

"That goddamn cow blood again?" Bobby D asked.

"No, we're doing fat tonight," Diana said.

"So, that means whoever ain't the altar has got to smear herself with that crap," Bobby D said, thinking it over, the pros and cons, to be the altar and get tickled, or rub animal fat all over her body and have to walk around like that until she could get under a hot shower. "So, okay, I'll be the altar," she finally said.

When everything was set up to Diana's satisfaction she told Bobby D to take off her clothes and get up on the draped crates and to be sure not to knock over the cross like she did once before, almost ruining the pitch when they had that rich couple in from Detroit over to Rahab's studio looking for kinky thrills.

"Where's Ray?" the two Bobbys asked.

"I'm doing the high priestess number tonight," Diana said, "and he'll make an appearance later on."

"I hope it ain't nothing heavy," Bobby L said. "Sometimes he scares the shit out of me."

"So whatever he does just go along," Diana said. "Let's do it and get it over with so we can all go home as early as we can."

"I got to leave by two-thirty the latest. I got a regular coming in from Downey," Bobby L said.

"You got to keep your regular clientele sweet," Bobby D said, getting out of her bra and step-ins. "Christ, look at that, will you? I already got goose bumps."

"You ready, Billy?" Diana called.

The dwarf popped out of the shadows behind a bank of lights covered with blue gels and said, "I just want to set the baby." He was a grip over at the studios and always talked in film lingo, naming the various lights and filters as he went along. He toddled out in a pair of silver thong sandals and a black gown studded with foil stars and a crescent moon that was split at the sides. When he whirled in place, the parts of the gown spun out and lifted up, revealing his stunted, beastlike legs and a cock thicker and nearly as long as the stud's. He was sometimes asked to perform on the bodies of one of the Bobbys—who had an affectionate regard for him—and had even, upon occasion, been asked to mount some matron from Des Moines.

"Set the fucking baby and let's get going," Bobby D said, climbing up on the rickety altar and nearly knocking over the goat's head. She lay flat on her back and straightened out her legs. Diana laid the knife on her belly with the blade pointing to her crotch and arranged the blossom of the paper rose between her breasts with the stem splitting her belly in half and touching the black handle of the knife.

"Would you mind warming your finger, doctor, before you stick it up my twat?" Bobby D said, and started to giggle, causing the knife and rose to bounce around.

"For God's sake, be serious," Diana said.

They could hear the rising babble of the crowd beyond the curtained stage.

"If I don't make a joke about this, Diana," Bobby D said, "I'll be running the hell out of here. This feels different."

"It's just the size of the crowd," Diana reassured her. "You ready, Maude?" she whispered harshly. "Will you stop fucking with your makeup? This ain't *The Wizard of Oz.*"

"There wasn't any giants in *Wizard of Oz,*" Billy Bottle said. "In *Gulliver's Travels* they had giants."

"We going to talk movies now? Is that what we're going to do?" Diana complained. "Take your places and hit the goddamn gong."

She went over to the light board and fiddled with the lights, setting them the way she wanted, then took her place as Bottle replaced her at the console and hit a button that electronically reproduced the booming brassy sound of a temple gong. It reverberated on the air for a long time as the audience hushed again.

The curtains flowed open around the stage. From the audience they saw a marble slab altar and a massive black cross standing behind it upside down. A great square of green stone, dressed with a white cloth, a copper bowl, a skull and a black knife stood in front and off to one side of it.

The illuminated walls faded. The room became so dark it was as though they had been transported outside onto the beach beneath the night sky. The altar was suddenly lit from above with a dozen concealed spotlights. The effect drew gasps from the crowd.

Spots lit up Mike, the stud, standing off to one side urging Jeanne to walk onto the stage. She took five steps, with him right behind her, and then he touched her on the shoulder and she stopped, holding herself with her arms, using one hand every now and then to bat away the vagrant lock of hair.

He leaned over and whispered, "Take off that goddamn cape."

Jeanne shook her head and wrapped it more tightly around her.

He looked at Diana, who had entered from the other side and was waiting for them, her naked body shining through the transparent drapery she wore. She gave a little nod and Mike unbelted the trench coat he was wearing. He looked like an actor in a very old-fashioned pornography flick, standing there naked with his raincoat opened down the front, still wearing his socks and oxford shoes. She frowned a little and he caught the message, balancing himself on one foot and then the other like an awkward crane while he removed his shoes and socks and finally shucked aside the coat.

There was a ripple of laughter in the audience, people secretly relieved that the terrifying effects had been mitigated by the clumsiness of those who were clearly actors.

Diana saw that the stud was already getting an erection. You had to hand it to old Mike, she thought, he was always up and ready. That's what made him such a pro. She'd done a little X-rated acting in her time—though the camera didn't love her as it loved some and she hadn't gotten very far in the profession—and she'd seen the contracts the male actors had to sign guaranteeing erections and ejaculations. Men might have the edge in a lot of things but when it came to sex the women had the easy ride. It was no effort at all to go, "Ooo ooo ooo, Oh oh oh, Aggggh!" simulating orgasm. It was the boys who had to stand and deliver. She wanted to giggle at the foolishness of it all. It was something you had to watch every minute when you were asked to play a part in one of these Black Masses. She'd been told that there were satanists who took it all very seriously. Just like her mother and grandmothers had taken going down on their knees in front of a man hanging from a cross and begging favors from a plaster statue of the Virgin Mary seriously.

She'd been told that a lot of evil, even murder, was sometimes done. You read about it all the time and she'd even read about this Cardinal Somebody—O'Connor—from New York, a big shot in her own Holy Mother Church, announcing from the pulpit that two exorcisms had been performed in his archdiocese that year. Thinking about that and some other things, maybe she shouldn't be so flippant and casual about joining into these rituals. She didn't think it was more than a scam for Ray, even if he did call himself Rahab—"dragon of darkness"—and scrootched around in a beard that made him look like a devil. Except that he'd cut Kenny Gotch's throat and God knew what else?

The thing for her to do was get this performance over with and get the hell out of there, not even staying long enough to turn a couple of quick tricks in some dark corner with two or three of that horny mob.

"Naked came we into the world, and naked are we in the shadows of the night, and naked we must be upon introduction to Lucifuge, prime minister of the infernal spirits, commander of Bael and Agares and Marbas, also known as Lucifuge Roficale, minister to the Lord of Flies, and so must you be naked before him and before them all," she intoned, pleased to have gotten it right.

Bobby L and Maude helped Jeanne Millholme get out of the clothes she wore under her cape and tied a scarlet cord around her waist, but she wouldn't let them carry away the cape, and when they left her standing there she draped it around herself again.

Bobby D squirmed on the altar.

"Don't sneeze," Diana said under her breath, turning her head slightly toward her shoulder.

"Well, speed it up, will you?" Bobby D whispered.

Diana glanced off into the wings and saw Rahab standing there with a masked figure in a scarlet satin cape. They were struggling with something between them. She squinted her eyes—she'd have to do something about that, she was getting nearsighted—and saw that there was a body of a naked man hanging upside down on a cross, which could be trundled around on a set of wheels.

As they pushed the man and contraption out onto the stage she could see blood running down his chest toward his face and, unless she was very much mistaken, his heart had been ripped from his chest and lay exposed on his belly.

There were screams of horror and appreciation from the audience. The directors and producers of this extravaganza were tearing the line between reality and fantasy into fragments.

# 45

For Christ's sake, that's Isaac Canaan hanging up there," Whistler said.

Essex put his hand on Whistler's arm. "Give it another minute."

Up on the altar Diana did some fumble-mumble with the knife and rose, frowning down into Bobby D's grinning face and then asked Jeanne, the acolyte, to approach and kneel before the altar of female flesh with the man hanging on the cross beside her.

Bobby L came and knelt beside her, dressed in nothing but a cold chain around her waist and a pair of sweat socks because her feet were cold.

Diana picked up the chalice in her two hands and lifted it

in imitation of the priestly gesture in the Catholic celebration of the mass.

"Emperor Lucifer, master of all the rebellious spirits, I beg you to be favorable in the invocation that I make to your great Minister Lucifuge, as I wish to make a pact with him," she intoned.

Jeanne stared at Canaan, who was blinking the sweat and tears out of his eyes. He was alive and conscious, the heart, she could now see, tied to his belly with a piece of string.

"You're going to have to get rid of that cape," Bobby L whispered.

"I conjure you, O spirit, to appear within a minute by the power of the Great Adonai, by Eloim, by Ariel, Johavam, Agla, Tagla, Mathon, Oarios, Almouzin, Arios, Membrot, Varvis, Pithona, Magots, Silphae, Rabost, Salamandrae, Tabost—"

There was a flash of flame and a burst of smoke from the side of the stage.

Well, the hell with this, she thought, hardly hearing the gasps of dismay and fright from her fellow actors, there goes Ray stepping on my lines. He wants me to do an acting job, he should let me say all the words. He's going to blow it, if he tries to speed things up. These idiots want a performance. She turned her head.

Ray—Rahab—was standing there, in front of the crucified man, in his long black robe, one hand held high over his head. It held a long knife.

Whistler yelled out a warning, as though Canaan could defend himself, and ploughed headfirst through the crowd in front of the stage.

Jeanne Millholme let go a muffled scream that was like the sound of orgasm.

She scrambled to her feet, Bobby L dragging at her cape to keep her down on her knees.

Rahab stood in front of Canaan, who hung upside down like a steer waiting for the knife.

Jeanne jerked the cape away from Bobby L, fumbling in the inner pocket, coming out with a small gun, blue steel barrel and black grip.

Essex had his head down and was bulling his way through the crowd almost shoulder to shoulder with Whistler, and then he got jammed up behind two heavyweights who wouldn't give way, who turned around scolding him, telling him to mind his manners, he'd get to see it all.

Diana screamed because she knew none of it was part of the performance.

Rahab looked over his shoulder, the knife coming down in what looked to Whistler like slow motion, a camera trick meant to emphasize the action, string out the suspense.

He swung his head, almost expecting to see the lights and camera crane and a crew standing by, filming this latest horror flick soon to be visiting your local theater.

The woman with the gun in her hand was standing there with the weapon pointed directly in front of her in one trembling hand.

Christ, Whistler thought, she hasn't been watching much television or she'd know to support the wrist of the gun hand by circling it with the fingers of her other hand. She'd know enough to spread her legs and bend her knees a little for balance.

Rahab was holding the backward glance, grinning at the woman, as though he were daring her to fire. Then he turned his glance to Whistler as the knife kept coming down.

Whistler climbed up onto the stage and threw his arms around the half-naked woman from behind, grabbing the gun and her hand in both of his hands, turning her so that the angle of fire was oblique and the bullets wouldn't pass through Rahab and catch Canaan.

The gun popped, scarcely heard above the cheers and comments of the crowd.

Rahab's eyes changed, lost focus. He turned around, as though startled more by the sound than the impact. He flinched as each bullet struck flesh and bone. The knife clattered to the floor, unheard amidst the din.

Whistler squeezed Jeanne Millholme's finger on the trigger over and over again until the clip was empty.

He gave up his embrace. Jeanne stood there with the gun dangling loosely at her side, as though her arm had grown too weak to hold it. Bobby L was screaming now, either through genuine fear or because she thought Diana's scream had been a cue.

Whistler started loosening the bonds tying Canaan to the cross. Essex, finally reaching them, got down on his knees and humped his back so that Canaan wouldn't fall to the floor in a heap. As Whistler covered the old man's naked body with his jacket he looked across the stage and saw Kilroy standing in the wings, dressed in scarlet satin, staring at the rescued Canaan. Whistler could read the look on Kilroy's face. Their eyes met. Everything was known and understood.

Kilroy turned and ran.

The thought went through Whistler's head that Kilroy couldn't run fast enough or far enough to escape the vengeance of Isaac Canaan, the Wizard of La-La Land.

The guests applauded.

# 46

**Where'd** you find Kilroy?" Rialto asked.

"Up in the hills at his house in Agoura. Him and the kid who was the caretaker. Both of them hanging from the rafters in the barn," Canaan said.

"How you going to figure it?" Rialto said. "What'd they think they could get away with, wheeling Isaac out there in front of five hundred people like a lamb to slaughter?"

He looked at Canaan as though asking for the answer to a question in a game of trivia, the truth of what had happened being a little too much to handle except as a common, if screwball, everyday affair.

"Most of the crowd would think it was part of the production. Just another special effect, the blood pouring out of me. Just another actor doing a job," Canaan said.

"Academy award performance," Bosco remarked, as though praising Canaan for hanging there upside down, bare-assed naked. "Ain't we all just actors doing a job?"

"Oh, stuff a sock in it, will you?" Canaan grumbled. "I could've ended up buried somewhere under the basement floor or taken out to sea and dumped. Gone missing."

"Which one of them gazoonies grabbed you?" Rialto asked.

"The one that looked like Howdy-Doody, the red-headed gazooney. The one that killed my brother's baby. You can take a lesson. Don't ever hunt when you're full of rage." He looked at Whistler. "Hunters have to be cool. No, hunters have to be cold."

He, himself, was talking as though what he'd been through was a game that had suddenly gone too far, a play that had gotten out of hand.

"Rahab and Kilroy," Whistler said, "those two were feeding each other's craziness—"

"How crazy is crazy?" Canaan commented, just an aside, wondering about what madness is, a question society and the law have been struggling with for centuries.

"—trying to top each other, doing each other one better."

"Folie à deux," Bosco said, thoughtfully.

"Huh?" Rialto grunted.

"A psychosis shared by two or more persons," Bosco explained.

"How many more?" Canaan asked.

Bosco shrugged.

"How many more before you've got a whole society that's crazy?"

"The nuts running the madhouse," Whistler added.

"Maybe that's what we got. Maybe that's what it's always been, the way people act," Bosco said.

"So, never mind if it's the crusaders walking behind a flag with a cross on it and killing everybody in sight just to make sure no infidels get away," Bosco said. "Never mind if it's the IRA, the Red Army Brigade, the Stern Gang, the what-ever. What you're dealing with mostly here is power players, gangster types who don't like to play by the rules. Bullies and killers. They wised up to the fact that if you yelled loud enough that what you were doing was for God or country or to make things better in the sweet by and by, you could always find an army ready to follow you and cut babies up into one-inch cubes. That's the way it is and that's the way it's always been."

"That was a speech," Canaan said. "You should run for something."

The four of them, Isaac Canaan, the pious Jew, Whistler, the lapsed Roman Catholic, Mike Rialto, the nonpracticing Baptist and Bosco Silverlake, the secular humanist, stared out the window looking for something they could build their hopes on.

Mary Bucket walked through the door and sat down next to Whistler, her hip comfortable against his. She knew what they were sad about without even having heard. She understood better than they the true nature of humanity, the woman's way, the witch's way; you lived the hour, you walked through the night picking up the pieces and nourished what you could through the day.

"I heard it on the news," she said. "We can expect a first-stage smog alert this afternoon."

They all nodded.

"Thank Gaea for the good times," she said.